Date: 4/29/14

LP FIC JOHNSTONE
Johnstone, William W.,
Flintlock

FLINTLOCK

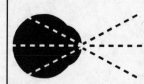

FLINTLOCK

WILLIAM W. JOHNSTONE
WITH J.A. JOHNSTONE

THORNDIKE PRESS
A part of Gale, Cengage Learning

GALE
CENGAGE Learning·

Farmington Hills, Mich • San Francisco • New York • Waterville, Maine
Meriden, Conn • Mason, Ohio • Chicago

GALE
CENGAGE Learning®

LIBRARY OF CONGRESS CATALOGING-IN-PUBLICATION DATA

Johnstone, William W.
  Flintlock / by William W. Johnstone with J.A. Johnstone.
    pages cm (Thorndike press large print western)
    ISBN-13: 978-1-4104-6694-5 (hardcover)
    ISBN-10: 1-4104-6694-9 (hardcover)
    1. Large type books. I. Johnstone, J. A. II. Title.
  PS3560.O415F59 2014
  813'.54—dc23   2013046806

Published in 2014 by arrangement with Pinnacle Books, an imprint of Kensington Publishing Corp.

FLINTLOCK

CHAPTER ONE

"I'm gonna hang you tomorrow at sunup, Sam Flintlock, an' I can't guarantee to break your damned neck on account of how I never hung anybody afore," the sheriff said. "I'll try, lay to that, but you see how it is with me."

"The hammering stopped about an hour ago, so I figured my time was near," Flintlock said.

"A real nice gallows, you'll like it," Sheriff Dave Cobb said. "An' I'll make sure it's hung with red, white and blue bunting so you can go out in style. You'll draw a crowd, Sam. If'n that makes you feel better."

"This pissant town railroaded me into a noose, Cobb. You know it and I know it," Flintlock said.

"Damnit, boy, you done kilt Smilin' Dan Sedly and just about everybody in this valley was kissin' kin o' his. Ol' Dan was a well-liked man."

"He was wanted by the law for bank robbery and murder," Flintlock said.

"Not in this town he wasn't," Cobb said.

The sheriff was a middle-aged man and inclined to be jolly by times. He was big in the belly and a black, spade-shaped beard spread over the lapels of a broadcloth suit coat that looked to be half as old as he was.

"No hard feelings, huh, Sam?" he said. "I mean about the hangin' an' all. Like I told you, I'll do my best. I've been reading a book about how to set the noose an' sich an' I reckon I'll get it right."

"I got no beef against you, Cobb," Flintlock said. "You're the town lawman and you've got a job to do."

"How old are you, young feller?" the lawman said.

"Forty. I guess."

"Still too young to die." Cobb sighed. "Ah well, tell you what, I'll bring you something nice for your last meal tonight. How about steak and eggs? You like steak and eggs?"

"I don't much care, Sheriff, but there's one thing you can do for me."

"Just ask fer it. I'm a giving, generous man. Dave Cobb by name, Dave Cobb by nature, I always say."

"Let me have my grandpappy's old Hawken rifle," Flintlock said. "It will be a comfort to me."

Doubt showed in Cobb's face. "Now, I don't know about that. That's agin all the rules."

"Hell, Cobb, the Hawken hasn't been shot in thirty, forty years," Flintlock said. "I ain't much likely to use it to bust out of jail."

"You're a strange one, Sam Flintlock," the lawman said. "Why did you carry that old gun around anyhow?"

"Call me sentimental, Cobb. It was left to me as a legacy, like."

"See, my problem is, Sam, you could use that old long gun as a club. Bash my brains out when I wasn't lookin'."

"Not that rifle, I won't. Your head is too thick, Sheriff. I might damage the stock."

Cobb thought for a while, his shaggy black eyebrows beetling. Finally he smiled and said, "All right, I'll bring it to you. But I see you making any fancy moves with that old Hawken, I'll shoot your legs off so you can still live long enough to be hung. You catch my drift?"

"You have my word, Sheriff, I won't give you any trouble."

Cobb nodded. "Well, you're a personable enough feller, even though you ain't so well set up an' all, so I'll take you at your word."

"I appreciate it," Flintlock said. "See, I'm

named for that Hawken."

"Your real name Hawken, like?"

"No. My grandpappy named me for a flintlock rifle, seeing as how I never knew my pa's name."

"Hell, why didn't he give you his own name, that grandpa of yourn?"

"He said every man should have his father's name. He told me he'd call me Flintlock after the Hawken until I found my ma and she told me who my pa was and what he was called."

"You ever find her?"

"No. I never did, but I'm still on the hunt for her. Or at least I was."

"Your grandpa was a mountain man?"

"Yeah, he was with Bridger an' Hugh Glass an' them, at least for a spell. Then he helped survey the Platte and the Sweetwater with Kit Carson and Fremont."

"Strange, restless breed they were, mountain men."

"You could say that."

"I'll bring you the Hawken, but mind what I told you, about shootin' off a part of yourself."

"I ain't likely to forget," Flintlock said.

CHAPTER TWO

"Pssst . . ."

Sam Flintlock sat up on his cot, his mind cobwebbed by sleep.

"Pssst . . ."

What was that? Rats in the corners again?

"Hell, look up here, stupid."

Flintlock rose to his feet. There was a small barred window high on the wall of his cell where a bearded face looked down at him.

"I see you're prospering, Sammy," the man said, grinning. "Settin' all nice and cozy in the town hoosegow."

Flintlock scowled. "Come to watch me hang, Abe?"

"Nah, I was just passin' through when I saw the gallows," Abe Roper said. "I asked who was gettin' hung and they said a feller with a big bird tattooed on his throat that goes by the name of Sam Flintlock. I knew it had to be you. There ain't another ranny in the West with a big bird an' that handle."

"Here to gloat, Abe?" Flintlock said. "Gettin' even for old times?"

"Hell, no, I got nothing agin you, Sam. You got me two years in Yuma but you treated me fair and square. An' you gave my old lady money the whole time I was inside. Now why did you do a dumb thing like that?"

"You had growing young 'uns. Them kids had to be fed and clothed."

"Yeah, but why the hell did you do it?"

"I just told you."

"I got no liking for bounty hunters, Sammy, but you was a true-blue white man, taking care of my family like that." Roper was silent for a moment, then said, "Sally and the kids passed about three years ago from the cholera."

"I'm sorry to hear that," Flintlock said. "I can close my eyes and still see their faces."

"It was a hurtful thing, Sam, and me being away on the scout at the time."

"You gonna stick around for the hanging, Abe?" Flintlock said.

"Hell, no, and neither are you."

"What do you mean?"

"I mean there's a barrel of gunpowder against this wall and it's due to go up in" — Roper looked down briefly — "oh, I'd say less than half a minute."

The man waved a quick hand. "Hell, I got to light a shuck."

Flintlock stood rooted to the spot for a moment. Then he yelled a startled curse at Roper, grabbed the rifle off his cot and pulled the mattress on top of him.

A couple of seconds later the Mason City jail blew up with such force its shingle roof soared into the air and landed intact twenty yards away on top of the brand-new gallows. The jail roof and the gallows collapsed in a cloud of dust and killed Sheriff Cobb's pregnant sow that had been wallowing in the mud under the platform.

A shattering shower of adobe and splintered wood rained down on Flintlock and acrid dust filled his lungs. He threw the mattress aside and staggered to his feet, just as Abe Roper kicked aside debris and stepped through the hole in the jailhouse wall.

"Sam, get the hell out of there," Roper said. "I got your hoss outside."

Flintlock grabbed the Hawken, none the worse for wear, and stumbled outside.

As Roper swung into the saddle, Chinese Charlie Fong, grinning as always, tossed Flintlock the reins of a paint.

13

"Good to see you again, Sammy," Fong said.

"Feeling's mutual, Charlie," Flintlock said.

He mounted quickly and ate Roper's dust as he followed the outlaw out of town at a canter.

Roper turned in the saddle. "Crackerjack bang, Sammy, huh? Have you ever seen the like?"

"Son of a gun, you could've killed me," Flintlock said.

"So what? Who the hell would miss ya?" Roper said.

"Somebody's gonna miss this paint pony I'm riding," Flintlock said.

"Hell, yeah, it's the sheriff's hoss," Roper grinned. "Better than the ten-dollar mustang you rode in on, Sam."

"Damn you, Abe, Cobb's gonna hang me, then hang me all over again for hoss theft," Flintlock said.

"Well, he'll have to catch you first," Roper said, kicking his mount into a gallop.

After an hour of riding through the southern foothills of the Chuska Mountains, the massive rampart of red sandstone buttes and peaks that runs north all the way to the Utah border, Roper drew rein and he and

Flintlock waited until Charlie Fong caught up.

"Where are we headed, Abe?" Flintlock said. "I hope you've got a good hideout all picked out."

He and Roper were holed up in a stand of mixed juniper and piñon. A nearby high meadow was thick with yellow bells and wild strawberry, and the waning afternoon air smelled sweet of pine and wildflowers.

"We're headed for Fort Defiance, up in the old Navajo country. It's been abandoned for years but the army's moved back, temporary-like, until ol' Geronimo is either penned up or dead."

Flintlock scratched at a bug bite under his buckskin shirt and said, "Is that wise, me riding into an army fort when I'm on the scout?"

"There ain't no fightin' sodjers there, Sammy, just cooks an' quartermasters an' the like," Roper said. "All the cavalry is out, lookin' fer Geronimo an' them."

"We gonna stay in an army barracks?" Flintlock said. "Say it ain't so."

"Nah, me an' Charlie got us a cabin near the officers' quarters, a cozy enough berth if you're not a complainin' man."

Roper peered hard at Flintlock's rugged, unshaven face and then his throat. "Damnit,

15

Sam, I never did get used to looking at that big bird, even when we rode together."

"I was raised rough," Flintlock said. "You know that."

"Old Barnabas do that to you?" Roper said, passing the makings.

"He wanted it done, but when I was twelve he got an Assiniboine woman to do the tattooing. As I recollect, it hurt considerable."

"What the hell is it? Some kind of eagle?"

Flintlock built his cigarette and Roper gave him a match. "It's a thunderbird." He thumbed the match into flame and lit his cigarette. "Barnabas wanted a black and red thunderbird, on account of how the Indians reckon it's a sacred bird."

"He wanted it that big? Hell, it pretty much covers your neck and down into your chest."

"Barnabas said folks would remember me because of the bird. He told me that a man folks don't remember is of no account."

"He was a hard old man, was Barnabas, him and them other mountain men he hung with. A tough, mean bunch as ever was."

"They taught me," Flintlock said. "Each one of them taught me something."

"Like what, for instance?"

"They taught me about whores and whis-

16

key and how to tell the good ones from the bad. They taught me how to stalk a man and how to kill him. And they taught me to never answer a bunch of damned fool questions."

Roper laughed. "Sounds like old Barnabas and his pals all right."

"One more thing, Abe. You saved my life today, and they taught me to never forget a thing like that."

Roper, smiling, watched a hawk in flight against the dark blue sky, then again directed his attention to Flintlock.

"You ever heard of the Golden Bell of Santa Elena, Sam?" he said.

"Can't say as I have."

"You will. And after I tell you about it, I'll ask you to repay the favor you owe me."

CHAPTER THREE

"Are you sure you saw deer out here, Captain Shaw? It might have been a shadow among the trees."

"Look at the tracks in the wash, Major. Deer have passed this way and not long ago."

"I see tracks all right," Major Philip Ashton said. He looked around him. "But I'm damned if I see any deer."

"Sir, may I suggest we move farther up the wash as far as the foothills," Captain Owen Shaw said. "Going on dusk the deer will move out of the timber."

Ashton, a small, compact man with a florid face, an affable disposition and a taste for bonded whiskey, nodded. "As good a suggestion as any, Captain. We'll wait until dark and if we don't see a deer we'll leave it for another day."

"As you say, sir," Shaw said.

He watched the major walk ahead of him.

Like himself, Ashton wore civilian clothes but he carried a regulation Model 1873 Trapdoor Springfield rifle. Shaw was armed with a .44-40 Winchester because he wanted nothing to go wrong on this venture, no awkward questions to be answered later.

Major Ashton, who had never held a combat command, carried his rifle at the slant, as though advancing on an entrenched enemy and not a herd of nonexistent mule deer.

Shaw was thirty years old that spring. He'd served in a frontier cavalry regiment, but he'd been banished to Fort Defiance as a commissary officer after a passionate, though reckless, affair with the young wife of a farrier sergeant.

Shaw wasn't at all troubled by his exile. It was safer to dole out biscuit and salt beef than do battle with Sioux and Cheyenne warriors.

Of course, the Apaches were a problem, but since the Navajo attacked the fort in 1858 and 1860 and both times were badly mauled, it seemed that the wily Geronimo was giving the place a wide berth.

That last suited Captain Shaw perfectly. He had big plans and they sure as hell didn't involve Apaches.

The wash, dry now that the spring melt

was over, made a sharp cut to the north and the two officers followed it through a grove of stunted juniper and willow onto a rocky plateau bordered by thick stands of pine.

In the distance the fading day painted the Chuska peaks with wedges of deep lilac shadow and out among the foothills coyotes yipped. The jade sky was streaked with banners of scarlet and gold, the streaming colors of the advancing night.

Major Ashton walked onto the plateau, his attention directed at the pines. His rifle at the ready, he stopped and scanned the trees with his field glasses.

Without turning his head, he said, "Nothing moving yet, Captain."

Shaw made no answer.

"You have a buck spotted?" the major whispered.

Again, he got no reply.

Ashton turned.

Shaw's rifle was pointed right at his chest.

"What in blazes are you doing, Captain Shaw?" Ashton said, his face alarmed.

"Killing you, Major."

Owen Shaw fired.

The soft-nosed .44-40 round tore into the major's chest and plowed through his lungs. Even as the echoing report of the Winchester racketed around the plateau, Ashton fell to his hands and knees and coughed up a bouquet of glistening red blossoms.

Shaw smiled and shot Ashton again, this time in the head. The major fell on his side and all the life that remained in him fled.

Moving quickly, Shaw stood over Ashton and fired half a dozen shots into the air, the spent cartridge cases falling on and around the major's body. He then pulled a Smith & Wesson .32 from the pocket of his tweed hunting jacket, placed the muzzle against his left thigh and pulled the trigger.

A red-hot poker of pain burned across Shaw's leg, but when he looked down at the wound he was pleased. It was only a flesh wound but it was bleeding nicely, enough to make him look a hero when he rode into Fort Defiance.

Limping slightly, Shaw retraced his steps along the dry wash to the place where he and Ashton had tethered their horses. He looked behind him and to his joy saw that he'd left a blood trail. Good! There was always the possibility that a cavalry patrol had returned to the fort and their Pima scouts could be bad news. The blood would help his cover-up.

He gathered up the reins of the major's horse and swung into the saddle. There was no real need to hurry but he forced his horse into a canter, Ashton's mount dragging on him.

It was an officer's duty to recover the body of a slain comrade, but Ashton had been of little account and not well liked. When Shaw told of the Apache ambush and his desperate battle to save the wounded major, that little detail would be overlooked.

And his own bloody wound spoke loud of gallantry and devotion to duty.

Lamps were already lit when Captain Owen Shaw rode into Fort Defiance, a sprawling complex of buildings, some of them ruins, grouped around a dusty parade ground.

He staged his entrance well.

Not for him to enter at a gallop and hysterically warn of Apaches, rather he slumped in the saddle and kept his horse to a walk . . . the wounded warrior's noble return.

He was glad that just as he rode past the sutler's store, big, laughing Sergeant Patrick Tone stepped outside, a bottle of whiskey tucked under his arm.

"Sergeant," Shaw said, making sure he sounded exhausted and sore hurt, "sound officer's call. Direct the gentlemen to the commandant's office."

"Where is Major Ashton, sir?" Tone said,

his Irish brogue heavy on his tongue. Like many soldiers in the Indian-fighting army, he'd been born and bred in the Emerald Isle and was far from the rainy green hills of his native land.

"He's dead. Apaches. Now carry out my order."

Tone shifted the bottle from his right to his left underarm and snapped off a salute. Then he stepped quickly toward the enlisted men's barracks, roaring for the bugler.

Shaw dismounted outside the administration building, a single-story adobe structure, its timber porch hung with several large clay ollas that held drinking water. The ollas' constant evaporation supposedly helped keep the interior offices cool, a claim the soldiers vehemently denied.

After leaning against his horse for a few moments, the action of an exhausted man, Shaw limped up the three steps to the porch, drops of blood from his leg starring the rough pine.

He stopped, swaying slightly, when he saw a woman bustling toward him across the parade ground, her swirling skirts lifting veils of yellow dust.

Shaw smiled inwardly. This was getting better and better. Here comes the distraught widow.

Maude Ashton, the major's wife, was a plump, motherly woman with a sweet, heart-shaped face that normally wore a smile. But now she looked concerned, as though she feared to hear news she already knew would be bad.

Maude mounted the steps and one look at the expression on Shaw's face and the blood on his leg told her all she needed to know. She asked the question anyway. "Captain Shaw, where is my husband?"

As the stirring notes of officer's call rang around him, Shaw made an act of battling back a sob. "Oh, Maude . . ."

He couldn't go on.

The captain opened his arms wide, tears staining his cheeks, and Maude Ashton ran between them. Shaw clasped her tightly and whispered, "Philip is dead."

Maude had been a soldier's wife long enough to know that the day might come when she'd have to face those three words. Now she repeated them. "Philip is dead . . ."

"Apaches," Shaw said. He steadied himself and managed, "They jumped us out by Rock Wash and Major Ashton fell in the first volley."

Maude took a step back. Her pretty face, unstained by tears, was stony. "And Philip is still out there?"

Boots thudded onto the porch and Shaw decided to wait until his two officers were present before he answered Maude's irritating question.

First Lieutenant Frank Hedley was in his early fifties, missing the left arm he'd lost at Gettysburg as a brevet brigadier general of artillery. He was a private, withdrawn man, too fond of the bottle to be deemed fit for further promotion. He'd spent the past fifteen years in the same regular army rank. This had made him bitter and his drinking and irascible manner worsened day by day.

Standing next to him was Second Lieutenant Miles Howard, an earnest nineteen-year-old fresh out of West Point. His application for a transfer to the hard-riding 5th Cavalry had recently been approved on the recommendation of the Point's superintendent, the gallant Colonel Wesley Merritt, the regiment's former commander.

Howard had a romantic view of the frontier war, his imagination aflame with flying banners, bugle calls and thundering charges with the saber. He'd never fought Apaches.

"Where is the major?" Hedley said.

"He's dead," Shaw said. "We got hit by Apaches at Rock Wash and Major Ashton fell."

Hedley turned and saw the dead officer's

horse. "Where is he?"

Shaw shook his head and then stared directly and sincerely at Maude. "I had to leave him. The Apaches wanted his body but I stood over him and drove them away. But I was sore wounded and could not muster the strength to lift the gallant major onto his horse."

Lieutenant Howard, more perceptive and more sympathetic than Hedley, watched blood drops from Shaw's leg tick onto the timber.

"Sir, you need the post surgeon," he said.

"Later, Lieutenant. Right now I want you and Mr. Hedley in the commandant's office," Shaw said, grimacing, a badly wounded soldier determined to be brave.

CHAPTER FOUR

"Something going on with the soldiers," Charlie Fong said. He stood at the open door of the cabin, smoking a black cheroot. "They got cooks and clerks lined up with rifles and the headquarters building's all lit up."

Sam Flintlock stepped to the door and looked over Fong's shoulder.

A dented moon hung high in the night sky and spilled weak, white light across the parade ground. The air was cool and smelled of dust kicked up by the dozen troops who stood at shabby attention outside the commandant's office, spiced by the faint horse odor of the empty cavalry stables.

Flintlock turned his head and looked at Abe Roper, who sat at smiling ease on a wooden rocker by the iron stove, a glass of whiskey in his hand.

"They ain't coming fer you, Abe, are they? Or me?" Flintlock said.

"Hell, no, we ain't done nothing in this neck o' the woods," Roper said. "Well, me an' Charlie drove a few rustled head down into Mexico a couple of weeks back, but that shouldn't bother the army none."

"The doctor's wearing his white coat and he just went into the major's office at a trot," Fong said.

"Maybe the major's feelin' poorly," Roper said. "Don't he get the croup now and then?"

"Hell, they wouldn't turn out the troops fer the croup," Flintlock said.

"If you're so all-fired interested, why don't you wander over there an' see what's goin' on, Sammy," Roper said. "Could be Indian trouble."

"God help us if ol' Geronimo attacks the fort," Flintlock said. "You should see what's passing for soldiers out there."

"It's funny," Charlie Fong said, grinning. "Hank Long the mess cook's out there and he can't button his soldier tunic over his big fat belly. Looks like that young Lieutenant Howard is yelling at him."

"He's a good cook though, Hank is," Roper said. "When he puts his mind to it, like, and stays sober."

"I hope he's a better cook than he is a soldier," Flintlock said. Then, after a moment, "Hell, I'm going over there."

"Wait, Sammy," Roper said. "You better take a real gun with you. If Geronimo attacks, your old Hawken won't do you any good. Hey, Charlie, give him Vince Lawson's guns."

As Fong stepped inside the cabin again, Flintlock said, "Won't ol' Vince need his guns?"

"Not in hell, he don't," Roper said. He read the question on Flintlock's face and added, "Vince got hung by a hemp posse."

"Friend of yourn, Abe?" Flintlock said.

"Business associate."

"Ah, then that explains it," Flintlock said.

Fong opened a brassbound trunk, unwrapped an oily green cloth and produced a blue Colt with a yellowed bone handle. The barrel had been cut back to the length of the ejector rod and there was no front sight.

"It's handy," Roper said. "You'll find cartridges on the shelf over there by the door."

Fong handed the Colt to Flintlock and laid a Winchester on the rough pine table. "Both .44 caliber, Sam'l. There's no leather for the revolver on account of how ol' Vince was a waistband-carrying man."

"Hell, if it was good enough for ol' Vince

that got hung, then it's good enough fer me." Flintlock examined the Colt and the rifle, then said, "I reckon I owe you twenty-five dollars, Abe."

"Sammy, you're gonna help make me rich, so forget about it," Roper said. "Call them guns a gift out of the goodness of my heart."

"You getting rich? You talking about the Golden Bell of Saint What's-Her-Name?" Flintlock said.

"Yeah, but we'll discuss it later, if the Apaches don't scalp us afore then."

Flintlock shoved the Colt in his waistband then pulled his buckskin shirt over the handle. "Then I'll mosey over to the soldiers and find out what's happening," he said.

"I'd load that revolver first if'n I was you, Sammy," Roper said.

"Damn, I plumb forgot," Flintlock said.

"You been carrying that damned Hawken too long, you ask me," Roper said.

Sam Flintlock walked into the moon-splashed night, past the tall wild oak that grew, despite all the odds, at the edge of the parade ground.

He was thirty-eight that spring, not forty as he claimed, short, stocky and as rough as a cob. A shock of unruly black hair showed under his battered straw hat and his eyes, gray as a sea mist, were deep set under shaggy eyebrows. His mustache was full, in the dragoon style, and he walked with the horseman's stiff-kneed gait. If he'd chosen to, he could've sold his clothes, including his boots, for ten cents.

Flintlock was tough, enduring, raised to be hard by hard men. But there was no cruelty in him, much honesty of tongue, and he had a quick, wry sense of humor. He liked whores, children and dogs and was kind to all of them.

He'd killed eight men, three as a lawman, the remainder since he turned bounty hunter. None of those dead men disturbed his sleep of nights and the only ghost he ever saw was that of wicked old Barnabas.

But Lieutenant Miles Howard was aware of none of these things.

As Flintlock walked toward him that night he made the snap judgment that here was a typical frontier tough, all horns and rattles, a far cry from any kind of gentleman. The man's throat was grotesque, tattooed with a bird of some kind. He was not the sort the lieutenant would care to meet at any kind of social gathering.

Flintlock's opening words did nothing to dispel that opinion.

"What the hell's happening?"

31

Howard looked Flintlock up and down before he answered, taking in the man's stained woolen pants, down-at-heel boots, battered shapeless hat and buckskin shirt, shiny black at the armpits and chest from ancient sweat. He didn't like what he saw.

"And you are?" he said.

"Sam'l Flintlock, me and my two compadres just rode in. And your name, sonny?"

Howard was outraged and he noisily slammed his saber closer to his side. "Second Lieutenant Miles Howard at your service." Then, after a pause, "What can I do for you?"

"We saw all you soldier boys lined up and wondered what the hell happened," Flintlock said. "You borrowed yourself some Indian trouble?"

The soldier's disdain for inquisitive civilians showed on the lieutenant's face. "Hostile Apaches attacked a hunting party from this post," he said. "Major Ashton was killed in the engagement and Captain Shaw was wounded. We fear an imminent attack by the hostiles." Howard's next words sounded more like a question than a statement of fact. "Though Apaches don't fight at night."

"They do when it suits them, Lieutenant," Flintlock said. He waved toward the motley collection of soldiers, still standing at shambling attention. "Is that all you've got?"

"Yes. Should the hostiles attack, my flying column will be more than enough to mount a stout and spirited defense."

Flintlock shook his head. "Then God help us," he said.

CHAPTER FIVE

The defenders of Fort Defiance stood to all night.

There was no Apache attack.

However, just before dawn, the flimsy timber door of Roper's cabin was attacked, with considerable force, by a gloved fist.

"Go away!" Abe Roper yelled. "Or I'll shoot ya right where you stand."

"Open up! This is Lieutenant Howard."

"Who?" Roper said.

Flintlock sat up in his blankets and yawned. "He's the ten-year-old kid I told you about. The one the army calls an officer."

Roper put on his hat, got to his feet and padded across the floor in his long-handled underwear. He opened the door just as Howard raised his fist to strike again.

The young officer saluted smartly and said, "Good morning, sir. I have a favor to ask."

Roper's voice was hoarse from smoke and whiskey. "You wake up a man in the middle of the night and then ask him to do you a favor?"

Taken aback, Howard said, "But, sir, it's five o'clock. Didn't you hear reveille?"

"Boy, that's for soldiers, not civilians," Roper said. "Now, get to —"

"What can we do for you, Lieutenant?" Flintlock said, stepping to the door. Like Roper, he wore only his long johns and hat.

"Ah, yes, good morning, Mr. . . . ah . . . Mr. . . ."

"Flintlock."

"Yes, yes, indeed, Mr. Flintlock. It's nice to make your acquaintance again."

"Tell us what you want, soldier boy, or my friend here is liable to shoot you out of spite," Flintlock said.

Howard had changed from his kepi to a wide-brimmed campaign hat and faded blue shirt adorned with his shoulder straps. He'd ditched his saber and carried only a revolver in a flapped holster.

"I need your help," Howard said.

"What kind of help?" Roper said, his voice edged with suspicion.

"I'm detailed to recover Major Ashton's body and I've procured a wagon for that purpose," Howard said.

"So?" Roper said.

"It's a small wagon," Howard said.

"I'm not catching your drift, son," Roper said. He turned his head to Flintlock. "Do you catch his drift?"

"I think so. You can't carry soldiers in the wagon, and even if you could, you know you can't turn a bunch of company clerks into Apache-fighting infantry," Flintlock said. He smiled. "Is that about the size of it, Lieutenant?"

For a few moments Howard was lost for words, but he finally managed, "Sergeant Tone saw you gentlemen ride in last night and he said you appeared to be well mounted and armed with repeating rifles. If we engage the Apaches, I'd appreciate your fire support."

"Not a chance, soldier boy," Roper said, making to close the door. "We make it a rule never to fight Apaches or any other kind of Injun. Live longer that way and have hair to comb."

Howard stuck his foot in the doorway. "I'm authorized by Captain Shaw to pay you five dollars each to take part in the expedition, ten if we encounter hostiles."

Roper shook his head. "No deal, boy. Now you run along like a good little soldier and tell Captain Shaw where he can stick his

36

five dollars."

"Very well," Howard said. Then, louder, "Sergeant Tone, burn down this cabin. It's been condemned as unfit for human occupation by the authority of Captain Shaw."

"Hey, you can't do that," Roper sputtered. "This is my cabin."

"The dwelling is on army property, so you're trespassing," Howard said. "Sergeant Tone, carry out my order."

A torch flared in the morning half-light and the big noncom marched toward the cabin, the flaming brand in one hand, a can of coal oil in the other.

The soldiers, looking more unkempt and sloppy after standing to all night, had their rifles trained on the door, and they seemed mean enough and angry enough to cut loose if they had to.

"Wait!" Roper yelled. "All right, we'll join the . . . whatever the hell you called it. Pat Tone, you damned mick, get away from here with that torch before you burn us all to death."

"Saw the light, huh, Abe?" Tone grinned. "It's about time and damn ye fer a benighted heathen."

"Damned micks, damned army, damned officers, damned Apaches," Roper said. "Then let's get it done." He made a stand, a small act of defiance. "But I ain't going nowhere without my coffee."

Howard said, "And you . . . ah . . . Mr. . . ."

"Flintlock."

"Yes, of course. Will you join us?"

"It ain't my cabin."

"Sam, if you don't ride with us to wipe the noses of the soldier boys, I'll take it hard," Roper said. "Besides that, I'll shoot you the first chance I get."

"You got a way with words, don't you, Abe?" Flintlock said.

"Well?"

"What's in it for me?"

"The golden bell."

"Ring-a-ding-ding," Flintlock said.

"What the hell does that mean?"

"It means I'll ride with you, Abe. But if the bell turns out to be a big windy, it's me who will shoot you the first chance I get."

"I suggest you gentlemen save your ammunition for the Apaches," Howard said. He looked at Roper. "There's coffee in the mess hall, and be quick about it."

"Thank God the hostiles didn't get a chance to mutilate Major Ashton's body," Lieutenant Howard said. "Captain Shaw was right, the major was indeed a gallant officer."

38

"Ain't he though," Flintlock said. "Hell, the major looks as good as new, lying there."

Howard chose to ignore that and said, "The spent cartridges tell the story. See how Captain Shaw stood over the major's body and drove off the hostiles with steady and courageous rifle fire."

"He deserves a medal," Flintlock said.

"And I'm sure he'll be awarded one of the highest order," Howard said, a single tear rolling down his plump young cheek. "He's a hero, like the gallant Custer."

"Hey, how come I scouted this whole meadow and didn't see any blood?" Flintlock said.

"Yeah, strange that," Charlie Fong said, chewing on a stem of grass.

"What do you mean?" Howard said.

"Well, if the captain done all this here shootin' and drove away Apaches who don't quit easy, you'd at least think he winged a couple."

"No blood on the grass," Fong said. And again, "Strange that."

The air was hot and close and smelled of distant rain.

"The reason is obvious to a thinking man," Howard said, slightly angry. "Obviously Captain Shaw put up such a stout defense that, despite suffering no casualties, the cowardly hostiles fled in confusion."

"Soldier boy, the Apaches are many things, most of them bad, but being cowards ain't one of them," Abe Roper said.

"Then I beg to differ," Howard said. "Fort Defiance drove off with ease attacks by hostiles twice in half a dozen years. Note, I say, with ease, Mr. Roper."

"Lieutenant, those were Navajo," Roper said. "When it comes to sand and meanness, a hundred of them don't stack up to a single Apache."

"I'm here to return Major Ashton's body to the fort, not to argue the point about savages," Howard said. He turned to the two sullen privates who'd come with the wagon. "You men, load the major's body. He's an officer and a gentleman, remember. Treat him with all due respect for his rank."

As the two soldiers struggled to load the major's body into the wagon, Roper took Flintlock aside.

"What do you reckon, Sammy?" he said.

"The captain never fit Apaches here, I reckon that much. No bloodstains in the grass out there, no horse tracks, no spent shells."

"Why the hell would he lie about it?"

"Well, he and the major were deer hunting. Shaw might've plugged the man by accident and then skedaddled."

"Yeah, after he fired a few rounds over Ashton's body to back up his Apache story and then shot himself in the leg," then added, "Makes sense," Roper said. "What do you think, Charlie?"

"Good an explanation as any," Fong said. "Sam's right, there's no sign that Apaches were ever here."

"He could've done it on purpose," Roper said.

"You mean Shaw murdered him?" Flintlock said.

"Maybe so."

"Why?"

Roper shrugged. "Who knows?"

"A woman maybe?" Flintlock said.

"You seen Ashton's wife? Shaw didn't murder his commanding officer over her."

"Then it was an accident."

"I don't know what it was," Roper said. "Do we care?"

"No, I guess not," Flintlock said. "But I got the feeling there's something mighty strange goin' on around here."

Roper grinned. "I declare, Sammy, you're like an old maiden aunt who hears a rustle in every bush."

"Maybe I am," Flintlock said. "Or maybe I'm not."

Chapter Six

"So, how you like the Old Crow sippin' whiskey, Sam'l?" Abe Roper said.

"Besides Robert E. Lee, it's the best thing that ever came out of the South," Flintlock said.

He set his glass on the floor beside his rickety chair, one of only two in the cabin. "Abe, tell me about the bell," he said.

"Gettin' gold fever, Sam?" Charlie Fong grinned.

"Gettin' curious, Charlie," Flintlock said.

"That's what killed the cat, Sammy," Roper said.

"So let the cat out of the bag and we'll see what happens," Flintlock said.

"All right, first the story, then I'll tell you where it happened. That set fine by you?"

"Story away."

"Once upon a time . . ."

"I like it already," Flintlock said.

"There was a Spanish mission, at a place

north of here," Roper said. "For two hundred years the holy monks took care of the local Indians, converted them to the one true faith and did many good works."

Flintlock ran an oily cloth over the barrel of the Hawken. "You should've been a preacher, Abe," he said. "When you try, you're a fine-talking man."

"Thought about it for a spell, but then I figured I was more suited to the bank-robbing profession."

"You were cut out fer that, all right, Abe," Charlie Fong said.

"Thanks, Charlie, I appreciate it," Roper said, bowing his head in acknowledgment of the compliment.

"So, the holy monks are going about baptizing folks and doin' good works, then what?" Flintlock said. His entire attention seemed to be focused on scraping a speck of rust off the Hawken's barrel with his thumbnail.

"Well, suddenly the monks was in a heap of trouble," Roper said. "Bad stuff comin' down, if'n you catch my drift."

"You don't say?"

"I do say. See, how it come up, over the years the Indians brought the monks all kinds of gold as presents, like. I mean, they knew how all white men love gold and the

43

monks were no exception."

"Just like us, Abe," Charlie Fong said.

"Truer words was never spoke, Charlie," Flintlock said. "I hate to break it to you, but you're not just like us. You ain't a white man, Charlie."

"No, I'm a yellow man."

"Close, but no ceegar," Flintlock said.

"Now where was I? Oh yeah, the gold the Injuns was bringing was raw, nuggets and dust most likely, not golden rings and chalices an' the like," Roper said. "The monks ended up with quite a poke, but then they got nervous."

"How come?" Flintlock said. "I never seen a nervous monk."

"Well, them old monks was nervous right enough. It seems that the king o' Spain's tax collector got wind of the stash and it was in his mind to . . . what's that word, Charlie?"

"Confiscate."

"Oh yeah, confiscate the gold and send it back to Spain for the king to spend on women and whiskey."

Flintlock laid the now gleaming Hawken across his knees. "Harsh thing that, robbin' holy monks who did nothin' but good works," he said.

"It was all of that. But then the monks

44

put their heads together and came up with a plan."

"This is when the story gets good," Fong said, grinning.

"So let me tell it, Charlie, huh?" Roper said.

"Go right ahead, Abe. Sorry, but I always get excited at this part."

Roper glared at Fong for a few moments, then said, "Well, anyhoo, the monks did two things — they made a cast for a bell —"

"What kind of bell?" Flintlock said.

"A big bell. How would I know what kind of bell?"

"Well, there's a hand bell and a —"

"A big bell, like I said. Sammy, it was a big bell, all right?"

Flintlock nodded. "Fine. A church bell. Go right ahead, Abe."

"I swear, you're a worse interrupter than Charlie," Roper said.

"So the monks melted down the gold an' cast it into a bell," Flintlock said.

"Yeah, that's what they did all right, made a big bell."

"Wouldn't the tax collector notice a big golden bell?" Flintlock said. "I mean, it would be pretty obvious."

"The monks thought of that. They painted the bell black, rubbed rust onto the surface

45

and then hung it above the entrance to the mission. The tax collector rode under the bell and never knew it was made of solid gold."

Flintlock built a cigarette and without looking up, said, "How heavy was the big bell?"

"I knew you'd get around to askin' that, Sam'l. Are you ready fer this?"

"I guess I am. But I'm holding my breath."

"It weighs two thousand pounds of pure, shining gold."

"How much is that in American money?" Flintlock said.

"Tell him, Charlie," Roper said. "I want to see his face."

"Sixty-five thousand dollars and a few cents, more or less," Fong said. "Big bell, big money, Sam."

"How did they get it up there?" Flintlock said.

Roper was puzzled. "Get what up there?"

"The big bell. If it weighs as much as you say it does, how did they hang it above the mission gate?"

"Pulleys and willing hands," Roper said. "How the hell should I know? Sammy, you sure ask some dumb questions."

"All right, then here's another dumb question: Where do I come in?"

"That ain't dumb, it's a true-blue question as ever was," Roper said.

"Then answer it," Flintlock said.

"We need your gun, Sam'l. That's how come I saved you from gettin' hung. I mean, once I knowed it was really you."

"I smell a rat," Flintlock said. "Damnit, I'm sure I smell a rat."

"And no wonder. By anybody's reckoning, it's a real big rat," Charlie Fong said.

"How big?" Flintlock said. For the first time that night he felt uneasy.

"How about Asa Pagg big?" Roper said.

Those words hit Flintlock like five hard jabs to the belly.

"You've got to be joking," he said. "You want me to say ha-ha, right?"

"No joke," Roper said. "He's in this neck of the woods. How we know, we heard he'd killed a man at a settlement down in the Zuni Buttes country of the New Mexico Territory."

"Asa always operates south of the Mogollon Rim," Flintlock said. "It's his home range and he never budges."

"He's budged," Roper said.

"He still run with Logan Dean an' Joe Harte an' them?" Flintlock said.

"I don't know."

"Why is he here, Abe?" Flintlock said.

47

He figured he already knew the answer to that question and Roper confirmed it. "We think, me an' Charlie, that maybe he heard about the golden bell."

"How?"

Roper looked at Charlie Fong.

"Sam, the way it was told to us, a prospector was up in the Red Rock Valley when he got caught in a snowstorm," Fong said. "Well, he headed west into the Carrizo Mountains and took refuge in a cave."

"And he saw the bell," Flintlock said.

"Yeah . . . a huge bell made of solid gold. He says the sight of it made him sick and he didn't stay long."

"Was he sober?" Flintlock said.

"Sober enough to know he couldn't move two thousand pounds of gold by himself," Roper said.

"So he came to you," Flintlock said.

"Nope, we happened on him by chance in a saloon down Silver City way," Roper said. "That was a two-month ago."

"And he told you the story about the monks and the gold and you believed him?"

"Not right off, we didn't. Ain't that right, Charlie?"

"Damn right . . . until the old-timer showed us a map he'd made of the mountains and an *X* marking the cave," Fong said. "Then we figured he was telling the truth."

"Tinpans tell big stories, everybody knows that," Flintlock said. "How much did you pay him for the map?"

"Not one thin dime," Roper said. "He said his time was short, on account of how he couldn't breathe, and if we found the bell and sold it, we were to send some of the money to his widowed sister in Richmond. Give us a paper with her address an' all. Said the lady's husband wore the gray and fell at Gettysburg. A man doesn't lie about a thing like that."

"Then how did Asa Pagg get wind of the bell?" Flintlock said.

Roper smiled as he admired the amber glow of his whiskey.

"Sammy," he said, "a man can have an *affaire d'amour* with the wife of the president of these United States and keep it a secret. But if a man strikes pay dirt in a wilderness, within a week he finds himself in the middle of a gold rush."

"In other words, when gold's involved, word gets around," Fong said.

"So your dying prospector got drunk an' blabbed," Flintlock said.

"Maybe so," Roper said.

"Where the hell did you pick up fancy

words like *affaire d'amour?* You goin' back to school or something?" Flintlock said.

"Nah, an El Paso whore teached that to me," Roper said. "I took a shine to it, like."

"Educated whore," Flintlock said.

"No, she wasn't. She was a French gal, from up Canada way, and she was as dumb as dirt."

"All right, then why me, Abe?"

"Call yourself a gift from heaven, Sam'l. I knowed it when I sprung you from that rube jail —"

"Blew me up, you mean."

"Don't be so harsh, Sam," Charlie Fong said. "We figured you had one chance in ten of surviving the gunpowder. Them's better odds than the hangman would've given you of walking away after the drop."

"To anybody but a Chinaman, them's lousy odds," Flintlock said. "But go ahead, Abe. Why me?"

"Because I can't shade Asa Pagg, but you can," Roper said. "Charlie, can I say it any plainer than that? Am I right or am I wrong?"

"No, sir, you're right and you can't say it plainer," Fong said.

"And study on this, Sammy," Roper said. "If for some reason we don't find the big bell, last time I looked, Asa had a five-thousand reward on his head, dead or alive. Gun ol' Asa and in a manner of speakin' you'd be mixing business with pleasure. Ain't that right, Charlie?"

"Truer words was never spoke," Fong said.

"So what do you say, Sam'l?" Roper said.

"Like you said, I'll study on it," Flintlock said. "I admit that the bounty on Asa Pagg kinda tilts the scales in your favor."

"Just don't sit on your gun hand too long," Roper said. "We're riding out as soon as Jack Coffin gets here."

"I never liked that breed," Flintlock said. "He still collect trigger fingers?"

"As far as I know," Roper said. "You don't have to like him, Sammy. Who the hell does? But if the tinpan's map ain't exact, he'll find that cave for us."

"I may gun him," Flintlock said. "He's a disgrace to the bounty-hunting profession."

"Sure, but wait until after he finds the cave."

"And the golden bell," Charlie Fong said.

CHAPTER SEVEN

Captain Owen Shaw sat his horse in a moonlit glade among the pines.

Nearby an owl asked his question of the night and in the distance a pair of hunting coyotes yipped one to the other in the shadowed foothills. The shallow depth of the meadow's lilac light did not extend beyond the trees, and darkness lay among them like spilled ink.

Through this gloom appeared a rider who bulked large in the saddle, his mount picking its way like an antelope through the pines.

Shaw let the man come. He'd left his revolver behind so as to present no threat, real or imagined.

The rider drew rein. He was a tall, bearded man, the upper half of his face lost in shadow under his wide-brimmed hat. He wore a long, Confederate army greatcoat, much frayed and patched, and his two

Remingtons in shoulder holsters made his wide chest look even broader.

Now he lifted his head to the moonlight, smiling, wrinkles at the corners of his eyes drawn tight as cheese-cutting wire.

"Howdy, Captain Shaw," the rider said. He smiled. "Fancy meeting you here."

"Asa. Good to see you again."

"The feeling's mutual, I'm sure," Asa Pagg said. "You got a bandage on your leg. You stop a bullet?"

"Had to make the killing of Major Ashton look good."

Pagg took time to light a cigar, then said, "Talk to me."

"Everything is going to plan, Asa. We take the money at the fort, head for Mexico and live high on the hog for the rest of our lives."

"What are the chances of the cavalry coming back?"

"None. They're still in the field and will be for another month at least."

"Unless they catch up with Geronimo."

"They won't."

"How many fighting men at the post?"

Shaw snorted a laugh. "Fighting men? None."

"Don't bandy words with me, Captain," Pagg said, his voice edged. "How many?"

"Two officers and fourteen enlisted men,

three of them in sick bay."

"I don't like the odds."

"Clerks, cooks and malingerers," Shaw said. "Like I told you, they're not fighting men." His horse tossed its head and the bridle chimed. "How many of your boys can I expect?"

"Just me and two others."

"That's it? That's all?"

"If your garrison is as useless as you say, it's enough."

"What about the escort?"

"We'll take care of them first."

Shaw looked worried. "Asa, I don't like it. We're too thin on the numbers."

"Then there's more to go around, I say," Pagg said. As though he'd suddenly made up his mind about something, he added, "I'm coming into the fort."

Shaw looked more worried still. "Is that wise?"

"Who the hell knows me at Fort Defiance, a damned wart on the ass of the U.S. Army? I need to get the lie of the land, see what I'm facing once the shooting starts. Maybe I'll organize a few killings to whittle down the numbers, like."

Pagg stared at Shaw, then grinned. "Look at you, a fine officer and a gentleman so scared you're about to piss your pants. What

54

did you expect when you threw in with the likes of me?"

"Maybe we're wrong about this, Asa. Maybe it's too big for us."

"It ain't too big. A hundred thousand dollars split four ways ain't too big."

"If I'm caught, the army will hang me," Shaw said.

"Yeah, well it's too late for second thoughts. If I figure you're turning yellow on me I'll —"

"I'll stick, Asa," Shaw said. "It's . . . it's . . . maybe it's just that killing Major Ashton was easy, but the rest seems so hard."

"Hell, it's always easy to kill a man," Pagg said. "But you're right, making money is hard."

"When will you come into the fort, Asa?"

"Right now seems as good a time as any. You got a place for me and the boys to spread our blankets?"

"Yes, there's a civilian cabin you can have. Only problem is that three men are already living there."

"That's not a problem. We'll take care of it."

Pagg turned in the saddle and trilled a bird call.

Two men rode out of the trees and Pagg

said to Shaw, "You remember my associates, Mr. Logan Dean and Mr. Joe Harte?"

"I remember," Shaw said. He was uneasy — Dean and Harte were both named and deadly gunmen. He'd set this scheme in motion with the murder of Major Ashton, but now it seemed to be moving too fast, slipping beyond his control.

Two weeks before, after Asa Pagg had responded to Shaw's wire and agreed to meet him in Gallup in the New Mexico Territory, the railhead for the Atlantic and Pacific Railroad, Pagg had taken him aside and warned him about the gunmen.

"Logan Dean will cut any man, woman and child in half with a shotgun for fifty dollars," he'd said. "Step careful around him. He's poison with the Colt, lightning fast on the draw and shoot. Same goes for Joe Harte. He's a quiet one all right, reads poetry an' such, but he's a contract killer and to my certain knowledge he's gunned eighteen white men."

Asa Pagg himself was a man to be reckoned with, an outlaw and sometime lawman who was fast on the draw and had killed more than his share. If he'd ever had a conscience it had shriveled up and died a long time ago. He was a hard, merciless man and there was no kindness in him.

Used to disciplined soldiers who obeyed his commands without question, Shaw was suddenly faced with men who would not accept orders and would choose their own way.

Could he control such men?

The captain had no answer to that question and it troubled him greatly.

"Well, Captain Shaw" — Pagg waved a hand toward the fort — "shall we proceed?"

"Asa, I need a drink," Logan Dean said. He looked like a cross between a man and a rat. Then, to Shaw, "You got a saloon in your fort, soldier boy?"

Shaw let the disrespect go. Later there would be bigger things to argue about.

"There's a sutler's store with a bar," he said.

"Suits us," Pagg said. "First a drink or two then we'll move into our cabin."

CHAPTER EIGHT

"The sutler is a Scotsman by the name of Angus McCarty," Abe Roper said. "He's a fair man, but I don't know how much he'd charge you for powder and ball."

"Well, I want to shoot the old Hawken, so I'll have a word with him," Sam Flintlock said.

"He's got an old powder horn. I seen it hanging on his wall. He might sell it cheap."

"Ol' Barnabas could shoot a squirrel off a tree branch at a hundred yards with the Hawken," Flintlock said. "Of course, there wasn't much left of the squirrel after he got hit with a .50 caliber ball."

"Talk to McCarty, Sam'l," Roper said. "He'll do you right."

"I sure will after I get a few bucks ahead. Damn sheriff took all my money. Said it would pay for my bacon, beans and coffee."

"Damned bandit," Charlie Fong said. "Lawmen are all damned bandits."

"Hell, Sammy, I'll stake you," Roper said. "You can pay me back when we find the golden bell."

Flintlock shook his head. "Nah, Abe, borrowing money doesn't set well with me. Barnabas always told me, 'Neither a loaner nor a borrower be.' "

"It's an investment, Sammy, not a loan. If that old cannon shoots as well as you say, it could come in handy if we run up against Asa Pagg an' them."

"And besides, a stroll over to the sutler's will do us all good," Charlie Fong said. "Get us some fresh air, like."

"All right, Abe, but it's a loan," Flintlock said. "I'll pay you back once I'm flush."

"Hell, Sam, there's sixteen balls to the pound an' powder's cheap," Fong said. "We're not talking about a fortune here."

Flintlock nodded. "Charlie, for a Chinaman sometimes you sure make sense."

Four soldiers sat at a table and McCarty, a tall, lean man with cool gray eyes and a stern set of jaw, stood behind the bar, dusting bottles.

"What can I do for you gentlemen?" he said. There was no friendliness in his voice, but no hostility either.

Flintlock laid the Hawken on the bar. "I

need powder and ball for this here rifle," Flintlock said. "I was told you have some."

"A fine weapon," McCarty said. "And well cared for."

"Yeah, and it's in .50 caliber."

"Young man, back in the olden days, the mountain men did not speak of caliber." McCarty picked up the rifle. "This rifle was referred to as a thirty-five gauge or a sixteen-balls-to-the-pound Hawken. Its caliber is in fact fifty-one, not fifty."

"Well, McCarty, do you have any of them kind of balls?" Roper said.

"I do indeed. Old stock, since there's not much call for them nowadays."

"And powder and patches?" Flintlock said.

"Yes, I can supply those," McCarty said. He eyed the thunderbird that covered most of Flintlock's throat, his worn buckskin shirt, battered hat and general shabbiness and added, "If you have the wherewithal to pay."

"He can pay," Roper said. "And how much for the powder horn on the wall over there?"

"Ah, a rare item indeed," McCarty said. "That one is made from buffalo horn and it's seen some use."

He crossed the floor, took the powder horn from the wall and returned to the bar.

The horn had yellowed from age, and carved into its side it bore the legend:

THOS. WATSON HIS HORN

"Ever hear of Thos Watson, Sam'l?" Roper said.

"He wasn't one of Barnabas's cronies," Flintlock said.

"How much?" Roper said to McCarty.

"For a horn like that, with a name on it and all, I couldn't let it go for any less than twenty dollars," McCarty said.

"I'll give you five."

"Done."

Roper stuck out his hand. "And done."

McCarty shook Roper's hand, then said, "Now I'll fill the rest of the order."

But he stayed where he was when the door opened and three men stepped inside.

Asa Pagg stopped in the doorway for a moment, glanced at the soldiers and gave a little grunting laugh of contempt. His eyes swept the sutler's store and settled on Abe Roper.

Pagg nodded. "Abe."

"Howdy, Asa," Roper said. "Fer piece off your home range, ain't you?"

"You could say that. I got business in this neck of the woods." He waved a hand. "You

61

know my associates."

"Howdy, Joe. Logan."

"How's things, Abe?" Logan said.

"Oh, keepin' busy, Logan. You know how it is."

"I know how it is."

"Chinese Charlie, ain't nobody shot you fer bein' an uppity Celestial yet?" Pagg said.

"Not yet, Asa," Fong said, smiling. "I'm still here as ever was."

"Maybe that's just as well. Be a pity to gun a good cook," Pagg said.

Pagg walked to the bar and said, "Three whiskeys." Without turning his head, he said, "Howdy, Sam. Still got the thunderbird, huh?"

"Good to see you, Asa," Flintlock said. "I can't get rid of the bird, unless I get skun."

"Maybe Geronimo will oblige you. The bird would look good on his rifle stock." Now Pagg glanced at the Hawken lying on the bar. "Armed to the teeth, I see."

Dean and Harte grinned, and Flintlock said, "It's a family heirloom."

"Don't go shootin' off a thumb with that thing," Pagg said.

"It's happened," McCarty said.

Pagg looked at the Scotsman as though seeing him for the first time. "How would you know?"

"I heard."

"Yeah, well, you're here to serve drinks, so shut your trap when white men are talking."

McCarty, used to dealing with drunk and belligerent soldiers, would not step back from any man and his anger flared.

Flintlock moved quickly to defuse what could easily turn into a killing situation.

"What brings you to Fort Defiance, Asa?" he said. "If you don't mind me asking."

Pagg scraped his eyes away from McCarty, but they were still burning with black fire as he looked at Flintlock and said, "A business opportunity."

Flintlock was aware of Roper and Fong exchanging glances.

"What kind of business?" Flintlock said. "Anything that might ring a bell with me?"

The expression on Pagg's face didn't change. "Still a questioning man, ain't you, Sam? Well, my business here is confidential." Then, a nod to Flintlock's own commercial interests. "I'm not hunting a bounty on this trip."

"Glad to hear that, Asa," Flintlock said. But Pagg was already talking over him. "Abe, you the feller that lives in a cabin here at the fort?"

"Sure do, Asa, me and Charlie and Flint-lock," Roper said. "We'll be moving on in a couple of days."

"The captain feller told me I could have that there cabin," Pagg said. "Me and the boys need a place to bed down, like."

Like a man stands on his porch and sees the lightning coming, Flintlock was suddenly wary. If Pagg pressed a claim to the cabin, Roper would resist and guns would be skinned.

Mentally, Flintlock calculated what could happen next.

The sutler's store was small, close and windowless, lit by three oil lamps that hung from the ceiling. If shooting started the concussion of the guns would blow out the lamps and six men would gunfight in pitch darkness.

If there was anybody left standing after McCarty opened his door to let the smoke clear, it would be a miracle.

But Asa Pagg was no fool. He knew as well as Flintlock did what pushing a gunfight might mean.

Abe Roper was good with a gun, Flintlock better, and the Chinaman could be sneaky. All three had sand and there was no back-up in any of them.

"Well, hell, we got an empty old fort here," Pagg said, smiling, as though he was everybody's friend. "I'm sure the captain

64

can find us another place to bunk."

Roper, a thinking man, figured that for now at least he should extend an olive branch. "You're welcome to bed down with us, Asa," he said. "But six men in my small cabin could be a crowd."

"Nah, I'll talk to the officer." He drained his glass. "Let's go, boys."

Pagg stepped to the door, then turned. "Hey, Sam," he said, grinning, "I ain't near as stupid as you think. Anything that might ring a bell with me, you said. Well, that tickled me. The story of the golden bell is just that, a story, and only a rube would fall for it. If you boys reckon you'll find it, think again. The army and every damned gold hunter in the West has searched for the bell for years and nobody's found it yet."

Pagg grinned. "And you know why? Because it ain't there."

He followed Dean and Harte out the door, but before slamming it shut behind him he turned his head and threw over his shoulder, "Go home, boys. You're wasting your time."

CHAPTER NINE

The boy led the old man to the cave entrance where the woman waited.

When the man appeared, the woman bowed low and extended the round loaf of bread she held.

"For you, great lord," she said. "It is but a small offering."

The boy took the bread and placed it in the old man's hands because he was nearly blind and his eyes were the color of milk.

After a while the man smelled the bread and he smiled. "It is a fine gift," he said.

"The loaf is made from the finest wheat flour and I baked it myself, great lord," the Mexican woman said. She bowed again. "I hope you will enjoy the bread, lord, and I ask that you do not enter my home where my husband lies very sick."

"Why do you ask me this thing, child?" the old man said.

"Because you are the Angel of Death sent

by the holy Santa Muerte to collect the souls of those who have passed away. This is well-known in my village and it has been so for many years."

The woman was very afraid, but she said, "Aiii, you are truly a great and powerful lord and I beg you not to take my poor husband from me."

The old man wore the rough, brown robes of a monk. He was very thin and the skin of his face was tight to the bones so that he bore the same features as the holy Santa Muerte . . . a yellow skull.

"Woman, don't you know why the great lord is here?" the boy said. He was ten, with a shock of black hair and eyes of the same color.

"Yes, *chico,* he guards the golden bell that the devil cast down from heaven in a rage," the woman said. "But he is also the *Angel de la Muerte* and is to be feared by such as me and mine."

"Woman, you have nothing to fear from me," the old man said. "Go back down the mountain to your village. No harm will come to your husband. He will rise from his bed and be well again."

The woman bowed. "Thank you, great lord."

"I will say a prayer for him," the old man

said. "I will ask our God that your husband will soon be in good health."

The old man watched the woman walk through spring wildflowers down the hill that led to the cave, her bright red skirt eddying around her legs in the high country wind.

That same wind tossed the old man's white, shoulder-length hair as he placed his hand on the boy's head and said, "We will go into the cave. I have a story to tell."

"You must eat first, Grandfather," the boy said.

He led the old man inside the cave and settled him into a finely carved chair that once belonged to a noble Spanish conquistador. He tore a piece from the bread and then found some goat cheese. These he placed in the old man's hands. His hands were the color of ivory, seamed with blue veins.

"Eat," the boy said. "You must keep up your strength, Grandfather."

And so the old man ate, and when he was finished he said, "I had a dream last night that troubled me so much, I woke from sleep with a start and felt afraid."

"What kind of terrible dream could trouble you so?" the boy said.

"I saw a man, a fearsome man who bore

an ancient rifle."

"And what did this man say to you?"

"Nothing. He said nothing."

"Then what did he do, this man?"

"He sat in a chair, as I sit in this one, and the rifle leaned against the chair and the rifle stock was bright with polished brass."

"Aiii, it was a fine rifle."

"Indeed, little one, a very fine rifle and of great age. But the man did not touch the rifle because he held a green apple in his hands and he peeled the skin with a sharp steel knife."

"But this is not a bad dream, Grandfather," the boy said.

"Until then, it was not. But I walked into the room where the man sat and he wore a shirt of animal skin and his eyes were the color of smoke."

"Ah, then he was a fearsome man," the boy said.

"Yes, and he turned to me and he smiled and said, 'Soon I will come and steal your bell.'"

"And what else did he say?"

"Nothing more, for then I woke in the dark and was afraid because the man had a great thunderbird tattooed on his throat and it was a terrible sight to see."

The boy reached out and took the old

man's frail hand in his. "We will fight him," he said.

"I am too old to fight, and you are too young. But I will pray that I find a way to defeat this man."

The boy was silent for a while, and then he said, "The holy bell of Santa Elena is very precious, is it not?"

"Yes, it is. We will guard it until the day the Spanish monks return and take it away."

"Then God surely will help us," the boy said.

"A green apple," Abe Roper said. "Is that your breakfast?"

Flintlock shook his head. "There's a barrel of them in the sutler's. I figured I'd give one a try."

He finished peeling the apple, held a slice between the Barlow blade and his thumb and popped it into his mouth.

"Ahh . . . hell . . . the damned thing's sour enough to pucker a hog's butt," Flintlock said, making a face.

"Them green apples are for pies, Sam," Charlie Fong said. "They need sugar. You should know that."

Flintlock grinned and threw the apple at Fong's head. "Then make a pie with that one, Charlie."

Fong ducked, the apple hit the wall, and Roper said, "I hope your aim with the Hawken's better than that."

"I didn't much reckon on shooting it," Flintlock said.

"Hell, after you got all that powder and ball, you're gonna shoot it," Roper said. "After breakfast we'll head out and see how you do with the old smoke pole." He smiled. "Make your old grandpappy proud, Sam'l."

"Barnabas had a good eye," Flintlock said as he pulled on a boot.

"So do you, Sam," Fong said.

"Yeah, at spittin' distance. All the men I've killed, I killed real close."

"Like me, you're a draw fighter, Sammy," Roper said. "Real close goes with the profession. I never met a one that was any good with a long gun, an' that includes ol' Wild Bill hisself."

"Close up, you look into a man's eyes when your bullet hits him, right at the moment he knows it's all up with him," Flintlock said. He shook his head. "That's not a sight for a white man to see." He looked at Charlie Fong. "Or for a yellow man to see either."

"Like I said, it goes with the profession," Roper said. "Bang-bang, close enough to hug each other."

"Don't it bother you none, Abe?" Flintlock said.

"Nope. And if it did, I'd get into a different line of work." He stared hard at Flintlock. "Bother you?"

"I don't know. Maybe there's something to be said for killing a man at a distance. You can't see his damned eyes."

"Then let's shoot the old Hawken. Mc-Carty says it's sighted in at a hundred and twenty-five yards. Hell, Sammy, you can't look into a man's eyes at that distance."

After sharing the enlisted men's breakfast of salt pork, beans and hardtack, Flintlock and the others picked up some empty bottles from the sutler and walked into the foothills about half a mile from the fort.

"You ever walk behind a plow, Sam'l?" Roper said as they stepped through the clear light of the new aborning day.

"Can't say as I have," Flintlock said. "Old Barnabas knew nothing about farming."

"I did. My pa was a farmer, or he tried to be. Here's a word of advice, Sammy, never feel inclined to plow the land. All you see the livelong day is a mule's ass. Now, when a man works from the back of a horse he can see across the country as far as his eye is good."

"You done some cowboyin', Abe?" Flint-lock said. "I never knowed that."

"Sure I did. Went up the trail for the first time when I was fourteen."

"Hell, you think you know a man and it turns out that you don't," Flintlock said. "Doesn't that beat all?"

"There's a lot to know. Me, I've been a lawman, stagecoach guard, bank robber, back to lawman again, bounty hunter, and wunst I was a dishwasher at one o' them fancy restaurants in Denver. But that didn't last. I must have broke a hundred o' cups an' plates afore they cut me adrift."

"A man who washes dishes must know how to take care," Charlie Fong said. "Or he'll break many."

"Is that one o' your wise Chinaman say-ings, Charlie?" Roper said.

"Well, I just made it up, but I guess it is."

"Then pace off a hundred and twenty-five steps from here and set them bottles up," Roper said. "That's a wise white man sayin'."

They'd stopped in a grassy cut between two tall hills crested with aspen and a few scattered juniper. There was no wind and the morning was already hot, the sun climb-ing in a blue sky that looked like an up-turned ceramic bowl. Insects made their small music in the grass and jays quarreled in the tree branches.

Charlie Fong, taking giant steps, paced off the required distance then dragged a dead tree trunk from the brush. He set up six bottles on the trunk then yelled, "How's that?"

"Good, Charlie," Roper said. "Now get back here. We don't want Sammy shootin' an ounce of lead into you." He turned to Flintlock and in a normal tone of voice said, "You know how to load that thing?"

"Of course I know," Flintlock said. "Old Barnabas taught me."

"Then let's see if you can shoot it. I guess Barnabas taught you that as well."

Flintlock loaded the Hawken, drew a bead on the bottle on the extreme left and fired.

The glass bottle shattered into a shower of shards.

His ears ringing, Flintlock lowered the rifle and said, his voice sounding hollow in his head, "Dead center."

Roper said something, but the roar of a Winchester drowned out his words.

The remaining five bottles exploded, one after the other, in the space of a couple of seconds.

Asa Pagg took his rifle from his shoulder and grinned.

"Hell, Asa, what did you do that fer?" Flintlock said. "I wasn't done shootin' yet."

"It would take you all day to get five more shots off with that old blunderbush, Sam, and I've got news that can't wait."

"That was good shootin', Asa," Charlie Fong said. "An' we was just saying that gun-fighting men don't shoot a long gun worth a damn."

"Well you was wrong, an' me not even half tryin'," Pagg said. "Of course, a pistol fighter needs to get up close with a rifle."

He wore a faded red bib-front shirt, black bandana, and his brown wool pants were tucked into mule-eared boots. His hat was also black, with a wide, tooled-leather band edged with woven silver. Perhaps to appear less threatening, he'd set aside his revolvers. The little finger of his left hand bore a large gold signet, engraved with the words *"Mi amor,"* and overall, Pagg looked prosperous.

"When you get done with your braggin', Asa, maybe you'll tell us your news," Flint-lock said. The wanton destruction of his bottles still stung.

"Well, it's for Abe," Pagg said. "Guess who just rode into Fort Defiance as bold as brass?"

"I'd guess Jack Coffin," Roper said.

Pagg looked disappointed. "How did you know?"

"I'm hiring him. He's scouting for us."

It didn't take Pagg long to work it out.

"Hell, you want him to find the golden bell for you, huh?"

Roper said nothing and Pagg grinned. "I swear, if brains were dynamite you boys couldn't blow the wax out of your ears. You know the breed is liable to cut your throats in your sleep?"

"We'll take our chances," Roper said.

"Abe, Coffin is half Jicarilla Apache an' they don't come any meaner. His other half was ol' Hack Coffin, him that ate his Kiowa squaw one winter up on the Flathead River country to keep hisself from starving."

"That ain't quite true, Asa," Charlie Fong said. "Hack and the Kiowa squaw ate the lady's grandmother, is what happened. Ol' Hack always said the old woman was as tough on the teeth as wet rawhide. He got hung in Tombstone you know, ol' Hack, for always gettin' drunk an' being a damned nuisance."

"How you know so much about it, Charlie?" Flintlock said.

"I cooked for the Clantons an' them when they had a ranch at Lewis Springs, west of Tombstone. Hack used to stop by for a visit

76

and a feed, and he'd come into the cook-house for coffee and we'd get to talking."

"Then I stand corrected," Pagg said, his black eyes as hard as obsidian. "Just don't correct me too often, huh, Charlie?"

"Only setting the record straight, Asa," Fong said. "No offense."

Not for the first time, Flintlock wondered at Charlie Fong.

He was a small, thin man with expressive brown eyes and a ready, genuine smile. Charlie claimed to be about forty, but he could've been any age. He never openly carried a gun, but always had a .38 caliber Smith & Wesson about him somewhere. Apologetic and inoffensive, he spoke softly and never started or encouraged a quarrel.

Yet Charlie had consorted with hard, violent men and had been a member of the notorious Tong gang along San Francisco's Barbary Coast where shootings and cuttings were an everyday occurrence and life was cheap.

Flintlock teased Charlie mercilessly and when they met it was an ongoing thing between them. But he'd never pushed the little man to anger and never would.

Once a Tong, always a Tong, and behind Charlie Fong's mild Oriental façade was a man to be reckoned with.

Flintlock had his Colt in the waistband of his pants, otherwise he would've never asked the question that he did now.

"Asa," he said, "you make light of the golden bell. You wouldn't be after it yourself, would you?"

The stunned, disbelieving expression on Pagg's face answered Flintlock's question.

"Didn't I already tell you idiots that there is no golden bell?" he said. "It's a . . . hell, what's the word I'm looking for, Charlie?"

"Myth," Fong said.

"Yeah, that's it, a myth. The bell doesn't exist. It never existed. Now get that through your thick heads and go do something useful like robbing a bank."

Pagg shook his head, turned and walked away. The he stopped and said, "Abe, I'll tell Jack Coffin that you want him to go into the mountains and lead you to a giant golden bell."

He roared laughter through his words. "Hell, that ought to make him real happy."

His name was Kuruk, a sixteen-year-old Mescalero warrior with black, glittering eyes that had watched the white men shooting in the gulch.

When the men left he crouched among the aspen for a while, then rose and walked silently to his horse.

Geronimo would want to hear of this, that there were white men at the fort that had not been counted before.

Kuruk smiled. Geronimo would tell him he'd brought good news . . . that there were now more whites to kill.

CHAPTER TEN

The land that lay around Sergeant Tim O'Neil and Privates Oscar Werner and Jacob Spooner was vast; endless distances in all directions that had never been measured, dominated by the blue and red mesas and skyscraping cliffs that made up the Sonsela Buttes country.

The mirrors had been talking for the past hour and O'Neil was worried. That went double for the two eighteen-year-olds under his command.

Spooner was an orphan from New York's Five Corners, a towheaded runt who'd missed too many meals as a child, and Werner hailed from a cuckoo-clock village in the Bavarian Alps and could speak little English.

They were thirty miles north of Fort Defiance, in a land without shadow. The sun was lost in a brassy sky and about them heat shimmered as though the earth was melting.

"Well, they're here all right," O'Neil said. "Talking mirrors and Apache sign all over the place."

"Maybe the column will show up, Sarge, huh?" Spooner said. He'd only been west for three weeks and his nose and cheeks were burned red.

"Don't count on it, lad," O'Neil said. "Colonel Brent and the regiment may still be in the Red Valley. We must go to them."

O'Neil's orders had been to scout for hostiles as far south as Sonsela Buttes. If he encountered Apaches he was on no account to engage the enemy but to immediately report back to the main column.

O'Neil smiled to himself at that. He'd no intention of engaging the enemy, but it seemed the Apaches had a different idea about that.

Now, pinned down and with no hope of assistance, the noncom swept the landscape with his field glasses, bringing into close-up focus desert, brush and the eternal mesas just as immovable and majestic as the mountains. Nothing moved and there was no sound. A lizard panted on a flat rock on the sandy bank of the dry wash near where O'Neil lay, and in the distance a buzzard glided and quartered the land with its scalpel eyes.

"You think they know we're here?" Spooner said.

"We're the lads the mirrors have been talking about," O'Neil said. "Of course they know we're here."

"Will they attack?" Spooner said. He touched his tongue to his dry lips.

"Apaches are notional, and there's no telling what they'll do," O'Neil said. "But I reckon they'll at least feel us out, see if it's worth a throw of the dice."

Werner was farther down the wash holding the horses. He didn't understand the talk, but the sergeant's tone and Spooner's scared face told him all he needed to know.

He moved closer, bending low to take advantage of the cover of the bank.

Thirty minutes passed and the noon heat was unbearable. About a pint of water sloshed in each of the three canteens and O'Neil gathered them together. They might be in for a siege and the water would need to be rationed.

He was content to stay where he was. The wash made a U-turn around a large sandstone boulder, and over the years the spring runoff from a nearby mesa had cut it a good four feet deep. O'Neil and the others had taken a position at the bend of the U and the rock was at their back.

The way O'Neil had it figured, if the Apaches attacked, Werner, a good marksman with his Springfield carbine, would take a position next to the rock and guard the rear while he and Spooner took care of a frontal assault.

Of course, they were facing Apaches, and O'Neil knew it wouldn't be that simple. They weren't like the Plains Indians he'd fought before, a bunch of mounted warriors coming at you all at once. Apaches were just as brave as the Sioux and Cheyenne, but considerably more cautious.

As though to reinforce that opinion, a probing shot kicked up a startled exclamation point of dust on the bank three feet to O'Neil's left.

Beside him Private Spooner cut loose a shot from his carbine.

"Did you see the Apache?" O'Neil said.

The soldier shook his head.

O'Neil wasn't a cursing man by nature, but he yelled, "Then damn your eyes, don't shoot at shadows. You hear me? Conserve your ammunition."

"Sorry, Sarge," Spooner said.

Another shot. Close enough to shower dirt into O'Neil's face.

"They're taking our measure," he said. He

rolled over on his left side and called out to Werner. "Leave the horses. Take up a position next to the rock and guard our rear."

The German looked puzzled.

"Damnit, man!" O'Neil roared. "Learn how to speak American."

He got to his feet, grabbed Werner and dragged him to the rock. He pushed the man down into a crouched position. "There," he said.

Werner said nothing. But he looked frightened.

Behind O'Neil, Spooner fired again.

"I think I got him, Sarge!" he yelled. "Damnit, I reckon I nailed him. I'm gonna get a scalp for Custer!"

"Nooo!" O'Neil shrieked as he lunged for the soldier.

Too late.

Spooner climbed over the parapet and then sprang to his feet, grinning as he reached for the knife on his belt.

A bullet smashed the grin from his lips and the lower jaw from his skull.

His mouth a bloody cavern of blood, shattered teeth and splintered bone, the young trooper, his eyes wild, fell back into the wash. His booted feet gouged convulsively into the sand, once, twice . . . then he lay still.

Oscar Werner turned his head and saw the grotesque horror of what had once been Spooner's face. Far from his snow-capped land, surrounded by a scorching desert inferno and a skilled and ruthless enemy, the teenager broke.

He rose to his feet and ran past Sergeant O'Neil. Werner scrambled up the bank, raised his hands and ran in the direction of the hidden Apaches.

"Kameraden! Kameraden!" he yelled, his teenaged voice high-pitched and frantic.

But Apaches had no word for *comrade.*

Horrified, O'Neil watched as strong brown arms struck like copper snakes and pulled Werner to the ground.

Alive.

O'Neil had no time to act. He could only react.

He stood, thumbed back the hammer of his Colt and fired.

His bullet crashed into Werner's blond head and for a moment it looked as though the young cavalryman had pinned an exotic red blossom in his hair.

Sergeant O'Neil could not look longer.

Screaming their anger and frustration, half a dozen Apache warriors rose from the earth like the resurrection of the dead and charged him.

O'Neil shoved the muzzle of his Colt into his mouth, angling upward, and pulled the trigger. Blood, bone and brain fanned above his head as he collapsed.

The Apaches, outraged at what they took to be a sign of cowardice, pissed on O'Neil's corpse.

Geronimo, old, wise and wizened, stared at O'Neil's body. The soldiers had not fought well, and it seemed that the taking and burning of Fort Defiance was well within his means. He had thirty warriors, more than enough if this shooting scrape was an indication of the fighting prowess of the white soldiers.

But Geronimo was cautious, a man with a wait-and-see attitude that had earned him the Apache name *Goyathlay,* The Yawner.

He knew the young bucks were primed for war and would press for an immediate attack on the fort. But, though he was not a chief, Geronimo's medicine was powerful because he talked with the spirits of the dead, and the young men would listen to him.

It came to him then that he should postpone the attack for a couple more days until he was sure of a victory. . . .

The Yawner would wait and see.

CHAPTER ELEVEN

Jack Coffin did not scoff at the plan to find the Golden Bell of Santa Elena. He said only, "It is guarded by a specter. His name is Death."

Abe Roper smiled. "Do we believe that, Jack?"

"I believe it. What you believe is of no concern to me."

The breed's black eyes moved to Flintlock. "I feel your hate, Samuel."

"I don't hate you, Jack," Flintlock said.

"I think you do. You hate me because you fear me."

"We're all friends here," Charlie Fong said quickly. "I mean, ain't we?"

"I have no friends," Coffin said. "I had a few, many years ago, but I buried them."

"Well, we're not your enemy, Jack," Roper said. "Are we, Sam'l?"

Before Flintlock could answer, Coffin said, "You are white men. All white men are my enemy."

"Here, Jack, you ain't throwin' in with ol' Geronimo, are you?" Roper said. "If you plan to go on the warpath, wait until you find us the goddamned bell."

Coffin shook his head and his long black hair spilled over his shoulders. "Geronimo is doomed, as are all the Apaches. And me along with them."

For reasons known only to himself, the breed had adopted the costume of the vaquero, much faded by harsh weather. He wore a tight *charro* jacket, silver-studded leather pants, the cotton shirt of the vaquero, and a wide sombrero.

"Hell, Jack, you're only half Apache. You got nothing to fear," Roper said. "What's your white half?"

"I don't know. I don't care."

"Too bad. But I've got your daddy pegged as a Frenchy. Wunst I shacked up with a French gal in El Paso for a spell, and you got the look. The Frenchy look, I mean. Kinda swarthy an' all."

Coffin turned to Flintlock again. "What do you think, Samuel?"

"I'd say you're half skunk, but I could be wrong."

For the first time since he'd ridden into the fort, Coffin smiled. "Better a skunk than a Frenchman."

Roper, smiling affably, moved to smooth things over.

"Well, we all have different opinions, *n'est-ce pas*? That's what makes the world go round, I say. Now, Jack, will you find us the cave where the big bell is kept?"

"I will find it, but it will be my death," Coffin said. "This I know."

The breed was a tall man, wide shouldered and big boned, with the hard, lean face of a man who'd followed many desert trails. He had no softness in him and no deep well of human kindness waiting to be discovered. Ten years before, he'd buried his entire family, including his wife and three children, slaughtered by Mexican lancers, and he'd died a small death with every shovelful of dirt until only the hard shell of a man was left.

Jack Coffin, scouting for American lawmen or Mexican *Rurales,* had killed twelve men, all of them white or Mexican. He'd never killed or caused the death of an Indian. He was fast with the Colt on his hip, a man to be reckoned with.

But then, so was Sam Flintlock, as Coffin was well aware.

"How come you're so all-fired hung up on dying, Jack?" Flintlock said. "You got a hemp posse on your back trail?"

"I was told about my death in a dream," Coffin said. "An old man in a monk's robe came to me from a mist and told me I'd die before the summer wildflowers bloom. But the way of it, he would not reveal. He said there are secrets Death keeps to himself."

"Well, I wouldn't worry about it," Roper said. "We all have bad dreams, right, Charlie? Frijoles can do that to ya."

"A nightmare is a black dream because our soul wandered too far in sleep into a haunted place," Charlie Fong said. "When we wake, and sit upright in our blankets, our heart pounding, gasping for breath, it's only because our body rescued our soul and made it return home."

"Hell, Charlie," Flintlock said, "you're a strange one."

"I'm a Celestial, remember," Fong said. He winked at Flintlock.

"When I woke he was still holding my hand," Coffin said.

"Who?" Roper said.

"Death. He'd taken my right hand and he still held it when I woke. My hand was cold, as though I'd been carrying ice."

"Enough of this, Jack, you're spookin' the hell out of me," Roper said. "Let's get back to talking business, huh?"

"We will leave for the Carrizo Mountains at first light tomorrow," Coffin said. "Now our business is done."

He turned and moved toward the door, but Flintlock stepped in front of him, his face like stone.

"Jack, you try any fancy moves on this trip, I'll take it personal and I'll take it hard," he said. "And when I take stuff personal, I do bad things. Understand?"

"I have nothing to do with Geronimo," Coffin said.

"As far as I'm concerned, you're an Apache," Flintlock said. "That's enough for me. I don't trust you."

"Why do you hate me so much, Samuel?"

"You know why."

"You talk of Barney Glennon and Sonora."

"I talk of Santa Cruz."

"Glennon was a bandit, a bank robber. He was wanted by the *Rurales,* dead or alive."

"He was my friend and a white man and you killed him."

"Yes. In the Coyote Azul cantina. He drew down on me." Coffin's eyes met Flintlock's, clashed. "He'd been informed."

"He left a wife and two children back in Texas."

"How many of the men you killed left wives and children?"

"As far as I know, none of them. They were all trash like you, Jack."

"Don't push me any harder, Samuel."

Coffin's hand was close to his gun. He was as fast as chain lightning and hard to handle.

"Damn your eyes, I'll be the death you fear if you sell us down the river to your Apache friends," Flintlock said between gritted teeth. "Keep that in mind, breed."

"Sam'l, ease off, back up some," Roper said. "Jack says he'll lead us to the bell and that's all he'll do." He beamed and placed a hand on both Coffin's and Flintlock's shoulders. "Four even shares once we break up the bell. How does that set with you, Jack? True-blue, huh?"

"I don't care about the gold," Coffin said. "I go with you only because I follow my destiny."

The breed's highfalutin talk about death and destiny was beyond anything in Abe Roper's experience. He fell back on what he did know.

"I tell you what, boys, there's a dugout saloon with a hog farm just two miles west of here," he said. "Ain't that right, Charlie?"

"So I've heard, Abe. Sergeant Tone says the place is run by Saggy Maggie Muldoon, big gal, used to have her own house in Abilene. Tone says the whiskey is only twenty cents a shot and the gals are clean."

"There you go, boys, made to order fer lively young gents like yourselves," Roper said. "Why don't you two ride on over there and have a drink and a woman and let bygones be bygones?"

Charlie Fong nodded. "Words of wisdom, Abe. Yes, siree, words of wisdom as ever was."

Coffin said nothing. He reached for the door handle and Flintlock took a step to the side.

"One day soon I'll kill you, Samuel," the breed said as he opened the door and let a blast of hot, dusty air inside. "I will put a bullet through the thunderbird's head, depend on it."

"Not if I see you coming."

"You'll see me."

"Then I look forward to it."

"Hey, boys, don't forget Saggy —"

The slamming door cut off the rest of Roper's words, but Charlie Fong talked across the silence.

"Boy, this is gonna be a fun trip," he said.

CHAPTER TWELVE

The arrival at Fort Defiance of a middle-aged major and his young bride did nothing to ease Captain Owen Shaw's fears about the success of his enterprise.

Keeping Asa Pagg and his gunmen under control could prove to be difficult enough, but now the unexpected appearance of Major Andrew Grove threatened to upset the whole applecart.

To Shaw's irritation, Grove showed up like a potentate in a mule-drawn, army escort wagon converted for passengers, and an escort of five cavalrymen.

His annoyance grew when the major sat behind the commanding officer's desk, ushered his prim wife into the only other available chair, and before even uttering a greeting said, "Very sloppy, Captain. I wasn't challenged by a sentry on my way in and the fort is run-down. Mister, it looks like it's held together by baling wire and spit."

Shaw bristled. "May I remind the major that Fort Defiance has been abandoned for fifteen years and only recently has it been reactivated."

"That's no excuse, Captain. It's the commanding officer's duty to see that everything is shipshape and Bristol fashion."

"That's a nautical term, sir. It may apply to a British ship of war, but not to a United States Army frontier post."

"Damn your eyes, sir, don't bandy words with me," Grove said. "Where is your commanding officer?"

"He's dead, sir. I am . . . was . . . the commanding officer of this fort."

Grove raised a monocle to his right eye, an upper-class affectation Shaw loathed, then said, "Well? Identify yourself, man."

Shaw straightened to attention. "Captain Owen Shaw, at your service, sir."

"What happened to the other fellow?"

"Major Ashton? He was killed by Apaches, sir."

"How very careless of him." Grove's monocle glinted in the sunlight. "What happened?"

"He and I were hunting when the hostiles struck. The major fell in the first volley."

"Pah, hunting." Grove turned to his wife.

"Did you hear that, my dear Winnifred? The major was out hunting while his command was falling apart."

"It is easy to dodge our responsibilities, but we cannot dodge the consequences of dodging our responsibilities," the woman said.

Winnifred Grove had a V-shaped upper lip that overhung the lower one, but loosely, as though a button had once held it up and was now missing.

Shaw badly wanted to kill her.

"Once again your common sense educates us all, my dear," Major Grove said. "Is that not so, Captain?"

"Indeed, sir. A most edifying observation." Shaw relaxed a little from his stiff pose, aware that his blue shirt was dusty and smelled heavily of sweat. "Does the major wish to tell me why he's visiting Fort Defiance?"

"Yes, the major wishes to tell you. General Crook has informed his field commanders that all hostiles, and I include women, children and old persons in that description, are to be brought to this post. From here they will be taken south to Fort Grant for disposal. My orders are that I will lead the . . . ah . . . exodus, though there may well be others at a later date."

Shaw felt a surge of relief. It would take time to round up every Apache in the Arizona and New Mexico territories. More time than he needed.

But he asked the question anyway. "When can we expect the first of them, sir?"

"I'm told I should expect the women and children to arrive first, possibly in as little as two weeks. The young bucks will follow soon thereafter, those that are still alive."

Shaw nodded. He had plenty of time. Then another thought came to him that made him smile inwardly . . . *he had time to kill.*

Grove spoke again. "How many men in the garrison, Captain Shaw?"

"Two officers and fourteen enlisted men, sir. None of them are of the best quality."

"Does that include the officers?"

"Unfortunately, yes."

"Well, I'll soon whip them into shape, officers and enlisted men. I want the officers to join me and my lady wife for dinner tonight."

"Does that whipping into shape include me, sir?"

"Should it?"

"I do my duty, sir."

"Then your duty lies in getting this fort fit for the arrival of the hostiles. Do I make myself clear?"

"Perfectly. But there is the matter of Geronimo."

"What about him?"

"He could be a danger to this post, sir."

"I think with my escort and driver to reinforce the garrison, we have enough fighting men to deal with savages."

"As you say, sir."

Winnifred Grove coughed and her husband said, "Yes, my dear?"

"We haven't spoken yet of those important matters we discussed," the woman said. "Andrew, they are of the greatest moment."

The major feigned a look of surprise and his monocle popped out of his eye socket and dropped onto his chest. "How remiss of me, my dear," he said. "Please inform Captain Shaw of your wishes."

Winnifred sat on the edge of her chair with her knees pressed close together, as though guarding a treasure she considered constantly under threat. She had a pale, pinched face, muddy brown eyes, and the hair that showed under her straw bonnet was so blond as to be almost colorless.

"Captain Shaw, what I am about to say to you is of singular importance and, as I have already indicated, of the greatest moment," Winnifred said.

Shaw gave a little bow. "Your obedient servant, ma'am."

"Thank you, Captain. First, I wish to mention demon drink. Yes, Captain, those tools of the devil, the whiskey and beer that poisons the mind, pollutes the body, desecrates family life and inflames sinners to lustful fantasies." She tightened her knees. "I am against demon drink in all its forms and disguises."

Shaw bowed. "I understand, ma'am."

"Thank you, Captain. Secondly I am against the presence of loose women, and yes, I will say it, whores, on or near an army post. Without her purity, a woman is no woman, but rather a lower form of being, a fallen female, unworthy of the love of her sex and unfit for their company. A woman, even a married woman, must be willing to guard her sweet treasure with her life. Do you understand me, Captain?"

"Perfectly, ma'am."

"I will not tolerate any fallen . . . creatures . . . anywhere near this fort while my dear husband is in command. They may flaunt their" — Winnifred lightly touched her small breasts — "dumplings of the devil where'er they please, but not at Fort Defiance. I am very adamant on these matters and I assure you, so is Major Grove."

99

"Indeed I am, my dear," Grove said. "On that wondrous day we first became betrothed I vowed that my lips would ne'er touch alcohol or my loins be stimulated by impure or lecherous thoughts. Under your sweet guidance I have kept both those vows."

"And I have not forgotten that in whatever situation of life I find myself, from the cradle to the grave, a spirit of obedience and submission to my husband, as well as pliability of temper and humility of mind, are required of me."

"My darling," Grove said.

"Beloved," Winnifred said.

Shaw smiled. All right then, first the wife, then the major. When the time came he'd kill them in that order.

"Do you understand, Captain? No loose women and no alcohol are to be permitted at Fort Defiance. My lady wife has made her feelings clear on these critical points, has she not?"

"Indeed she has, sir, perfectly clear. I will obey your . . . wife's . . . orders, Major."

"Good, now take me on a tour of the fort. I wish to see how badly it's been run recently."

"Yes, sir," Shaw said.

And you'll get your bullet in the belly, Major.

CHAPTER THIRTEEN

It had been too late in the afternoon to send out a wood detail, and everybody at Fort Defiance knew it — except Major Andrew Grove.

He'd demanded that the woodpile be replenished so that there would be plenty at hand when the fighting soldiers returned with their prisoners.

"Gonna be dark soon, Lieutenant, and the wagon ain't half full yet," Sergeant Pat Tone said. He spat into the sand at his feet. "Damn desk major who knows nothing."

"Hold your tongue, Sergeant," Second Lieutenant Miles Howard said. "Major Grove is a fine officer and he'll bring discipline and order to the post, something that up until now has been sadly lacking."

"Yes, sir," Tone said. He scowled. Grove and the lieutenant were two of a kind.

Privates Liam Mahoney and Lee Webster were using a two-man saw to cut timber in a pine grove a mile to the east of Window Rock, an arched sandstone rock formation the Navajo held sacred. When the tree was felled, they'd use a shorter bucking saw to cut the trunk into logs.

It was hard, grueling work, especially for Webster, a forty-year-old who'd pushed a pen for years and had pimp-soft hands.

As the day began its slow summer shade into night, the only sound was the rhythmic rasp-rasp of the saw, Webster's quiet cursing, and the occasional jingle of harness when a mule moved impatiently in the traces.

A few lilac clouds hung motionless in the lemon sky and a breeze from the north was cool and smelled of freshly sawn lumber.

Tone lit his pipe then left the wagon to check on the progress of the sawers.

Lieutenant Howard struck a gallant figure. Mounted on his white charger, he had drawn his saber, the blade resting on his right shoulder, and patrolled the area at a walk. He had seen enough tintypes and drawings of battles during the War Between the States to know that this was how the ideal combat officer should act, straight in the saddle, saber drawn, eagle of eye.

That he was an ideal target for an Apache bullet didn't enter his thinking. But it would later, and by then it wouldn't matter.

The five Apaches were Chiricahua and a week before they'd broken off from old Geronimo's band to raid farther south, but had met with little success. The army was out in force and the lost, lonely land along the length of the Chuska Mountains had presented few opportunities for killing and horse stealing.

They'd slaughtered a few Mexicans and enjoyed their women for a while, but the peons were poor and although a donkey made a good feed, it was not a prize they could boast of in front of the others who'd remained behind with The Yawner.

But now the great god *Usen,* the Giver-of-Life, had smiled on them.

The soldier with the yellow officer straps rode a fine white horse, and there would also be guns and mules. Those were things worth fighting for.

And what of the coyote and the owl?

Surely those were good omens?

Last night a coyote bitch had walked into the Apache camp and stared into a tree where an owl called. There could be no better luck, for the bitch and the owl had been sent by *Usen,* to tell the Apache that they were mighty warriors and to be of good cheer. That great booty would soon come their way.

Thus emboldened the six warriors watched the wood detail and waited with the patience of hunting cougars for their chance.

"Be dark in an hour, Lieutenant," Sergeant Tone said.

"I'm well aware of that," Howard said. He checked his pocket watch, and then eyed the wagon. "Another half cord or so and we'll be on our way, so tell the men to put their backs into it."

"Yes, sir," Tone said. Mentally he added, *And may you go to hell and not have a drop of porter to quench your eternal thirst.*

Tone, his face stormy, stepped into the clearing to tell Mahoney and Webster the bad news.

Lieutenant Howard watched the sergeant go, then sat his horse and listened into the twilight's lilac silence. A thin gray mist hugged close to the ground, here and there tinged pink by the reddening sky. Soon the night birds would peck at the first stars and in the brush the members of the insect orchestra were already tuning their instruments. The air smelled only of wood and . . .

Apaches!

Howard swiveled his head in the direction of the clearing. After the first flurry of shots, the two privates were down; their bodies sprawled like rag dolls across the pine trunk they'd been sawing.

Sergeant Tone, his mouth and chin bloody, backed toward the wagon, his well-handled Colt bucking in his fist.

The Apaches came at him in a rush.

Howard saw the danger and dug his spurs into the flanks of his horse. He charged the hostiles, screaming a war cry without words or meaning, adding wild sound to an ancient race memory he'd torn from the time of his Anglo-Saxon warrior ancestors.

Not for nothing had the frontier army abandoned sabers as a weapon against Indians. The Apaches easily dodged Howard's slashing steel, and two of them dragged him from the saddle.

Tone, a professional soldier to the core, attempted to save his officer.

He leaned against the wagon and punched shells into his empty revolver. He'd been hit hard by a bullet high in the chest and it was weakening him. An arrow thudded into his left shoulder and he cried out in sudden agony. But he bit back the pain, pushed away from the wagon and tried to bring the Colt to bear.

But the gun was heavy . . . way too heavy . . . and he didn't know why.

Tone's vision tunneled until all he saw were the three Apaches running at him. He lifted the revolver with both hands. No good. The weight of the gun was beyond his strength and it dropped from his stiffening fingers.

A bullet thudded into Tone's belly just above his belt buckle. Another slammed into him. He heard an Apache shriek in triumph. . . .

And then he heard nothing at all.

The Apaches were disappointed in Lieutenant Miles Howard.

He had not died well. After only an hour of fire and the knife, he'd screamed like a woman in childbirth and had not borne the pain as a warrior should.

The coyotes were yipping in the hills and the moon was rising when Howard's spirit mercifully left his blackened, bloody body. No one sang his death song.

But the Apaches, especially the Chiricahua, were great pranksters. And here was an opportunity for mirth.

They had a flea-bitten Mexican burro in camp and they agreed that it was worth sacrificing the animal's meat to play a good joke on the soldiers at Fort Defiance.

Later, when they'd tell Geronimo about the joke he'd laugh and say they did well. And then he'd say, "After all, what is a white man useful for but to play good jokes on him?"

Yes, that's what he'd say.

Chapter Fourteen

Winnifred Grove had felt a familiar stirring in her loins and the budding of her breasts when she thought of Captain Owen Shaw. He was a fine-looking man. Of that there was no doubt, with his fine, sweeping cavalry mustache and soulful brown eyes, to say nothing of his broad shoulders and tight, horseman's hips.

But a lady, especially a married one, must never surrender to lustful fantasies, so Winnifred told her husband that she was stepping out onto the porch to catch a breath of fresh night air, now that the dust of the day had settled.

Andrew, ever solicitous, had at once jumped up from his chair to get her wrap and warned her not to spend too much time outdoors, "lest you catch a chill, my darling."

The night was indeed cool, but Winnifred was glad of that. She'd been a little overheated of late.

She sat on a wooden bench and looked out across the dark parade ground. Well, not dark, the bright moonlight made everything so opalescent, but shadows pooled everywhere, as deep and mysterious as Captain Shaw's eyes.

Winnifred noticed that there were beads of condensation on the brown surface of the hanging ollas, like sweat on the tanned shoulders of a lover who has exerted himself heroically in bed.

She shook her head. Lordy, she was in heat and Andrew couldn't satisfy her and never had. It was as though she was trapped in a burning building searching for an exit, knowing all the time that there was not one to be found.

There was no escape in sight. No relief.

Winnifred squeezed her knees together and for a few moments tried to think of other things. How about that ridiculous old bore, Maude Ashton?

The recent widow was going around dressed all in black, in heavy mourning for her dead husband, moaning and crying with a face as long as a Missouri mule's. Why, she looked like the pictures Winnifred had seen of old, widowed Queen Vic who'd been mourning for . . . what was it? . . . a hundred years or something. Maude was just as plain, just as dumpy, and just as po-faced as her majesty.

Finally she shook her head. Well, that didn't work. Thinking of Maude Ashton just depressed her.

Damnit, there was only one thing left to do. . . .

The large pocket of her day dress held two items, a round tin of strong English mints and a pint of rye.

She took out the bottle, popped the cork and slugged down several ounces. There, that was better. Winnifred wiped off her mouth with the back of her hand, put the bottle back in her pocket and then sucked on a mint so strong, it covered up the smell of whiskey.

However, there was no real need. It would never enter Andrew's thinking that, because of his inadequacies in the bed department, his wife was a secret drinker and an unfulfilled nymphomaniac.

Let him think that the façade of sexual prudery they presented to the world reflected his wife's true feelings.

Winnifred smiled to herself, her teeth like yellowed piano keys.

If only you knew, Andrew . . . if only you knew.

Perhaps it was whiskey courage or the closeness of her husband and the other officers, but when Winnifred heard the soft shuffle of a tired horse out in the darkness she felt no alarm.

It was probably that nice young Lieutenant Howard riding ahead of the wood wagon.

And it was Howard. Or what was left of him.

Winnifred rose, stepped to the edge of the porch and gazed into the moonlit gloom. The wind had sprung up and small veils of dust lifted from the parade ground. A night bird called from the ashy canopy of a wild oak and leaves rustled as it looked for a place to roost. The bird finally settled and then fell silent.

Winnifred Grove had to smile. All she could make out was the silhouette of man and mount, but the animal was tiny, a small donkey she guessed. Lordy, had the lieutenant's beautiful white destrier bolted, forcing him to return to the fort astride a burro?

Oh, what a delicious hoot! His brother officers would tease him unmercifully!

Winnifred stepped off the porch and walked onto the parade ground where she could greet the returning hero.

She smiled. "Why, Lieutenant Howard, I declare, how dirty you are."

The officer made no answer as the burro plodded closer.

Then Winnifred saw his face.

And she screamed. And screamed.

Alarmed, as sudden shrieks echoed through the silvered darkness, the night bird scattered leaves and twigs in its haste to scamper out of the oak.

Mercifully, Winnifred Grove fainted and her last horrified screech stilled in her throat.

Major Andrew Grove, dressed in a house robe, slippers and tasseled smoking cap, found his wife sprawled on the parade ground. A trickle of saliva ran from the corner of Winnifred's mouth and her eyes were wide open, as though the horror she'd seen had frozen them in place.

First Lieutenant Frank Hedley, half drunk, his boots on the wrong feet, pounded outside and demanded to know what in holy hell was going on. Captain Owen Shaw, wearing his gun, arrived a few moments later.

"Oh my God, look at that!" Major Grove exclaimed, the monocle popping out of his eye.

He staggered back, one hand pointing to the horror on the blood-soaked burro, the other clutching at his chest.

Then he too fainted.

CHAPTER FIFTEEN

The scream woke Sam Flintlock, but Abe Roper got out of his blankets and onto his feet faster.

"What the hell?" he said, to no one but himself.

"Some poor woman run into Jack Coffin in the dark?" Flintlock said.

"That ain't funny, Sam'l," Roper said. "We need that damn breed. I don't want him hung until after we get the bell."

Charlie Fong, scratching his belly, padded on bare feet and blinked at Roper. "What's going on, Abe?"

"I don't know, but I aim to find out. Get dressed, you two, and we'll go see. It might be Apaches."

Flintlock dressed, then shoved his Colt in his waistband. He slung the powder horn over his shoulder and picked up the Hawken.

"What the hell do you aim to do with that,

Dan'l Boone?" Roper said. He was only half awake and testy.

"It might come in handy," Flintlock said.

"You want handy, take a Winchester."

"The Winchester's my saddle gun, Abe. This here Hawken is fer show." He lifted his chin and scratched his unshaven neck. "Or something like that."

"You're nuts," Roper said. "You dream about ol' Barnabas again?"

"He was advisin', like he always does," Flintlock said.

"He tell you to take the Hawken?"

"He surely did."

"I'm surrounded by madmen," Roper said. He opened the door, stepped outside, and the others followed.

There was a commotion on the porch in front of the administration building and commanding officer's quarters.

Flintlock heard a man scream, "Take it away. Oh, dear God in heaven, take it away."

Then another man said, "Calm down now, Major."

Abe Roper ignored the officers on the porch and walked directly to the donkey and its grotesque burden.

After a while he turned to Flintlock and said, "Apaches all right. He's been skun."

Captain Owen Shaw, his caped greatcoat hurriedly thrown over his night attire, stood close by, but said nothing. He was deathly pale under his dark tan.

Flintlock and Charlie Fong stared at the body. It was braced upright on the donkey's back by a frame of pine branches, and Howard's purple and pink intestines spilled over the little animal's back and trailed in the dust.

"Hard to tell who he is, ain't it?" Roper said.

"Hard to tell if it was ever human," Charlie Fong said.

"It's human all right," Flintlock said. "It's the young lieutenant, or was."

"Damn, he died hard, didn't he?" Roper said. Howard's eyes were gone and his genitals had been cut off.

"I wouldn't wish that kind of death on my worst enemy," Flintlock said.

"Damned Apaches," Fong said, and spat.

Flintlock shrugged. "It's what they do, Charlie. They learned how to flog and flay a man from the Spanish, and how to burn him so it hurt for a long time." He glanced at Howard's body again. "Yup, it's what they do, all right."

"You fellows there!"

Flintlock turned and saw a man leaning

forward with both hands on the rail of the picket fence that surrounded the porch. He wore a smoking cap that was at a crooked angle on his graying head.

"Yes," the man said, "I'm talking to you."

"And who are you?" Flintlock called back.

"Damn your impertinence, sir." The man put a monocle in his right eye, as though trying to get a better look at Flintlock. "I'm Major Grove, the new commandant of this post."

"What can we do for you, Major?" This from Abe Roper.

"Take that horrible thing away," Grove said. "Take it away and bury it or burn it. I'll give each of you a dollar when the job is done."

Flintlock had no particular liking for Captain Shaw, but the man rose in his estimation when he took a few steps toward Grove and yelled, "Sir, this man was an officer in the United States Army and died on active duty. He should be buried with military honors."

A few soldiers had gathered around and by the expression on their faces they approved of what Shaw had said.

"Where are the other members of the wood party?" Grove said.

"Dead, I should imagine," Shaw said.

117

"And no wood?" Grove said. "You mean there's no wood?"

The man's voice was quivering, as though he teetered on the verge of hysteria.

"Hell, General, if your soldier boys were all kilt by Apaches they ain't likely to bring wood, now are they?"

Asa Pagg had emerged from the gloom and now he stood, hands on his hips, grinning at the major.

"That man is correct," Grove yelled. "Lieutenant Howard was clearly derelict in his duty. Now take that away and bury it somewhere in haste. A dollar for every man who volunteers."

At that point Winnifred Grove recovered from her swoon, helped by Maude Ashton fanning her face with a damp handkerchief. Winnifred pushed the woman away and fixed a stare on the nightmare astride the blood-splashed burro.

"We're taking it away, my dear," her husband said. "I'll dispose of it."

"Now," Winnifred said. "It's obscene, Andrew. Do it now."

"Of course, my precious."

Out on the parade ground, Flintlock's and Shaw's eyes met.

"Hell, we'll bury him," Flintlock told him.

Shaw nodded. "All the damned major has

done during his entire army career is count cans of beans and tubs of salt beef. He's never seen what Indians can do to a man."

"You can't let the Apaches get away with this, Shaw," Flintlock said. "If you don't head out after them they'll take it as a sign of weakness. They'll be back and next time Geronimo will go for your throat."

"In the event of an attack we have men enough to defend the administration building and possibly the sutler store," Shaw said. "At least for a while. We don't have the numbers to meet the Apaches in the open field. In any case, with the exception of the five cavalry troopers who formed his escort, the soldiers now under Major Grove's command are not fighting men."

Shaw glanced at the porch where Grove still yelled orders that now fell on deaf ears. "And we have two white women to protect," he said.

"What do you think, Sam?" Asa Pagg said, grinning. He seemed highly amused.

"Abe?" Flintlock said.

"I say we burn 'em, make them savages wish they'd never heard of Fort Defiance," Roper said.

"Count me in," Charlie Fong said.

Flintlock directed his attention to Pagg. "You heard it, Asa."

The big outlaw turned his head. "Joe? Logan?"

"I never fit Apaches before," Logan Dean said. "I've been meaning to give 'er a try."

"Me neither, but I'll give it a whirl," Harte said. " 'Half a league, half a league, half a league onward, all in the valley of Death rode the six hundred. "Forward, the Light Brigade! Charge for the guns!" he said. Into the valley of Death rode the six hundred.' "

"That one of them poetries you write, Joe?" Dean said.

"Nah, it was written by Alfred, Lord Tennyson, three score years ago," Harte said.

Abe Roper shook his head. "Seems to me there's some mighty strange folks gathered in this fort tonight," he said.

Pagg grinned. "Joe is mighty queer all right, but when the lead starts flying, he'll stand his ground and play the white man."

"Then let's saddle up and get it done," Flintlock said.

"You takin' that old smoke pole, Sam?" Pagg said.

"Seems like."

"Then Joe ain't the only one that's strange."

"I can't stop you men," Shaw said. Then, halfheartedly, "But I wish you'd reconsider."

The thought had occurred to Shaw that if Pagg stopped a bullet, he could handle Dean and Harte. "What about him?" he said, nodding in Howard's direction. The skinned body was already attracting flies and it smelled.

"I said we'd bury him," Flintlock said. "And we will."

CHAPTER SIXTEEN

"Damnit all, Sammy," Abe Roper said. "That thing following on behind us spooks the hell out of me."

"You ain't alone there," Asa Pagg said. "Way that burro follows us just ain't natural. Like it's being guided by the hands of a dead man."

"Let Lieutenant Howard be," Flintlock said. "He'll lead us to glory."

The donkey with its grisly burden had tacked on to the riders as they left the fort and it had kept up with the horses, Howard's dreadful body swaying on its back as though he was returning, tipsy, to his grave.

The trail was narrow and wound through rocks and trees, but twice Flintlock and the others had ridden past meadows thick with night-blooming wildflowers, moonlight covering the grass like a frost.

Here and there the tracks of the wood wagon were visible in the gloom and after an hour they swung west, into timbered hill country. The air was sultry and still and thick with insects that buzzed and bit.

Flintlock stepped from the saddle and walked back to the others.

"I smell smoke," he said.

"I don't smell it," Pagg said.

"Well, trust me, it's there," Flintlock said.

"How do we play this, Sam'l?" Roper said, his voice a hard whisper. "What did ol' Barnabas teach you about sneakin' up on Apaches?"

"Nothing. Barnabas never fit Apaches."

"Lucky for him," Roper said.

"The way I got it figured," Flintlock said, "is that we go from here on foot, except for Lieutenant Howard. He's riding."

Asa Pagg said, "Anybody catching his drift? I'm damned if I am."

"Then listen up, Asa," Flintlock said. "And I'll talk real slow so even you can understand."

"Why haven't I shot you afore this, Sam?" Pagg said.

"Because you're such a warm and compassionate human being," Flintlock said.

The irony flew right over Pagg's head. "Damn right I am. Too softhearted fer my own good. A lot of people have told me that."

123

"They still alive, Asa?" Charlie Fong said.

"Most of them are dead. Keep up with the lip, Chinaman, and you'll be joining them."

Fong laughed into his hand as Roper said, "All right, everybody, listen to Sam'l."

Flintlock outlined his plan and when he was done, Pagg grinned and said, "Hell, the poor soldier boy should get a medal for this."

"I'll talk to Captain Shaw about that when we get back," Flintlock said. He looked around him. "We can leave the horses right here."

"So what about the lieutenant?" Pagg said. "He's the hero."

"When we move out, the burro will follow us," Flintlock said.

But it didn't. The little animal wanted to stay with the horses.

Finally Charlie Fong, his face empty, went back and led the donkey forward.

Howard's body looked as though it had been splashed with red paint.

Booted and spurred white men don't sneak up on Apaches.

Unless the warriors were sound asleep in a treelined clearing because they feared no attack.

The Chiricahua sprawled around a small fire, a string of smoke lifting from its ashy coals. Standing next to the tethered Apache ponies and the army mules in the darkness, Howard's white charger looked like a ghost horse.

Abe Roper, Asa Pagg and his gunmen and Charlie Fong had shaken out in a line on the edge of the clearing and crouched low in thick underbrush that smelled of rotten vegetation and mold.

Fong was an unknown quantity, but Roper and the others were named gunfighters, and five of them made a force to be reckoned with. The distances were short and this would be a revolver scrape, the kind of fighting in which skilled gunmen excelled.

The quiet that had descended around the Apache camp was such an uneasy thing, Sam Flintlock wondered if that uneasy nature itself would shatter the silence with a bang of thunder or would prod a dozing screech owl into an outraged shriek.

But right then he needed silence. He needed a silence as quiet as the grave.

Rising from his crouch, Flintlock rose and stepped to the burro that stood head down, oblivious to anything happening around it.

Trying to avoid even a glance at the horror on its back, Flintlock led the burro forward. The body stank of blood and spilled guts, and now its mouth hung open, as though about to scream at this final indignity.

Flintlock froze at the edge of the clearing as a warrior mumbled in his sleep and restlessly flopped from his back onto his side. The man finally settled and lay still.

The thud-thud of his heartbeat loud in his ears, Flintlock led the burro into the clearing, as close to the sleeping Apaches as he dared. The little animal was placid, its huge brown eyes free of any thought or doubt, and it stood still when Flintlock dropped the lead-rope.

He backtracked into the brush and whispered, "Get ready."

There was no sound and no movement from the Apaches. Young men sleep sound.

Flintlock cast around and found what he was looking for, a piece of pine branch about a foot long. He measured the distance between him and the campfire, then chunked the branch. His aim was perfect. The branch thudded into the fire and shot upward an exclamation point of ash and flame.

Then three events happened very quickly, one tumbling after the other.

The Apaches woke, sprang to their feet

and grabbed for weapons.

The burro, a friendly creature, walked silently toward them on dainty feet.

The corrupt gasses that had built up in Lieutenant Howard's body escaped from his open mouth with a low, dreadful moan.

Their eyes as round as coins, the horrified Apaches gazed at the corpse. Not one of them moved and their rifles hung at their sides.

The man they'd tortured and skinned and killed had returned as a demon wraith to wreak his vengeance.

"Now!" Flintlock yelled.

He threw the Hawken to his shoulder and drew a bead on the Apache nearest him, a short, bandy-legged man wearing a blue headband that marked him as a former army scout.

Flintlock fired as six-guns hammered to his right, streaking orange flame. For a moment Flintlock's target was obscured by the cloud of gray smoke belched by the Hawken. When it cleared the Apache was sprawled, unmoving, on the ground.

Four other bucks were down, the survivor sprinting for the horses.

"Let him be!" Flintlock yelled. "Don't shoot!"

He heard Asa Pagg's puzzled shout. "What

the hell?"

As the Apache galloped away, his heels drumming on the ribs of a paint pony, Flintlock stepped into the clearing and said loud enough that everyone could hear, "He'll carry the word back to Geronimo not to mess with the soldiers at Fort Defiance, because even dead an' skun, they'll come back and even the score."

As he punched fresh cartridges into his Colt, Pagg stepped toward Flintlock and said, "Heard you touch off the old blunderbush. You hit anything?"

Flintlock glanced at the dead Apache. "Yeah, I killed my Indian," he said.

Abe Roper stepped out of darkness. He nodded in the direction of Howard's body. "What about him?"

"I'll take care of the lieutenant," Pagg said. "Least I can do since I'm takin' his hoss."

"It's army property, Asa," Flintlock said.

"Yeah, so it is. As though I give a damn."

Pagg walked to the burro, picked up the lead-rope and led the little animal into the trees at the opposite side of the clearing.

A moment later a single gunshot fractured the deathly quiet of the night, then Pagg emerged and walked toward the Apache horses, holstering his revolver.

He turned his head, cupped a hand to his mouth and yelled, "Lieutenant Howard is buried, boys." He laughed, his teeth gleaming white. "About now I reckon he's riding his burro through the gates of hell."

Roper said, "What say you, Sammy? Want to do it right?"

"Hell, no," Flintlock said. "Pagg said the man's buried, so he's buried."

"You're a hard one by times, Sam'l," Roper said. "I wonder if you're any better than Pagg."

"Sure I am," Flintlock said. "But not by much."

Roper and Charlie Fong walked across the clearing to collect the army mules. Pagg stood a distance away, showing off his new horse to Logan Dean and Joe Harte.

Old Barnabas, smoking a clay pipe, sat on a mossy log in the trees.

"Found your ma yet, boy?" he said.

"Still lookin', Grandpappy," Flintlock said.

"A man needs a name."

"I know it."

"Still got the old Hawken, I see," Barnabas said. There was no wind, but the old man's shoulder-length white hair tossed around his face.

"I won't part with it."

"More fool you," Barnabas said. "Get yourself a Henry."

"You came to me in my sleep and told me to carry the Hawken," Flintlock said.

"Then you're an eejit, heeding anything a dead man tells you in a dream." Barnabas puffed on his pipe, then said, "Ask me what I do, Sam."

"What do you do, Grandpappy?"

"I follow the buffalo, boy." Barnabas's lined face pruned in a frown. "I'll always follow the buffalo. It's a mountain man's hell, like."

"I'm sorry."

"Why? It ain't your fault."

Flintlock held out the rifle. "It shot well."

"Ain't no big thing to kill an Injun with a one-ounce ball at ten yards, boy."

"It was a good shot in the dark, Grandpappy."

"Know what I think of that?"

"No."

Barnabas cocked his ass and let rip with a tremendous fart.

"That was a good shot in the dark as well," he said.

"Sam'l, who the hell are you talking to?" Abe Roper said.

He stepped beside Flintlock and his eyes scanned the darkness.

There was no one on the mossy log. No one anywhere.

"Myself, I guess," Flintlock said.

"No, you weren't. You were talkin' to dead old Barnabas again," Roper said.

Flintlock thought about lying, but chose to be truthful. "He was here, asked me if I'd found my ma yet."

Roper shook his head. "Sammy, you're nuts and getting nuttier with every passing day. I'm gonna keep my eye on you."

Roper walked away, muttering, but Charlie Fong, his black eyes agleam with moonlight, stood beside Flintlock.

"Following the buffalo, isn't he, Sam?" Fong said.

Flintlock was shocked. "How do you know that?"

Fong smiled. "I have ears to hear. Eyes to see."

CHAPTER SEVENTEEN

"Sam Flintlock and them pulled out early this morning," Asa Pagg said. "Chasing their dream, I reckon."

"Leaves us shorthanded if Geronimo attacks the fort," Captain Owen Shaw said.

"He won't attack the fort," Pagg said. "He lost five young bucks last night. That'll scare him away for a spell and give us the time we need."

"I wish I had your confidence, Asa," Shaw said.

"Best Flintlock and Roper are gone," Pagg said. "With the job we got planned comin' down soon, them boys could have messed things up for us, lookin' fer a share, like."

"That idiot Grove has already messed things up," Shaw said. "He brought five men with him. Have you seen them? All of them have fought Apaches and there's isn't one that looks like he'd be a bargain."

"Me and Logan and Joe will take care of

them." Pagg looked at the two gunmen, who were lounging against a wall in the captain's quarters. "Ain't that right, boys?"

Joe Harte smiled and said, "We're a sight worse hell in a fight than Apaches."

"Damn right we are," Dean said. "A hundred times worse."

Pagg smiled. "See, Captain? The boys are primed."

"Where are Flintlock and the others headed?" Shaw said.

"A breed by the name of Jack Coffin is scouting for them, taking them north to look for a golden bell."

"What the hell is that?"

"It's a big windy tinpans tell, about a huge bell made of gold that the old Spanish men left in a cave." Pagg waved a negligent hand. "I wouldn't put any stock in the story and only idiots like Roper and Flintlock would."

Shaw smiled. "You're right. We have gold closer to home, Asa."

"No, we don't, not until the coins are lying heavy in our palms."

"The pay wagon will be here any day now," Shaw said. Because of his wound he'd been served breakfast in his quarters. He poured coffee into a cup from a silver pot, then said, "With the Apaches out, we can expect an escort."

"I can take care of them as well," Pagg said.

"You and those two, Asa?" Shaw said. "Maybe this job is getting too big, too complicated. Damnit, the fort is filling up and there's more on the way."

"You wouldn't yellow out on me, Captain, now would you?" Pagg said.

"I'm just saying —"

"I know what you're saying, that the job is too big for you. Well, it ain't too big, it's that you're too damned small."

"Hell, Asa, then reassure me," Shaw said. "Say something to make me feel better."

Pagg smiled. It wasn't a pleasant smile.

"Here's reassurance, Captain Shaw. I start to think that you're turning yellow on me and I'll kill you." He made a gun of his hand and dropped his thumb like a hammer. "Bang! Right between them pretty brown eyes. *Comprende?*"

"Harsh words, Asa," Shaw said.

"Yeah, and I meant every one of them."

A tense silence stretched taut and Joe Harte decided to lift the mood.

"Hey, Cap'n," he said, "would you do that Grove gal?"

Shaw was surprised. "I never really thought about it. No, I don't think I would."

"How about you, Asa?" Harte said.

"Maybe. If I was drunk enough."

"Is she worth saving after the killing starts?" Harte said.

"Hell, no. She has to die with all the rest. We're gonna blame this on Apaches, remember?"

"What about you, Joe?" Logan Dean said. "Would you do her?"

"A beautiful woman is a poem, Logan," Harte said.

"Mrs. Grove ain't beautiful," Dean said.

"No, she's not. And she ain't a poem either, she's newspaper prose."

"Well?" Dean said.

"Well, what?" Harte said.

"Damnit, man, would you do her?"

"Nah. Too scrawny."

"Did we get that settled?" Pagg said. "Or do you want to discuss it further, Logan?"

"Yeah, I guess we got it settled," Dean said. "I wouldn't do her either."

"Then I got the last word," Pagg said. "There are two women in this fort and when the time comes they die with the rest of them."

"Hell, Asa, shooting ol' Mrs. Ashton will be like killing my own ma," Dean said.

"You never had a ma, Logan," Pagg said.

"Everybody had a ma, Asa," Dean said.

Pagg said, "There are exceptions to every rule."

"And you're one of them, Logan," Harte said, grinning.

"Kiss my arse," Dean said.

Shaw picked up the coffeepot, looked inside and then let the lid fall, like a period at the end of a sentence.

"I think our business is concluded," he said. "Asa, we'll meet again when the pay wagon gets here and plan our strategy."

Pagg got to his feet. "I got a hundred thousand dollars riding on you, Shaw," he said. "Don't let me down."

"If they catch me, I'll hang," Shaw said.

"If they catch us, we'll all hang," Pagg said. He scowled at the captain like an unhappy schoolmaster. "You scared?"

"Of course I'm scared. What man can plan to murder a score of people, steal a pay wagon from the U.S. Army and not be scared?"

"Then learn to live with it, Captain," Pagg said. "It gets easier after a while."

"When the time comes, Asa, please, no killing until I give the word," Shaw said. "I want to be damned sure we wrap this up without any loose ends."

"Sure, Captain, sure," Pagg said. He shook his head. "God, you're a pathetic excuse for a man. A damned scared rabbit is what you are."

Pagg turned to Harte. "Hey, Joe, he denies it, but Captain Shaw here would do Mrs. Grove."

"Or she'd do him," Harte said.

CHAPTER EIGHTEEN

When a man reaches a certain age, he'll sometimes catch a glimpse of himself in a mirror and stop and wonder and ask himself, "Can that old coot really be me?"

Sam Flintlock was nearly forty, not quite old enough to seek out lying looking glasses, but his face reflected in the rock pool shocked him.

Despite a growth of stubble, the thunderbird on his throat stood out in stark relief. Grotesque was the effect, a startling image that caused children to run from him and women to take a step back and stare, fascinated yet half afraid.

Flintlock stared at himself, the reflection of the flaming scarlet sky framing his head like a man gazing into a mirror in hell.

Why had old Barnabas done this to him?

"So folks will remember you, boy," the old man had said. "A man folks don't remember is of no account."

Flintlock grimaced, as did the man in the rock pool.

They remember me all right, Barnabas. But for all the wrong reasons.

A rock splashed into the pool and threw water into Flintlock's face. He came up fast, the Colt that had been lying beside him in his hands.

Jack Coffin didn't flinch, only glared at him.

"Why the hell did you do that?" Flintlock said, angry. "I thought it was Apaches."

"If it had been Geronimo and his band, you'd be dead," Coffin said. Then, "Why do you stare into the water, Samuel? What pictures do you see?"

"This face. It was the only picture I saw."

Coffin looked behind him to where Roper and Charlie Fong were bent over, encouraging kindling to flame, then directed his attention back to Flintlock.

"The bird on your throat troubles you," he said. "I can see it in your eyes."

"Sometimes it does. Tonight. It troubles me tonight."

Coffin nodded. "The Lakota call the thunderbird *Wakiya.* It means —"

"I know what it means," Flintlock said.

"Then you know you bear sacred wings on your throat. It is not an evil thing."

139

Flintlock realized he still had the revolver pointed at Coffin. He shoved the Colt back into his waistband and said, "Why are you making this your business?"

"You will not die soon, Sam," Coffin said. "You will live long."

Flintlock smiled. "Well, that's good to hear."

"You have great tribulations ahead and you will suffer a wound. But the thunderbird will bring you luck and you will not perish."

"Hey, Sammy, fill the coffeepot and bring it here, like I told you," Roper yelled. "We got a fire goin'."

"Be right there," Flintlock said. He picked up the pot he'd left by the pool as Coffin said, "Old Barnabas had lived with Indians and what they saw in dreams, he saw. He knew the thunderbird would one day save your life. That is why he had the Assiniboine put it there."

"I guess it's good to think that way, Jack," Flintlock said.

He brushed past Coffin, but stopped and turned when the man said, "Samuel, will you steal the bell?"

"Ain't that why we're here?" Flintlock said.

"It is guarded by Death. That is what they say."

"So you told us already."

Coffin said nothing, but he nodded and walked into the pines.

"What were you and the breed jawing about?" Roper said.

"This and that. The bird on my throat, mostly."

"If that had happened to me, when I got big enough to hold a scattergun I would've cut that old man in half," Roper said.

"Coffin said Barnabas did it to save my life," Flintlock said.

"The breed is crazy, everybody knows that."

"Maybe so," Flintlock said. "How's the coffee?"

Roper lifted the lid of the pot, the firelight red on his face.

"We'll let it bile some more," he said. "She still won't float a silver dollar."

"What do you think, Sam, will Coffin lead us to the bell like he said he would?" Charlie Fong said.

"I believe he will. He says it's guarded by Death."

"Yeah, I know he says that," Roper said. He smiled. "I'll gun Death like I'd gun any

141

man who gets between me and sixty thousand in gold."

"Death can't be killed, Abe," Charlie Fong said. "He is not a man, he's an immortal god, and some say a demon."

Roper shook his shaggy head. "Never expect to get a lick of sense out of a Chinaman," he said.

"Well, I guess we'll find out soon enough," Flintlock said.

His eyes were troubled.

Often swept by a north wind, the Chuska Mountains are restless, and around Flintlock the pines rustled, and higher the aspen trembled, made uneasy by the whispering night. Gibbering things haunted the darkness and squeaking things scuttled in the long grass.

A slight summer rain ticked across the clearing where Flintlock lay awake in his blankets. Roper and Charlie Fong slept by the sputtering fire, but of Coffin there was no sign.

Flintlock closed his eyes and wished for sleep.

He was slipping into the dim twilight between wakefulness and slumber when he felt a rough hand shake his shoulder.

Flintlock was alert instantly and his hand

reached for the Colt at his side.

Jack Coffin held a forefinger to his lips then waved Flintlock to rise and follow.

Flintlock got to his feet and shoved the revolver into his waistband.

"What the hell do you want?" he said.

But Coffin, walking on feet that made no sound, had already stepped into the pines and Flintlock, wary and ready, went after him.

The misty rain did not penetrate the pine canopy but the way ahead was lost in gloom. Coffin set a fast pace and Flintlock followed him, dogtrotting through patches of aspen and unexpected open areas here and there where a few spruce grew.

The game trail Coffin followed left the aspen and again wound through pine, and Flintlock, his eyesight not keen in darkness, was slapped by low-hanging branches that stung his face and streaked cobwebs into his hair, and he cussed himself for ever leaving his blankets.

Coffin led the way to an open meadow. Then he angled to his left toward a high rock cliff that over the ages had eroded into the vague shape of a man's face — heavily lidded eyes, a wide mouth and a great V-shaped outcropping forming the nose.

As he trotted after the breed, Flintlock

fancied that the face had a passing resemblance to George Washington . . . or somebody's maiden aunt.

A moment later he saw the Apaches.

Five of them stood at the bottom of the cliff, shadowy figures lost in the gloom and slanting rain. Far off thunder boomed and to the north above the Carrizo Mountains lightning scrawled across the sky like the signature of a demented god. The night smelled of ozone and wet stone.

Alarmed, Flintlock's hand moved for the Colt in his waistband, but Coffin stopped him. "Geronimo will not harm you," he said. "He is honor bound to respect this truce."

"Why are we here?" Flintlock said. "What's going on?"

"I told him you were a great wonder and he wanted to see for himself."

"The bird?"

"It is powerful medicine. Geronimo says his body bears the scars of seven great battle wounds, but even those don't compare to a man with a thunderbird on his throat. Already he believes that the bird has flapped its wings with the noise of thunder and stirred the wind and rain. Geronimo will be afraid of you, but he will keep his fear hidden."

"I'll ask you again, Jack, what the hell are you up to?"

Coffin smiled, a rare event. "Barnabas says you're an idiot, and that's why you carry the old rifle. He told me you should meet with Geronimo, because he will spare your life one day."

"How did you speak to Barnabas?"

"He came to me in a dream. He's a rough old man and his ways are strange." Coffin's smile went away. "Now come, we will talk with the Apache."

"Geronimo says the thunderbird is a wondrous thing," Jack Coffin said. "He is afraid of your medicine and that is why his knees tremble so."

The old Apache peered through the darkness, his stare fixed on Flintlock's throat. The young warriors with him hung back, but their black eyes shone like obsidian and when thunder crashed they winced and clutched their rifles tighter.

And they glanced uneasily at the sky. The thunderbird in flight is a terrible thing.

Geronimo wore a Mexican peon's cotton shirt, breechclout and knee-high moccasins. His headband, as befit a medicine man, was bright red. Slanted across his chest he held a Springfield rifle, a barrier between him

145

and Flintlock's medicine.

The Apache said something and Coffin translated.

"Geronimo wishes to know if the thunderbird was placed there by *Usen,* the creator of all things," he said. "Humor him, Samuel, say it was. The Apaches don't hold the Assiniboine in high esteem."

"Tell Geronimo that *Usen* came to me in the night and after we talked of many and great things, he left the thunderbird as a gift," Flintlock said. "And damn me fer a liar."

"I won't translate the last part," Coffin said.

He spoke to Geronimo in his own language and the young bucks looked at Flintlock with wide eyes, though the old medicine man's face did not reveal his thoughts.

Geronimo talked again, then Coffin said, "Geronimo says he will remember you."

Lightning gleamed like steel on the wet cliff and the face in the rock was shadowed. Now it looked more like a grinning skull than George Washington or anybody.

There is no word in the Apache language for *good-bye.* Geronimo and his young men simply walked away and were soon swallowed by darkness and rain.

"You did a good thing this night, Samuel," Coffin said.

"I did nothing," Flintlock said. "I did nothing at all."

"Geronimo will protect you."

"From what?"

"From death."

When Flintlock returned to his damp blankets the rain had stopped but thunder grumbled in the distance and the black clouds shimmered with inner light.

Old Barnabas sat by the guttering fire, whittling a stick. He turned and stared hard at Flintlock and the blade of the Barlow gleamed in his right hand.

"Go away, old man," Flintlock said. "I've got nothing to say to you."

Barnabas rose to his feet with the athletic grace he'd possessed even when he was eighty years old. He turned and silently walked into the trees.

The old, lost smell of a great buffalo herd hung in the air.

CHAPTER NINETEEN

Captain Owen Shaw looked out the window of his quarters and was horrified at what he saw.

Drawn by four mules, the pay wagon had just rolled into Fort Defiance . . . but it was escorted by sixteen buffalo soldiers of the 10th Cavalry, fighting men who would not take a step back from anything or anybody.

Shaw cursed under his breath as officer's call sounded.

Like the idiot Grove's escort, the 10th were tough Indian fighters who'd stand their ground and be no bargain in any kind of fight.

Damn, Geronimo and his hostiles were the cause of this, all the damned soldiers riding into the fort.

He needed to talk to Pagg and hear the man's reassurances. They would make him feel better.

Damn, was his murder of Major Ashton

all for naught?

Despite his wound, Shaw was expected to attend officers' meetings. He dressed quickly, strapped on his Colt and hurried in the direction of the headquarters building.

The sun was full up in the sky and the day was already stinking hot. Shaw's boots kicked up puffs of dust as he walked along the edge of the parade ground where the flag hung listlessly in still air and the framing sky was the color of burnished copper.

Asa Pagg stood outside the mess hall, a cup in one hand, his first cigar of the day in the other.

He watched the buffalo soldiers obey their sergeant's order to dismount and like Shaw, he knew he was in a world of trouble.

He stared at the captain as he passed, but Shaw either deliberately ignored him or was too caught up in his own worries to notice.

First Lieutenant Frank Hedley, hungover and unshaven, met Shaw at the door to the commandant's office. He decided to pass on a "good morning," and instead said, "What the hell?"

"Something to do with the pay wagon, I guess," Shaw said. He stared at Hedley and said, "Stand closer to the razor next time you report for duty, Lieutenant. And for God's sake suck on a mint. You reek of whiskey."

Without waiting to hear what Hedley had to say, Shaw opened the door and stepped inside.

The corporal on duty waved in the direction of the door to Major Grove's office. "They're waiting for you, Captain," he said.

"Ah, Captain Shaw," Grove said as Shaw entered with Hedley close behind him. He waved to a young, red-haired major who sat near the desk. "This is Major Karl Jaeger of the 10th Cavalry. Major, allow me to introduce Captain Shaw and First Lieutenant Hedley."

Grove's disapproving eyes lingered on Hedley's stubbly, bloated face as he said, "Major Jaeger is in command of the pay wagon."

The major rose, smiled, and shook hands with both officers. He was a tall man, lean and slightly stooped, with the rakish, devil-may-care look of the fighting frontier cavalryman. He wore a fringed buckskin jacket, decorated by beadwork in the abstract, floral design of the Kiowa, a loosely knotted yellow bandana around his neck and on his head a wide-brimmed straw hat. Jaeger's eyes were navy blue in color and he spoke with a distinct German accent. He looked to be about forty years old, but could've been older.

Jaeger had fought with distinction in the Franco-Prussian War and, after some youthful indiscretions, had later served four years in the French Foreign Legion where he won a medal for gallantry, pinned onto his tunic personally by the great French soldier and patriot Marshal Patrice Mac-Mahon.

Shaw knew none of these things, but he'd pegged Jaeger as a first-rate fighting man and that did not bode well for his schemes.

For his part, Major Jaeger noticed that Shaw was disturbed but he took the wrong tack when he said, "Perhaps you're concerned that there is no paymaster present, Captain?"

Shaw played the game. "Yes, I did think it unusual, Major."

Jaeger smiled. "Orders. Somebody higher up decided that only fighting soldiers should accompany the pay wagon because of the Apache trouble."

Grove said, "Probably just as well. There's a hundred and twenty thousand dollars in gold and silver coin on the wagon."

"Indeed, Major," Jaeger said. Then, his tone joking, "If the word gets out to the lawless element I could have hell on wheels on my hands."

That drew a laugh from Grove and Hedley, but none from Shaw.

A hundred and twenty thousand was more than he'd expected.

But how to get at it? Once he thought it would be easy, but it was getting harder all the time.

Shaw forced himself to breathe easy again. Asa Pagg would have the answer. After all, robbing and killing was his line of work. He was the expert.

But even so, stealing the pay wagon was still a tall order.

Grove was talking again. "Where do you want to park the wagon, Major Jaeger?"

"Right outside where it is at the moment," Jaeger said. "I'll mount a twenty-four-hour guard. Have you any idea when the troops will start to bring in the Apaches? I reckon I'll pay out as the opportunity arises."

"Soon, I hope," Grove said. "I'm ordered to accompany the hostiles to Fort Grant and that can't come fast enough. My lady wife hates this godforsaken post and I don't blame her."

"Sorry to hear that, Major," Jaeger said. "Frontier outposts like this one are no place for women of gentle upbringing and refinement."

"You'll meet Winnifred at dinner tonight," Grove said. "I'm sure she'll be thrilled to hear of your exploits with the fighting 10th."

"Then I'll be delighted to entertain her," Jaeger said. "And I have tales from North Africa that never fail to enthrall the ladies."

"I'm sure Winnifred will add a piquant sauce to my poor table," Grove said. "Salt beef, boiled potatoes and onions followed by plum duff is hardly a fitting meal for a cavalry hero like yourself."

"Hardly a hero," Jaeger said. "And *meine Soldaten* . . . sorry, my soldiers . . . and I have been living on bacon and biscuit for weeks. Beef, even salt beef, will come as a welcome change."

Grove rose to his feet and inserted his monocle. "Then, until this evening, Major Jaeger. First Lieutenant Hedley will show you around the post and help with the disposition of your nigras and their horses."

"My *soldiers,*" Jaeger said, with heavy emphasis on the second word, "are experts at making do and will fend for themselves."

"As you wish, then," Grove, an insensitive man, said. "Just remember that we have two white women at Fort Defiance, Major, so keep your darkies in line."

Despite everything, Shaw was at heart a soldier, and a cavalryman at that. "I'm sure Major Jaeger's troopers will behave in an exemplary manner, as the 10th always does."

"Perhaps," Grove said, "but I just don't trust blacks not to sniff around my wife."

Jaeger and Shaw exchanged glances, the contempt, disgust and anger in their eyes mirror images.

CHAPTER TWENTY

After Shaw and Jaeger stepped outside, the major's face was still stamped with anger and his eyes, normally good-humored, were dark.

"I'm sorry about all that," Shaw said.

"I suppose I should get used to it, but I never do," Jaeger said.

"Grove is an idiot," Shaw said. "I wouldn't let him trouble you."

A disciplined soldier, Jaeger would not allow himself to belittle a fellow officer. He let his face go blank and said nothing.

"Lieutenant Hedley will show you around and help get your men settled," Shaw said. "Your quarters will be next to mine, Major."

Jaeger nodded his thanks, his eyes idly moving over his men, who were leading their horses toward the stables under the stern gaze of a graying sergeant whose skin had the color and sheen of polished ebony.

The troopers' mounts kicked up gray dust

that a hot wind drove across the parade ground like mist, filming the rusty old cannon that stood on guard under the flagpole.

"May I have your permission to attend to my duties, Major?" Shaw said.

"Yes, of course, Captain."

Shaw's right arm angled a snappy salute and he turned and walked back to his quarters. As he knew he would, Asa Pagg followed him.

"A hundred and twenty thousand dollars for the taking," Owen Shaw said. He was silent for a moment, fuming, and then spat out, "Only we can't take it."

"Who says we can't take it?" Asa Pagg said.

"Come again?"

"You heard me, Captain," Asa Pagg said. "And in case you didn't, I'll say it again. Who says we can't take it?"

"Did you see the size of the escort? Those are fighting soldiers and the man in charge is no fool," Shaw said. "How can we beat odds like that?"

"Geronimo."

The captain sank into a chair. "What the hell are you talking about?"

Pagg reached inside his coat and came up with a cigar. He bit off the end, spat it onto the floor and thumbed a match into flame. Holding the burning match in his fingers, he said, "We talk to Geronimo and ask for his help."

"And ask for his help? Asa, are you out of your damned mind?"

Pagg took time to light the cigar, then said through a cloud of blue smoke, "I'm talking massacree. The death of everybody in Fort Defiance, including them nigras that have you showing your yellow streak again."

"You're talking nonsense," Shaw said. "I mean, utter nonsense."

"Well, how about you shut your trap and listen, soldier boy," Pagg said. "We know the Apaches are in this neck of the woods, on account of how they done for Lieutenant Howard and we done for a passel o' them. Right?"

Shaw looked into Pagg's face, his eyes confused.

"Right?" Pagg said again.

"Yes, I guess that's right," Shaw said. "So what's your drift?"

"We meet with Geronimo and tell him we'll help him take Fort Defiance. All we want in return is the pay wagon. The Apaches don't set store by American money, so Geronimo won't give a damn about the wagon."

Shaw flinched, as though he felt a sudden pain.

"You mean . . . you mean we'll help savages murder everyone in the fort?"

Pagg smiled. "Yup, that's what the man said. Hell, do you care? All we'll kill is a bunch of folks you don't even like."

Shaw let his head drop into his cupped hands. His voice muffled, he said, "I'm an officer in the United States Army and I took an oath to protect our nation from all enemies, foreign or domestic. I can't break my oath and help a savage like Geronimo kill Americans."

"Hell, you broke that oath when you decided to steal the pay wagon and shot your commanding officer," Pagg said. "Don't sit there crying on my shoulder, Owen, boy. You're in all the way and your only way out is with me."

Shaw suddenly looked twenty years older. "There's got to be another way," he said. "We must find another way."

"There is no other way."

"Then we walk away from it, Asa. Let's just shake hands and part company. Maybe we'll have better luck next time."

"Like I told you, you're already in this thing too far to back out now. Hell, did you even think of your damned oath when you

158

shot Major Ashton, huh?"

"Geronimo won't talk to us," Shaw said. "He shoots white men on sight."

"We go in under a flag of truce. Geronimo has fought Mexicans long enough to know what a white flag means."

"He'll never go for it, Asa. We'll end up hanging upside down over a slow fire, dying by inches."

"He'll go for it. Hell, look what's in it for him . . . horses, guns, ammunition and the end of a fort that's been a pain in the Apache butt for years."

"He could be anywhere. We'll never find him."

"Yeah, you're right. He'll find us."

Shaw was silent for a few moments, then said, "It's thin, Asa. I think it's way too thin to work."

"Well, it's all we got."

"You don't even speak Apache."

"You soldier boys taught the Apaches to speak American pretty damn quick. We can get along."

Shaw said nothing, his head bent, a man being torn apart.

"Well?" Pagg said. "Is it a go?"

The captain nodded slowly and sighed, like a Judas in blue agreeing to the thirty pieces of silver.

"It's a go," he said finally.

"Hard times comin' down, Owen," Pagg said. "Just be ready."

Without looking up, Shaw nodded again.

Outside, brassy in the afternoon, the bugler sounded mess call.

CHAPTER TWENTY-ONE

Jack Coffin led the way across Buffalo Pass and then dropped down into the sandstone butte country at the southern end of the Red Rock Valley.

He turned in the saddle and said to Flintlock, "There is a trading post a mile ahead. We can get grub there and a place to sleep. And we need to rest the pack mules."

"Hell, Jack, there's a couple of hours of daylight left," Abe Roper said. "I say we press on. The mules are only carrying sledgehammers and pickaxes. It ain't a heavy load."

Coffin lifted his nose to the high mountain wind. "More rain coming. Best we take shelter soon."

"There ain't a cloud in the sky," Roper said. "It ain't gonna rain, trust me."

The breed ignored that and said, "We will find shelter at Gauley's trading post, and food."

161

"Sam'l, what do you reckon?" Roper said.

Flintlock answered that with a question of his own. "Jack, how far are we from the cave?"

"I don't know. Not far if the map is right. If the map is wrong, then who knows?"

"It's right," Roper said. "I'd stake my life on the map being right."

"Tomorrow, then," Coffin said. "We'll find the cave tomorrow."

Flintlock calmed his restive horse, then said to Roper, "Makes sense to hole up for the night, Abe. And the mules are getting tired."

"How's the whiskey an' the grub at . . . what the hell's her name?" Roper said.

"Chastity Gauley. The grub is good but I don't know about the whiskey."

"Girls?" Roper said.

"Sometimes."

"What about Chastity herself?" Roper said. "I've always liked that name for a woman, even though I never believed it."

"Chastity must dress out at around four hundred pounds," Coffin said. "He's a sight to see, even for an Indian."

"He? You mean a man who calls himself Chastity?"

"You'll find out, Roper," Coffin said.

"Ah well, if the grub's good, let's take

162

Sammy's advice an' give her . . . damnit . . . his place a whirl," Roper said.

"Just don't order the rabbit stew," Coffin said.

"How come?" Roper said.

"It ain't rabbit."

Coffin smiled and kneed his horse forward, and behind him, Roper said, "Anything else you feel the need to tell me?"

The trading post was an adobe building with a sod roof and a ramshackle porch out front with a painted, weathered sign that read:

BUFFALO PASS TRADING POST
~ CHAS. GAULEY, PROP.

The cabin was built like a fortress, with firing slits cut into its four walls, and the adobe was pock-marked with bullet holes, the calling cards of many Apache attacks. Behind the cabin was a smokehouse, chicken coop and what looked to be a two-holer outhouse, unheard of luxury on the frontier. There was also a pole corral with a lean-to shelter, a well, and a hundred yards farther back a small graveyard with a dozen crosses tilted over at all angles.

Roper drew rein, stared at the place for a

few moments, then said, "Well, it's homey, I guess."

"The coffee smells good," Charlie Fong said.

"Coffee always smells good, it's how it tastes that counts," Roper said.

"Then let's go make a trial of it," Flintlock said.

He held the Hawken high, swung out of the saddle and led his horse toward the hitching rail. The others followed him.

To the north the sky was gray with rain clouds and leaves blew out of the aspen groves and tossed like scraps of paper in the wind.

Flintlock opened the door of the post and stepped inside from light to the gloom of oil lamp and tobacco smoke.

But even in the semidarkness he knew he was in a heap of trouble.

A man often meets his destiny on the road he took to avoid it, and Sam Flintlock should never have run into Hiram Elliot . . . not then, not there, not ever.

Committed to stepping inside, getting pushed from behind by the impatient Roper, Flintlock walked into the cabin.

A gunfighter takes in a room at a glance and any potential dangers stand out like

164

diamonds in a coal scuttle.

That day Hiram Elliot, small, thin and fast with the iron, was the brightest diamond of all.

The man sitting at a table with him was a weasel by the name of Dark Alley Jim Cole, a blade artist who'd cut more throats than an abattoir slaughterer.

Elliot once had a brother, now greatly missed. Josh was his name, a killer and rapist, and Flintlock had put him six feet under after he'd tried to skip town to avoid arrest.

That Josh had made the serious mistake of skinning iron on Flintlock was neither here nor there to Hiram Elliot. A native of the Ozarks, he lived by the feud and the code of an eye for an eye.

There would be no back-up in him. Not that day or any other.

Flintlock knew a killing was on the cards and he'd no way of avoiding it.

Roper bellied up to the rough pine bar with Charlie Fong, and Flintlock joined them. He realized full well that the trouble wouldn't go away, but for now he chose to ignore it. The Colt in his waistband was tight and snug, its cold cheek pressed reassuringly against his skin, and he propped up the Hawken where it would be handy.

"Can we get service here?" Roper said,

thumping on the bar.

Out of the corner of his eye Flintlock saw that Cole's hand was on Elliot's forearm and he was talking earnestly to him, his mouth close to the other man's ear. Elliot's eyes were fixed on Flintlock's back, his mouth a tight, scissored gash.

Flintlock knew it was coming down. The only question was *when.*

A curtain rattled open on its rings and a . . . vision of ugliness . . . stepped behind the bar.

"What'll it be, gents?" Chastity Gauley said.

Flintlock, Roper and Charlie Fong didn't answer, but their jaws dropped to their belt buckles.

How else to react to a man who stood eight inches over six feet, sported a huge, black dragoon mustache and had eyebrows like hairbrushes . . . yet wore a woman's pink afternoon dress in the latest fashion, complete with bustle and heavily boned waist. A tiny hat, decorated with a faux millinery bird, perched on a scraggly blond wig and Gauley's thick lips were painted bright carmine, his cheeks rouged the same color.

Piling horror on top of horror, Gauley was enormously fat and he was sweating like a hog butcher after a frost.

Roper, more used to the vagaries of brothels and their denizens, was the first to recover.

"Three whiskeys," he said. Then, "You must be Chastity."

"Yes, indeed," Gauley said, his hairy fingers clenched around a whiskey bottle. "Chastity by name but not by nature. Afore I became a lady, my name was Charles."

"Hey, that's my name," Fong said. "I'm called Charlie."

"How wonderful for you," Gauley said, dry as dust.

He stared at Flintlock. "You have a bird on your throat."

"I know."

"It's . . . how should I say? Becoming?"

"Thank you."

"Spoils your looks though. It's just as well you weren't very handsome to begin with."

"Thank you," Flintlock said.

After Gauley poured the drinks and picked up Roper's silver dollar from the bar, he said, "When you feel like it, go through the curtain to the dry goods department. I have a wide selection of clothing and footwear for sale, including a consignment of gents' button-up ankle boots to be sold at cost. They were shipped to me from Denver and when they're gone, they're gone."

Flintlock heard a chair scrape behind him and he locked eyes with Hiram Elliot in the mirror behind the bar. The gunfighter hadn't moved but his stare met Flintlock's and promised hell.

Above the mirror hung a sign that read:

HAVE YOU WRITTEN TO MOTHER?

And to the right of that a railroad clock with a yellowed face ticked slow seconds into the room.

Gauley had a big, booming voice, like a blacksmith talking over the din of his forge, and he said, "You boys passing through?"

"Headin' north," Roper said. "We got a lot of country to see."

"Well, if you're passing this way again, I have a couple of young ladies come in on Thursday nights." He hesitated, then made a face as he said, "If you're interested in that kind of thing."

"Oh yes, we are, very much so," Charlie Fong said, the words tumbling out quickly.

"Pity," Gauley said. He winked at Fong, who suddenly found something of great interest at the bottom of his glass.

"Where's Coffin?" Flintlock said, raising his voice for the first time since he'd entered the post.

"Don't know," Roper said. "Probably outside scalping some poor sumbitch." He held up his glass. "Same again, Chas."

The sound of Flintlock's voice provided the catalyst that fanned the flames of Hiram Elliot's hatred and set him in motion.

He scraped back his chair, deliberately noisy, and got to his feet. Cole, a careful man, remained sitting, but he grinned like an ape.

Flintlock, knowing the time had come, set down his untouched whiskey and turned, his back against the bar.

Elliot wore his Colt high on his right side, in the horseman's fashion, its seven-and-a-half-inch barrel a potent reminder of his origins in the Ozarks.

"You be Sam Flintlock," Elliot said.

"You know it," Flintlock said.

"I been hunting you, Flintlock. A man with a bird on his throat who carries an old Hawken ain't too hard to track down."

"I got no beef agin you, Elliot."

"No dodger on me, you mean."

"I seen one. Had a good likeness of you on it. Said you was wanted for murder and rape, dead or alive."

"So you plan to kill me just like you did Josh. Only you ain't shooting me in the back

169

like you done him."

"He'd been notified but he still drew down on me. It was his mistake."

Elliot's hand moved closer to his gun. "No, it was your mistake."

The door swung open, letting in a blast of scorching air, and two dusty, bearded miners stepped into the room. Gauley, dropping all pretense to manhood, screeched, "Oh, Luke and Baldy, just in time. Please, take my mirror down." He pulled a scrap of lacy handkerchief from the pocket of his dress and fanned his face. "Ooh, this is terrible. There's going to be a gunfight."

The miners sized up the situation and one of them said, "That would kinda put us in the line of fire, Chastity."

"Ooh, men! I'll do it myself."

Gauley flounced to the mirror, which was large and heavy, and unhooked it from the wall as easily as a woman would take down a tintype of Mother. He hurried through the curtain again and before it swung back in place he started to sob.

Roper said, "Want me to take a hand, Sam'l? Hell, I'll gun him for you if'n you want."

"No. I guess I'll call my own play when I see how the cards fall."

"When you feel my bullet hit, remember

that it's for Josh," Elliot said.

"Are you trying to talk me to death, Elliot?" Flintlock said. "Make your play and get your work in."

"Josh got it in the belly," Elliot said. "And so will you, Flintlock." His eyes glittered. "An eye for an eye, a tooth for a tooth."

He made his move. Smooth. Practiced. Fast.

But not fast enough. Not even close.

Only one man in a thousand, perhaps in ten thousand, has the genetic potential and coordination between brain and hand to be lightning quick and deadly accurate on the draw and shoot.

Sam Flintlock was of that rare breed.

Elliot's long-barreled Colt was leveling when Flintlock's first bullet hit him.

The shot took the little gunman high in the chest, a severe wound that was enough to make him take a step back before he gritted his teeth and again got his revolver in play.

Elliot fired, but his bullet went wild as strength sapped out of him.

Flintlock, his Colt now held at arm's length, used the front sight and fired again. And again. Two hits, one to the center of Elliot's chest, the second, lower and to the right, plowed a furrow across the gunman's ribs, smashing bone.

Elliot went down on his knees, coughing blood. He stared hard at Flintlock and tried to lift his Colt. But he was done.

Dark Alley Jim Cole then made the last and worst mistake of his miserable existence.

He drew a .32 Smith & Wesson and two-handed it straight out in front of him, aiming at Flintlock.

Abe Roper drew, fired and blew the top of Cole's head clean off.

The man fell, perhaps wishing at the moment of death that he'd stuck to blades.

As Charlie Fong said later, "Jim Cole got his work in like a girl."

A gunfight is long in the telling but short in the doing.

The railroad clock on the wall tick-tocked only three times from the moment Elliot made his gun move to the death of Jim Cole.

But to Flintlock it seemed like an eternity.

He turned his head and his eyes met Roper's through a drift of gray gunsmoke.

Roper shrugged. "I thought I'd help out."

"You did," Flintlock said. "Thanks."

Chastity emerged through the curtain again, took one look at the dead men and promptly fainted.

When he hit the ground the trading post
shook.

CHAPTER TWENTY-TWO

The buffalo soldiers of C Troop, 10th Cavalry, had been on campaign against Apaches for two months and exhaustion showed on their faces as they prodded their equally weary captives south toward Fort Defiance under an iron-gray sky that blustered the threat of rain.

Once at full strength, ninety-five men, four civilian teamsters and two Piute scouts, detached duties and casualties had reduced the troop to just fifty-eight, half of them raw recruits.

Captain Robert Gibbs rode at the head of the column with Sergeants Fogarty and Ryan and the guidon corporal. Second Lieutenant Wilfred Mansfield rode drag, in command of herding the hostiles.

Captain Gibbs, a fine-looking soldier with a set of vast muttonchop whiskers, was distantly related to Ambrose E. Burnside and he'd adopted the general's style of facial hair as homage to the great man.

"Keeping Uncle Ambrose's whiskers in the family, don't ye know," he was wont to say. "I've recently heard men refer to them as sideburns, and I must say that it makes me quite proud."

But Gibbs was not a mere frontier dandy, he was a competent, brave officer and right now he was worried.

The black troopers, normally sympathetic toward the Apaches, were in a bitter mood. Earlier that morning, the discovery of the bodies of six miners and their womenfolk, and the killing of one of their own, had made them as hostile toward Apaches as any of their white comrades.

The screaming madwoman now riding in the supply wagon was a constant reminder of what they'd found, and with every hysterical shriek angry whispers were exchanged between the grim-faced troopers.

Gibbs decided his first order of business was to get rid of the woman and then hopefully the troop's anger would cool and with it the very real threat of massacred captives.

The troop had pushed forward ten miles since daybreak and then as the sun began its slow descent to the horizon they'd come on the dead miners.

Three wagons were scattered across a

grassy meadow that was thick with blue wildflowers, bordered by stands of pine and aspen. It was a pretty spot to be the scene of such a horrific catastrophe.

The Apaches had come out of the trees fast and struck hard.

According to the Piute scouts who read the signs, the miners had no time to mount a coordinated defense and most had been killed within minutes, right where they stood.

An older, gray-haired woman, perhaps the mother of one of the men, had been shot and had died quickly. The two other women, younger, had not been so lucky. Both had been raped and one of them, with bright red hair, was dead. The other wandered naked among the wildflowers and alternately screamed and muttered nonsense to herself.

Gibbs ascribed the death of the redhead as one of God's tender mercies. As for the other, she'd have to travel in the wagon all the way to Fort Defiance where the females at the post, who would understand the dreadful implications of what the girl had suffered, could care for her.

But then, disaster piled on disaster . . .

One of the young troopers, a raw recruit from the Boston slums, was detailed to help collect the naked bodies for burial, and along with five others he rode into the meadow.

The woman's screams were constant now, shrill and agonizing, and the trooper opened his mouth in horror and put his hands over his ears.

Captain Gibbs, who was there, later said he should've recognized the warning signs and relieved the man of duty, but didn't.

The trooper, a seventeen-year-old named Jackson, cried out like a man in pain and suddenly swung his horse around and galloped to the rear of the column. There eighty captive Apaches, all of them Chiricahua, sat in a circle, gazing at nothing. There were no warriors, just old men, women, several of them pregnant, and children.

Possessed by whatever demons the sight of the tortured, naked bodies had instilled in him, young Jackson rode among the captives and cut loose with his service revolver, shooting indiscriminately into them.

Sergeant Ryan said later that the trooper was screaming obscenities at the Apaches as he fired. He killed one old man, a woman and a couple of children before his Colt clicked on an empty chamber.

Jackson, raving, was reaching for the

carbine under his knee when Ryan shot him out of the saddle.

Trooper Jackson had been buried with the rest, but now the troop was seething with anger toward the Apaches and resentment directed at Sergeant Ryan, a decent enough man who'd stopped the killing the only way he knew how.

Captain Gibbs told his men it had been Ryan's duty to stop the killing, but it didn't help much.

With less than two hours of daylight left, under a threatening sky, a flurry of gunshots carried in the rising wind added to Captain Gibbs's woes.

He halted the column and said to gray-haired Sergeant Adam Fogarty, since Sergeant Ryan had been temporarily relieved of duty, "Apaches, d'ye think?"

Fogarty, who'd fought with the 10th in the 1880 campaign against Victorio, said, "Yes, sir. And to the south of us, I reckon."

"What's there, Sergeant? More wagons?"

"I doubt it, sir. But there's a trading post down that way."

"So the hostiles could be attacking the trading post?"

"Could be, sir. But the firing has stopped already."

"Maybe Geronimo got his fingers

burned."

"I couldn't say, sir."

"How far is the trading post?"

Fogarty looked around him, fixing landmarks. "Two miles, sir. No more than that."

Captain Gibbs was uncomfortably aware that this far from Fort Defiance if he brought on an engagement with Apaches he could expect no help. His orders were to duck a fight and deliver the captive hostiles in a timely manner. He'd been told that in any case the presence of so many blue coats would deter any attack.

But gunshots so close at least bore some investigation.

Gibbs nodded and said, "Sergeant, my compliments to Lieutenant Mansfield and ask him to join me at the head of the column."

A few moments later, Mansfield, a fresh-faced youth with clear blue eyes and a peach-fuzz mustache, brought his mount alongside Captain Gibbs.

"You heard the shots, Mr. Mansfield?" Gibbs said.

"Yes, sir."

Gibbs repeated what Fogarty had told him, then said, "Our orders are to escort the prisoners to Fort Defiance, not engage Apaches. But I will ride ahead to reconnoiter the situation with Sergeant Fogarty, one of the scouts and the first two pairs. You will bring on the rest of the column with all expedition."

Mansfield saluted. "Yes, sir." Then, "Ah, sir, the captives will slow us down."

A gust of rain spattered over the officers and distant thunder rumbled.

"Then make them walk faster, Lieutenant Mansfield," Gibbs said. He clapped his gloved hands. "Come on now, chop-chop."

CHAPTER TWENTY-THREE

At Chastity Gauley's insistence, Flintlock and Abe Roper carried out their dead in a drizzling rain and laid them under a nearby pine.

Gauley decided to have another fit of the vapors and flopped into a chair on his tumbledown porch, fanning his flushed face with a lacy handkerchief.

He was still there when a cavalry officer and six troopers rode up to the post, the red and white guidon of the 10th Cavalry snapping above their heads.

Before Captain Gibbs could speak, Chastity, an ox in a frilly dress, ran from the porch, waving his arms. "Murder! Murder!" he yelled.

Taken aback, Gibbs took a few moments to answer. Then he said, "Calm yourself, ma'am . . . sir . . ." He looked totally confused before the soldier in him reasserted itself. "What happened here? Was it

Apaches?"

Gibbs caught sight of Flintlock and his eyes lingered on his tattooed throat. Again he seemed bewildered.

"No, it wasn't Apaches," Gauley said. "Two dead men lie under the tree over there." He pointed to Flintlock and Roper. "Killed by those two."

"Well?" Gibbs said to Flintlock. His eyes telegraphed that he badly wanted to mention the bird, but as an officer and a gentleman that would be uncouth.

"Those two were hunting me," Flintlock said. "They found me."

"Are they lawmen?" Gibbs said, glancing at the bodies.

"No, they're skunks," Flintlock said.

"It was a fair fight, General." This from one of the miners. "Them fellers drawed down on these gentlemen and they defended themselves."

"That is a matter for the civil authorities, not the army," Gibbs said. "I have more important problems at the moment."

He glanced at Sergeant Fogarty, who sat his saddle stiffly, his face empty, then back to Gauley.

"I am Captain Robert Gibbs of the 10th Cavalry, escorting a number of hostiles to Fort Defiance. How do I address you?"

"Miss Chastity is fine, or just plain Chastity."

Gibbs gave an "ahem," then said, "Well, ah, Chastity, I have a favor to ask of you."

"Ask away, Captain, I'm always willing to help the army." Gauley looked around him. "Where are the Apaches?"

"With the main column, that should be here shortly," Gibbs said. "Now to the favor I need of you . . . ah . . . Chastity. Mine is a most singular problem, but it is of the greatest moment. It involves a young lady who was with a party of gold miners who were wiped out by Apaches."

Flintlock and Roper exchanged glances, and Charlie Fong spoke for both of them when he said, "Where was this, Cap'n? And did they have wagons?"

"A few miles north of here in the Red Rock Valley. And yes, they had three wagons," Gibbs said. "Why do you ask?"

"I just wondered," Fong said.

Roper looked agitated.

Gold miners with wagons in the Red Valley was bad news. Had they got wind of the bell?

Gibbs was talking again. "The young lady in question was ravaged most mercilessly by the Apaches and now, as a result, is quite mad. Her pitiful cries and screams are

183

undermining the morale of my men and I can no longer deal with her."

"So you want to leave her here?" Gauley said.

"In a word, yes."

"Soldiers can just about stand more'n they think they can, Captain," Chastity said.

"My troopers, for reasons I won't go into here, are already on edge," Gibbs said. "The woman is making things much worse."

The captain's shoulders slumped. "If you can't take her in, I'm afraid all I can do is abandon her to her fate. I can't let her undermine morale any longer."

"Is she a white woman?" Gauley said.

"Yes. And very pretty . . . or she was."

"You can't leave a white woman by the trail at the mercy of Apaches and wild animals," Gauley said. "All right, then bring her here. It will be nice to have another woman I can talk to."

"Yes. Quite." Gibbs's saddle creaked as he adjusted his seat. "But I'm afraid all she does is scream. She won't talk."

"Never underestimate the power of a woman," Gauley said.

Gibbs had no idea how to take that, but he was spared the need to reply when Fogarty said, "Column coming up, sir."

■ ■ ■ ■

Heads bent, C Company came on through a lashing rain. Above the troopers the sky looked like sheets of curled lead, branded by dazzling scrawls of lightning. Clouds blanketed the Carrizo Mountains like black gauze, but here and there green pine tops arrowed above the gloom.

Lieutenant Mansfield, wearing a slicker that gleamed in the fading light, rode at the head of the column, behind him the troopers, then the wagons and bringing up the rear the Apache prisoners, chivvied forward by soldiers just as wet and miserable as they were.

Because of the coming darkness and bad weather, further travel was impossible. Gibbs ordered Mansfield to bivouac the men in the trees and keep the Apaches under strong guard. He warned the lieutenant that the captives were to be fed only hardtack and water so that, according to his orders, "The hostiles should thus be rendered weak, passive and pliable, present no threat and be incapable of either fight or flight."

The old were already weak, as were the children. Only the young women had any reserve of strength, but the bread and water diet and the hard trail were steadily draining them.

Sam Flintlock and Abe stood on the post porch, rain ticking from the rickety roof, when a couple of troopers brought a woman from one of the wagons and headed in their direction.

She wasn't screaming, not then, but she walked with empty eyes, unseeing, uncaring. The woman, a girl really, was pretty, with a mass of auburn hair and dazzling blue eyes. Her calico dress was torn and stained and she bled from a cut on her forehead.

As she passed Flintlock she pointed at herself and said, "Seventeen." Then the soldiers took her inside.

"She ain't ever gonna be right again," Roper said. "Apaches can do that to a woman."

"She's pretty," Flintlock said.

"Yeah, but she won't stay like that much longer."

Captain Gibbs left the bivouac in the trees and stepped onto the porch.

"Did you see the madwoman?" he said.

"Yeah," Flintlock said, "she's inside."

"A tragic case," Gibbs said.

"I reckon," Flintlock said.

Flintlock saw the soldier's eyes go to his face, then his throat and slide away quickly as though they'd been burned.

"It happened when I was a boy," Flintlock said.

Gibbs looked relieved that he could finally mention the bird. "Who did that to you?" he said.

"Well, I reckon the Assiniboine," Flintlock said. "But it was my grandpappy's idea. He was a retired mountain man, rode with Jim Bridger an' them."

"He should've been horsewhipped," Gibbs said. "Even wearing a cravat, you can never appear in polite society. Did he realize that?"

"I don't know," Flintlock said. "Ol' Barnabas didn't know any polite society."

"What did your parents say?"

"They weren't around back then."

"You have my sympathies."

"Thank you, but I've grown used to it and so have my friends," Flintlock said. "Ol' Geronimo says the thunderbird on my body is good medicine."

"You met him?" Gibbs said, surprised.

"Only once."

" 'Good medicine' . . . it's the kind of thing a painted savage would say."

"When I met him he wasn't wearing paint."

Gibbs smiled. "They say he's so evil, he's grown horns. But I don't put any stock in that."

"Hell, Captain, he's got a spread like a Texas longhorn," Flintlock said.

Gibbs's gaze searched Flintlock's face, saw a crooked, amused smile, then he said, "You had me going there for a minute." He laughed. " 'A spread like a Texas longhorn.' Good. Jolly good." He touched the brim of his kepi. "Now, if you will excuse me."

After Gibbs brushed past and stepped into the post, Roper said, "Them two dead men need buryin'."

"Come morning I'll ask the captain if I can get a couple of his boys to help," Flintlock said.

Roper was about to say something but the words died in his throat.

Jack Coffin was walking toward them through the rain, his face like thunder.

CHAPTER TWENTY-FOUR

Lieutenant Colonel Tyne Martin was a hard, unforgiving man.

And that was why the Apache named Gosheven, the Leaper, kneeled on the wet ground and sang his death song.

A hemp noose hung from the limb of an ancient cottonwood, surrounded by caped infantry with fixed bayonets. Near the soldiers stood Gosheven's wife and three children, one of them a babe in arms.

Behind her huddled a dozen old women, their faces networked with deeply cut lines. Their black eyes were empty and tearless, drained by all the violent deaths they'd already seen.

The cottonwood stood in the high desert country, on the bank of a narrow stream that had its origins somewhere near Beautiful Mountain. The volcanic peak, a solitary outpost of the Chuska range, lay a mile to the west of the execution site, but it was lost behind shifting sheets of racketing rain.

"You think he knows why he's dying, Colonel?"

"Yes, Major Lowery, he knows," Martin said. He was a tall, thin man with a lined face as friendly as a honed hatchet blade.

"Seems a hard thing to kill a man for stealing some hardtack and a bag of flour," Lowery said.

"Since when did Apache bucks become men, Major?" Martin said.

Lowery made no answer and Martin said, "If the thief had gotten away with the food, some of my soldiers would've gone hungry. That is tantamount to treason. I hang men for treason."

"He was trying to feed his wife and children, sir."

Martin glared at his subordinate, his eyes as cold and unfriendly as lead bullets in the cylinder of a Colt. "I don't give a damn who he was trying to feed. Do I make myself clear?"

"Yes, sir. I understand your feelings perfectly."

"Good. Then enough of this damned heathen chanting. Proceed with the execution."

Lowery saluted and as he stepped away he called out to his men to get the Apache on the back of the horse that stood head-down under the swaying noose.

Gosheven was manhandled onto the horse and there was a pause as Colonel Martin drew his sword and, as though he was on parade, marched closer to the condemned man to give the signal.

The Apache's eyes met his wife's and he managed a smile.

I remember, Ela, when I played the courting flute outside your father's wickiup and how beautiful you looked when you stepped outside and smiled on me. I remember the birth of our first son and the way —

"Broke his damned neck clean," Martin said, sheathing his sword.

"Indeed, sir," Lowery said. "He didn't suffer."

The colonel snorted. "He didn't suffer! God save us from bleeding hearts."

But Lowery said nothing. He was staring across the flat ground to a patch of piñon and juniper.

Colonel Martin followed his gaze, then said, "Who the hell are they?"

"I don't know, sir. Looks like a monk and a young boy."

"Spies for Geronimo, likely," Martin said. He called out to the nearest junior officer, "Mr. Jerome, those two in the trees! Bring

191

them to me!"

The young lieutenant stared into the pines, then saluted. "Yes, sir."

"A strange business, Major Lowery," Martin said as he watched a dozen soldiers with fixed bayonets follow the lieutenant into the juniper. "What's a monk doing in this wilderness?"

Lowery shook his head. "I can't even hazard a guess, sir."

"Out trying to convert the heathen Apache, do you think?"

"It might well be, sir."

"Impossible task, I should imagine," Martin said. He thought for a few moments, then said, "No, they're spies, and by God they'll swing on the same rope as the Apache."

"Gone, sir. It's as though they vanished off the face of the earth."

"Did you search thoroughly, Lieutenant?" Colonel Martin said.

"Sir, if they were within a mile of here we'd have found them."

"Damnit, two people don't just vanish. Incompetent searching, I'd say."

Lieutenant Jerome looked miserable, the rain falling around him.

"Sir, we searched everywhere, behind

every tree, under every bush. There was no sign of them."

"Gone to ground, the rascals," Martin said. "Well, it doesn't really matter."

He turned to Major Lowery. "Get the hostiles on their feet and we'll resume the march. And take those damned wailing women away."

"What about the Apache, sir?" Lowery said.

"What about him?"

"Should I cut him down?"

"No, leave the beggar swinging. It will serve as a warning to others."

"A warning to which others, sir?" Lowery said.

"Don't be so damned impertinent, Major," Martin said. "A warning to whoever needs a warning."

The old man and the boy had walked through rain and crashing thunder for an hour before the boy spoke.

"Why didn't they see us, Grandfather?" he said.

"We were hidden by the trees."

"But they should have seen us. Is it because you are a great lord and they fear you? Is that why they didn't see us?"

The old man smiled. "You ask too many

questions, child."

"The Apache died well," the boy said.

"Yes, he did. His soul is now with his god."

After a long silence broken only by the old man's heavy breathing and the dragon hiss of the rain, the boy said, "What of the man you saw in a dream?"

The old man didn't answer, and the boy said, "The one who wears animal skins and has a bird on his throat."

"He comes," the old man said.

"Will he take the bell?"

"I don't know."

The boy looked at the lowering clouds and made a face, "Pah, why does it rain, Grandfather?"

"Because the sky weeps over the death of the sun."

"Will you weep for the bell if it is stolen?"

"Heaven will weep for the bell if it is stolen," the old man said.

CHAPTER TWENTY-FIVE

"They're penned up like cattle," Jack Coffin said. "Old men, women and children guarded by rifles. Half of them won't live to see Fort Defiance."

"*Vae victis,*" Charlie Fong said.

Coffin looked at Abe Roper. "What the hell is your Chinaman saying?"

"Hell if I know," Roper said.

"It's Latin and it means 'Woe to the conquered,' " Fong said.

"The Apache are not conquered," Coffin said. "Geronimo is still in the field."

"But they are a conquered people," Flintlock said. "Soon the Apache will go the way of the Comanche and the Cheyenne."

Coffin's anger would not let it rest. "Go where? The San Carlos?"

Flintlock shook his head. "No, Jack, far worse than even the San Carlos. Old Barnabas said the Indians would be defeated and then sent to the 'land of starvation.' "

"Where is this land?" Coffin said.

"I don't know."

"That's because you are a white man and know nothing."

Coffin's black eyes fixed on Roper. "How can we help the Apache?"

"How many of them are there?"

"I think a hundred. Maybe more."

"Then there ain't nothing we can do to help them," Roper said. "We came here for a reason, Jack, and that reason wasn't to help Apaches. Or have you forgotten?"

"The golden bell. I haven't forgotten. I'll find it for you."

"Right joyful to hear that," Roper said.

"Is there no one to help the Apache?" Coffin said.

"I can't bring dead men back to life," Roper said.

"I've heard rumors of a new dance that will resurrect all the dead Indian warriors and bring back the buffalo herds," Flintlock said.

Coffin nodded. "I have heard of this also. Among the Piute it is called the Ghost Dance."

Roper grinned. "Well, there you go, Jack. There's hope for your people yet."

Coffin said nothing. He turned and walked away toward the bivouac where the Apaches were held.

"Hard to figure a breed," Roper said, watching him go.

"Seems like," Flintlock said. Then, "Damn, I need a drink."

When Sam Flintlock stepped into the post he caught the sawed-off end of a conversation between the miners.

". . . still worth taking with us is all I'm sayin'."

"I don't know, Luke," the other man said. "Depends what Chas wants for her. Women don't come cheap in this country."

The man called Luke, big and burly with a bushy red beard, said, "What about it, Chas. How much will you take for her?"

Chastity Gauley glanced at the girl who sat silent on a chair, her head bowed, thick waves of hair tumbled over her face. Her torn dress had fallen away from her shoulders, revealing the milky swelling of the tops of her breasts.

"I dunno," Gauley said. "A woman like that don't come cheap here or anywhere else."

"Hell, man, she's crazy. Why do you want her?" Luke said.

"Why do *you* want her?" Gauley said.

Luke sighed his exasperation. "Why do

you think?"

"The lady isn't for sale," Flintlock said.

"Sez who?" Luke said.

"Sez me," Flintlock said.

Luke sized up the man with the bird on his throat and the Colt in his waistband and decided he wanted no part of him. He'd seen him use that Colt once and had no desire to see it again.

He backed off. "Sorry, mister, I didn't know she was already took."

Flintlock ignored that. He didn't blame the miners none. Any man would get horny who hasn't seen a white woman in months.

"Gauley," he said, "you got a bathtub?"

"Yes. But it's for my own personal use."

"Then I'm borrowing it for the lady. Get it ready, good and hot."

"Why?" Gauley said.

"She needs to get the smell of Apache bucks off of her, that's why."

"Chas, twenty dollars if we can watch her bathe," Luke said.

Flintlock smiled, but only with his mouth. "Luke, after the lady is finished, I suggest you take a bath yourself. A cold one."

To his credit, the miner saw the humor in that and laughed. "Takin' baths can kill a man quicker'n scat. Hell, everybody knows that."

Flintlock nodded. "You obviously do." He looked at Gauley. "You keep women's fixin's back there in the store?"

"I sure do. Got some gingham dresses, shoes and boots and cotton undergarments. All for sale at cost."

Flintlock studied the girl, who seemed to be in another place and time, and said, "I guess I can size her. Now get the bathtub ready" — he glared at the miners — "in a private place. I'll be right back."

He stepped through the curtain and into the store.

At first bewildered by the array of female fashion, aimed at pioneer women headed farther west and ranchers' wives and daughters, Flintlock recalled the whores he'd known and based his choices on them.

He settled on a blue gingham dress, bloomers, a camisole and a pair of highbuttoned boots. He added some hair ribbons and a brush and comb set.

Meanwhile Chastity Gauley had been rushing in and out, carrying buckets of water to the tub that was set up behind a strung blanket screen.

Finally the man stopped and said to Flintlock, "I put one bucket of hot water in the tub. If I'd try to heat them all, we'd be

199

here all day."

He handed Flintlock a bar of yellow lye soap and a scrap of white towel.

"Is that the only soap you got?" Flintlock said. "I want her washed, not skun."

"Ain't much call for any kind of soap in this neck o' the woods," Gauley said. He rubbed his unshaven chin. The front of his dress was wet.

"I have my own private stock," he said. "It's Pears soap, all the way from London town. It's the kind the divine Miss Lillie Langtry uses. And me, of course."

"Well, if it's good enough for you and Lillie Langtry, let's have at it," Flintlock said. "Leave it beside the tub."

He pushed aside the curtain and stepped into the saloon area.

Abe Roper and Charlie Fong stood at the bar, their fingers hooked around shots of whiskey.

"Sam'l, what the hell are you doin'?" Roper said.

"Arranging a bath for the young lady and buying her some clothes," Flintlock said.

"You don't have any money to pay for women's fixin's, remember," Roper said.

"No, you're right, I don't. That's why you're paying for them."

Gauley was taken aback at Flintlock's insolvency.

"Ahem," he said, "one ladies' dress, gingham, a dollar-fifty, camisole, cotton, fifty cents, bloomers, cotton, fifty cents, one bristle brush, seventy-two cents, an unbreakable rubber comb, two dollars and twenty-five cents and a pair of ladies' boots, button, square toe, one dollar and fifty cents. That comes to a grand total of six dollars and ninety-seven cents."

Gauley looked from Flintlock to Roper and back again. "Who's paying?"

Flintlock had stepped beside the girl. He looked at Roper and said, "Pay the man, Abe."

"Sam'l, I'm starting to regret saving your neck," Roper said. "I should've let you get hung."

"I'll pay you back, Abe," Flintlock said.

"When?"

"Oh, someday."

"Yeah, that's what I figgered."

Flintlock put his hand under the girl's elbow and helped her to her feet but she was totally unresponsive, her dead eyes staring into nothing.

"I've prepared a bath for you," Flintlock said. "It will make you feel better."

"Hell, Sammy, you're floggin' a dead

hoss," Roper said. "That little gal is loco now she's been with the bucks and now she'll never be anything else but loco."

"I'm taking her with us, Abe," Flintlock said, walking the girl slowly toward the curtain. "She can't stay here."

"The hell we are taking her with us," Roper said. "She's a madwoman, Sammy. She'll cut our throats in our sleep."

"She won't do that, I think," Charlie Fong said. "She walks in darkness, but perhaps Sam can lead her into the light again. It will take time, but patience is the wisdom of waiting."

Roper stared at Fong. "Charlie, you're as nuts as she is," he said. Then, to Flintlock, "She ain't goin' with us, Sammy." And, to rub his point home, "And why the hell did you buy her boots at a dollar-fifty the pair?"

"She's barefoot, Abe. Or didn't you notice?"

"Well, what's that to us?"

"Well, since she'll be with us, we may have to introduce her to folks," Flintlock said. "We can't do that if she's got no shoes."

Roper looked from Flintlock, to Charlie Fong and then to the girl. "God help me, I'm surrounded by lunatics," he said.

"Get used to it, Abe," Flintlock said. "We're all in this together."

■ ■ ■ ■

"Got the bath all ready for you, lady," Flintlock said, smiling. "And fancy English soap donated by Lillie Langtry. And I got you new clothes and shoes."

The girl stood beside the zinc tub, her face expressionless, eyes registering nothing.

"So you strip off now and relax in the warm water, huh?" Flintlock said. "Do you good, and I'll wait outside."

From the girl . . . no response. A marble statue.

Flintlock stood in front of her and stared into her beautiful blue eyes, but the girl didn't see him. It seemed that she'd retreated to a hushed place where no one could ever hurt her again.

"Given me a problem, haven't you?" Flintlock said. "Yup, now I study on it, there's no doubt about that, missy."

The female body holds no secrets for a man who has been much around women, and Flintlock knew his course of action was clear.

Quickly, efficiently, he undressed the girl and then helped her sit in the bathtub. He washed her thoroughly, using the Pears soap that fascinated him because he could see right through it.

After ten minutes he judged that the girl was as clean as a newborn.

Chastity Gauley concurred.

"She's just as sweet and pretty as a speckled pup," he said.

When Flintlock helped the girl from the tub Gauley sprinkled her liberally with perfume from a tiny bottle. "This is my favorite," Gauley said. "It's French, you know."

Flintlock thought the stuff smelled like a New Orleans bawdyhouse, but he let it go. The man was only trying to help.

Dressing the girl was like putting clothes on a doll. She didn't cooperate in the least and Flintlock's fingers weren't made for dainties. Gauley took over the chore and when everything was hooked and buttoned, he sat the girl on a chair and began to brush her hair.

"Us ladies will be out when we're ready," he said. "There's no need for you to wait."

Flintlock nodded and pulled the screen blanket aside.

He turned, looked at the girl . . . and she smiled shyly at him.

Chapter Twenty-Six

It was in Geronimo's mind that he head south into the high desert plateau country, then swing east to the Zuni Mountains and wait there for more warriors to join him.

He now had twenty young men with him, a formidable force to be sure, but not sufficient to hurt the soldiers badly enough that they'd withdraw, licking their wounds, from this part of the country.

Behind the warriors rode six young women and with them a few boys who laughed and jeered and tugged on the rope that was tied to the wrists of a soldier.

Tonight, after the fires were lit, they would watch the women test the man's courage, though he was young and already cried and slobbered and begged the Apache for mercy, ridiculous words that did not bode well.

Geronimo rode deep in thought, wondering if his decision to retreat to the Zuni Mountains was the right one, or should he raid with the men he had and teach the whites a lesson they'd never forget?

Faugh, it was a puzzle, and one that would bear more consideration. Perhaps the spirits would come to him in a dream and show him the way.

The sight of the scout galloping toward him roused Geronimo from thought. The young warrior pumped his rifle above his head, a sure sign of excitement.

The warrior drew rein on his buckskin pony and words fell from his mouth like rocks tumbling down a mountainside after an earthshake.

There were white men, three of them, camped in the open not a mile ahead. They had a fire and — this was a great wonder — a white flag hung from a pole near where they sat.

Geronimo listened and wondered what to make of this.

Were they soldiers surrendering?

The warrior shook his head. No, not soldiers.

Was it a trap set for the Apache?

No. There were just those three. None others.

His warriors gathered around him as Geronimo thought of this strange thing.

White men were not smart, as everyone

knew, but could they really be so foolish as to think that the Apache had any respect for a white flag?

None of the young men had an answer for that.

The lines on Geronimo's face drew fine and deepened. Such a thing had never happened before. Even the Mexicans weren't this stupid.

Finally he made up his mind.

They would go and take a look at these white men, and if there was no sign of a trap, kill them and take their horses and guns.

The young men agreed with this strategy.

But it was still a great marvel that the white men were there.

The scout led the way to the white men's camp, located in foothills at the western end of the Tohatchi Flats, where the featureless brush country meets the Chuska Mountains.

Fort Defiance lay just ten miles to the west, but Geronimo had no fear of soldiers being in the vicinity in force. The cavalry and infantry regiments were still well to the north and fully occupied rounding up Apache women and children.

But he was a cautious man and his warriors rode on the alert, their eyes everywhere.

Under a sky the color of cardboard, the Apaches dismounted and left the horses and their prisoner with the boys and women.

They fanned out and surrounded the white men's camp, eyes on fire, hungry as wolves.

Three good horses were tethered in a clearing within a clump of cedar and piñon and the white men carried repeating rifles and belted Colts.

Such men were worth killing.

"They're all around us, Asa," Logan Dean said. "Just settin' out there, watching."

"I know it," Asa Pagg said. "Keep your hand away from your gun and grin from your butt to your eyebrows."

"I don't like it," Dean said. "They're planning to lift our hair."

Pagg smiled. "Could be. But it's too late to do anything about it now."

"What's the call, Asa?" Joe Harte said.

Pagg said, "Like I just said, keep your hands away from your guns and grin like the Apaches were visiting kin."

"Hell, I knew this was a big mistake," Dean said. "I figured we were riding into trouble."

"Just shut your trap and think of the army payroll," Pagg said. "Keep your mind occupied, like."

"Yeah, well I'm scared, Asa," Harte said.

Pagg nodded. "Apaches will do that to a man."

He took a step for ward, cupped a hand to his mouth and yelled, "Geronimo! I want to talk to you. Got a deal for ya."

Pagg knew better than to declare his friendship. The Apaches didn't have a word for *friend,* because they never had any. Mention of a deal might swing it.

A silence settled on the foothills and even the crickets were still. Rain clouds crowded the sky to the north and a breeze picked up but as yet made no sound in the trees.

Unnerved by the quiet, Pagg yelled, his voice no longer as confident, "Geronimo, did you hear me? We got things to talk about, you and me."

A bullet kicked up a fountain of dirt an inch in front of Pagg's left boot and the rifle's flat statement echoed among the hills.

He heard the slap of hands on leather and yelled, "No! Stay as you are."

"Hell, Asa, they tried to kill you," Dean said.

"If they wanted to kill me I'd be dead right now," Pagg said.

To Geronimo, he yelled, "That was a good joke. Now come out and talk. We have business to discuss." He threw in the kicker. "It's about Fort Defiance."

A minute ticked past, taut as a fiddle string, then another. Thunder rumbled, still far off, and Asa Pagg listened to the thud of his heartbeat in his ears.

Brush rustled and a couple of Apache boys appeared, dragging a white soldier behind them by a rope. The man was obviously terrified. Then Geronimo and a couple of warriors seemed to rise out of the ground like ghosts from a grave.

The oldest of the bucks, a squat, wiry man with bowlegs and mean eyes, wore a broadcloth vest decorated with silver pesos. It was him who did the talking.

He held up two fingers. "The soldier for two rifles. This is Geronimo's deal."

Pagg shook his head. "No deal. The soldier means nothing to me."

"Please, mister, help me," the trooper said. He was no more than a boy and had already been badly abused. His face was cut and bruised by blows from the Apache boys' cudgels and his blue eyes were frightened.

The warrior and Geronimo exchanged words and the warrior said again, "Two rifles."

Asa Pagg was smarter than most of his kind. By demanding the Winchesters, he knew Geronimo was trying to weaken his defensive power at no cost in Apache blood.

"Mister . . . please . . ." The soldier whispered. "For God's sake don't let them torture me."

"The hell with this," Pagg said.

He raised his rifle and shot the young man between the eyes. The soldier dropped to the ground like a puppet that just had its strings cut.

"Tell Geronimo I'm serious," he said to the warrior. "I'm not playing around here. I want to cut a deal on Fort Defiance, not his damned prisoners."

Geronimo heard this and understood, but his weather-worn face showed not the slightest trace of emotion.

After a few moments' thought, he said in the English he'd only recently mastered, "We will talk. But remember this . . . I hold your lives in my hand."

Pagg didn't scare worth a damn, but he knew his life was on the line.

It was a time for some slick, and fast, talking.

Only Geronimo and the warrior with the fancy vest sat by the fire. Both kept their

Springfield rifles close across their thighs.

Pagg had offered them coffee, which they'd accepted, and whiskey, which they'd refused.

After talking for ten minutes, Asa Pagg said, "So it comes down to this, Geronimo: You attack with your warriors and we'll be inside taking care of as many defenders as we can."

"I do not understand this, taking care," Geronimo said.

"Kill. I mean we'll attack from their rear and kill defenders. It will make your task easy."

"Battle is never easy," Geronimo said.

"Well, as easy as we can make it."

The Apache's black eyes shifted to Dean and Harte and lingered on them for long moments. He seemed to be satisfied with what he saw.

"Why do you turn on your own kind like a ravenous wolf?" Geronimo said.

Pagg had been called worse and he smiled as he told the Apache about the pay wagon, then said, "We can share the money if you want, Geronimo."

"Gold and silver?"

"Yeah, and a lot of it."

"We use gold and silver to decorate our weapons and make necklaces for our women," Geronimo said. "Pah, you can keep your gold and silver."

"Then remember what I told you earlier," Pagg said. "You'll take many horses and many guns, and women too, if you want them." He smiled again, trying to make himself seem sincere. "And with our help you can burn Fort Defiance to the ground."

Geronimo sat in deep thought, head bowed, until Pagg became convinced he'd never talk again. But then the Apache looked up and said, "Pagg, you are a snake, a wild beast who kills its own kind, and to make a treaty with such as you hurts my heart. But I have thought of this and I know I must do what is best for the Apache."

Now Pagg was eager. "Then you agree? When will you attack?"

"Before the soldiers bring in our women and children. If I wait longer, there will be too many soldiers at the fort. Yet, I will wait awhile until more young men join me."

"Damnit, so when? Give me a time, Geronimo."

"I will wait five days."

"But I need a time of day, morning, noon or night? How will I know when your attack is coming?"

"You will know."

Geronimo rose stiffly to his feet, a man

pained by old wounds.

"There is a full moon in five days. Expect me when it rises."

"I thought Apaches didn't fight at night."

"The full moon makes the night as day."

Pagg stuck out his hand. "Well, put it there . . . pardner."

Geronimo ignored the gesture and he and his warrior walked back toward the brush. Then Geronimo stopped, nodded in the direction of the soldier's body and said, "Bury your dead, Asa Pagg."

CHAPTER TWENTY-SEVEN

With the help of Captain Gibbs's cavalry-men, Flintlock and Roper buried Elliot and Cole, and the captain himself said the words over the shallow graves.

It had rained the whole morning and by the time they returned to the trading post everybody had mud on their boots.

"How is she?" Flintlock asked Chastity Gauley.

"Still the same," the man said. "Cleaner and prettier dressed, but the same. She won't talk and she won't eat."

"Well, she ain't gonna get any better," Abe Roper said. "That's for damn sure."

"She will. In time," Flintlock said. "She's young and that will help."

"She's a crazy woman and she ain't worth it. Leave her here, Sam'l," Roper said.

"Damnit, Abe, I said no and I mean no."

"Easy, Sammy," Roper said. "Don't get mad at a man who knows better'n you do.

It ain't his fault."

Flintlock opened his mouth to speak, but Captain Gibbs stepped beside him, saluted and said, "We're pulling out, gentlemen. Thank you for caring for the madwoman so well."

"We're taking her with us, Captain," Flintlock said. "We've decided we can't leave her here."

"Yes. Well, do whatever you think is best." A trooper brought the officer his horse and he mounted.

Gibbs seemed to think about something, then he bent down to Flintlock from the saddle and said quietly, "Regarding your throat, Mr. Flintlock, doctors learned so much during the war that they do wonders nowadays with disfigurements. I strongly urge you to contact a physician and ask him what modern medicine can do for you."

"I'll sure keep it in mind," Flintlock said.

"Well, the best of luck to you," Gibbs said.

He swung his horse around and joined his departing column, galloping past the Apache captives who were even more weak and miserable than they'd been a day earlier.

Roper watched the man leave, then said, "Does it trouble you that much, Sam'l?"

"What?"

"You know what. The big bird on your throat."

"It troubles me some, some of the time."

"Folks who know you look past it."

"What about folks who don't know me?"

"Then you have a problem."

"A doc would have to skin me," Flintlock said.

Roper nodded. "Seems like."

"Then the bird stays where it is."

Jack Coffin walked toward them through the rain, his hair hanging lank and wet across his shoulders. He led his horse.

"Time you boys saddled up," he said. He looked around him. "Where's the Chinaman?"

"He's here somewhere," Roper said.

"Better tell him," Coffin said.

"We're taking the girl with us," Flintlock said.

Coffin said only, "She got a hoss?"

"She'll ride double with me," Flintlock said.

The Apaches, in common with all other Indians, had no concept of insanity as a stigma, nor did they have a word for a crazy person. The closest they came was "someone who makes me laugh" or "a person who can't be reasoned with."

Coffin, raised by the Apache, accepted the

presence of the madwoman without further question.

"Tell her we're leaving, Samuel," was all he said.

Charlie Fong's horse was gone, and of the man himself there was no sign. A search of the area around the post by Flintlock and the others turned up nothing.

"Has he wandered off before, Abe?" Flintlock said.

"No. Not like this."

"Maybe he left with the soldiers," Coffin said.

"Charlie's his own man," Roper said. "He'd have told us if he planned on doing that."

"Do we search for him, or go on?" Coffin said.

"This is wild country," Flintlock said. "He could be anywhere."

Roper vented his frustration. "Damned Chinaman," he said. "I could never tell what he was thinking."

"I say we go on and find the golden bell," Coffin said. "He will catch up if that's what he wishes."

"Sam'l, what do you think?" Roper said.

"I agree with Coffin."

"Hey, I just remembered that Charlie has

the map," Roper said.

"Then he wants the bell for himself, maybe so," Coffin said.

"No matter." Roper tapped the side of his head. "I got the map here."

"Then we go on?" Coffin said.

"Yeah, we go on," Roper said. He looked at Flintlock. "Sammy, since you're so all-fired determined to take the madwoman with us, I'll carry the grub sack, make more room for you."

"True-blue of you, Abe," Flintlock said, smiling.

But Roper wasn't listening. He stared off into distance.

"Where the hell is that damned China-man?" he said.

"You're coming with us," Flintlock said to the girl.

She smiled at him, but made no response, her eyes vague.

"You look real pretty this morning," Flintlock said.

The girl remained silent.

"Hell, I've got to call you something," Flintlock said. "Can you tell me your name?"

After a few moments of quiet, he said, "All right, then I'll call you Ayasha. It's a Chey-

enne name and it means 'Little One.' "
Flintlock smiled and said, "Because that's
what you are, Ayasha, just a little one. Do
you like that?"

The girl stared at Flintlock for a long
time, then she reached out and touched his
throat. "Bird," she said.

"Yeah, it's a bird," Flintlock said. "Ayasha,
we'll have you talking again real soon, huh?
Bird is a real good start."

Roper stepped into the post. "Sam'l, we
got to ride," he said. "Save your pretties for
later."

"Soon as I find a slicker for Ayasha, we'll
go."

"Who the hell is Ayasha?" Roper said.
"You haven't found another crazy female?"

Flintlock grinned and put his hand on the
girl's shoulder. "No, she's Ayasha. In Cheyenne it means 'Little One.' "

"Oh yeah? Well you tell Ayasha she ain't
getting a cut of the golden bell. Not even a
little one."

"You're all heart, Abe," Flintlock said.

"I know. I've always been too softhearted
for me own good. It'll be my downfall one
day."

CHAPTER TWENTY-EIGHT

"So, it's all set," Asa Pagg said. "The full moon is in five, no four days now, and that's when Geronimo will attack."

"And us?" Captain Owen Shaw said.

Strain showed on him and made him look older than he was.

"Us? Hell, you know the answer to that. We'll hit the defenders from the rear. It will be all over in a few minutes."

"I'll take no part in the killing, Asa. I won't shoot my own soldiers."

Pagg's face stiffened. "So what will you do? Sit back and then take your share of the payroll?"

"Maybe I've decided I want no part of it," Shaw said. "It was a bad idea to begin with and now the Apaches are involved, it's gone from bad to worse. I don't like it."

"Like I told you before, Shaw, you're in too deep to back out now." Pagg watched uncertainty waver in Shaw's eyes. "You'll deploy your men badly, set them up for Geronimo. That way you don't have to dirty your hands with direct killing. Savvy?"

"It's wrong, Asa," Shaw said. "Something about the whole plan is wrong. For starters, Major Grove will deploy the men, not me."

"Then I'll gun the major first. It don't make any difference to me."

"Nor me," Logan Dean said. "I never shot me a major before."

"Hell, I ain't never even shot a private," Joe Harte said.

"You'll get to shoot all the privates you want in a few days," Pagg said. Then, his eyes like flint, "Maybe even a captain."

"If I go down, so do you, Asa," Shaw said. "Don't ever forget that. We could swing from the same gallows."

"I know you're threatening me, Shaw, but I'm not catching your drift."

"A few days ago I sent a letter to my sister in Boston, to be opened only on the notification of my death," Shaw said. "It's all there, Asa, enough to hang you."

Pagg looked out the window of the captain's quarters to the parade ground. The flag hung listless in the humidity that followed the rain and a cavalry trooper walked a bay horse back and forth.

"Got it all laid out, huh, Captain Shaw?"

Pagg said without turning his head.

"I like guarantees," Shaw said.

Now Pagg turned. "Here's my guarantee, Shaw . . . if you try to cross me on this payroll deal I'll kill you, letter or no." He rose to his feet, the butts of his guns showing under his armpits. "Now, do you catch my drift?"

Joe Harte normally stayed out of Pagg's discussions. He reckoned he was paid for his gun, not his opinions. But now he said, "Hell, Cap'n, you sound like an old maid trying to hold on to her virginity at the devil's hootenanny. You tied in with us and now you got thirty thousand dollars at stake, enough to keep you on easy street for the rest of your life."

Harte stabbed his finger at Shaw. "It's too late to play coy."

"That much money will ease your guilty conscience pretty damn quick," Dean said.

Pagg grinned. "Hell, my boys say it better than me, Captain."

After a few moments, Shaw said, "I guess I'm already in too deep to back out now."

"Damn right," Pagg said.

"But once we split up the money, I never want to see any of your ugly faces for the rest of my life. Is that clear?"

"Clear as ever was, Captain," Pagg said.

"You stated how you feel straight up an' honest and true. There's no doubt about that, says I."

"And if anything happens to me, say, when it comes to the sharing, don't forget the letter I sent," Shaw said.

"I ain't likely to forget," Pagg said. "But you got no worries on that score. Share and share alike is the deal, and I'll stick to it like stink to a skunk's tail."

"I still won't do the killing," Shaw said.

"Hell, me and my boys and Geronimo will do the killing. Just put those soldier boys in harm's way and in a few days your pockets will be stuffed with double eagles."

"Blood money," Shaw said, his eyes bleak.

"Yeah, the best kind," Pagg said.

Asa Pagg smelled his salt pork sandwich, made a face and let it drop to his plate. He looked around the mess hall and said to the dozen soldiers who'd lingered after lunch, "How the hell do you boys eat this crap?"

A cavalry corporal with a beard as long as Pagg's said, "After a while you get used to it, mister. The first ten years are the worst."

Pagg picked bread crumbs out of his beard. "Hell, I'd never get used to it."

"If you don't like the food, don't eat it," hovered on the tip of a young trooper's tongue. But when he looked into Pagg's eyes and saw black iron staring back at him, he changed his mind and lapsed into silence.

"As to your question, Logan," Pagg whispered, "we need him until the fort is taken and we roll out of here with the payroll."

"All right, Asa, why?" Harte said. "We can kill him tonight and stash his body where it will never be found."

"That will come later," Pagg said. "Now listen to this . . . you know who's in Boston town, don't you?"

Harte shook his head and Dean said, "I dunno."

"Bill Blood, that's who. Good ol' Scarface Billy Blood as ever was."

"I haven't seen Billy in years," Harte said. "I thought he was in New York City."

"Nah, a while back he cut up a feller that turned out to be some politician's grandson and had to skip town with the law breathing down his neck," Pagg said. "He ended up in Boston town and he's prospering. There ain't a ship leaves the harbor that the owner hasn't paid Billy to keep the longshoremen in line."

"Billy's a heller, as good a man with the blade as ever I knew," Dean said. "It was him that cut Sand Baker from nose to navel, remember that, Asa? Ol' Sand died with his guts spilling out all over the floor of the Alamo saloon in El Paso."

"Aye, and Sand was fast with the iron," Pagg said. "He put a few lively lads in the grave."

"Yeah, but Billy was faster with the steel," Dean said.

Harte smiled. "He was a rum one, was ol' Billy Blood."

Pagg leaned across the table and dropped his voice to a conspiratorial whisper. "Now listen up, both of you. Here's what I want you boys to do . . . scout around and get a name and address for Shaw's sister. Drop some money on the clerks if you have to, but I want that address by tonight."

Dean grinned. "I get it. Captain Shaw ain't the only one who can write letters."

"Damn right, Logan," Pagg said. "I'll write to ol' Billy this very night and drop it in the soldiers' mail. Billy will do the rest. He owes me some favors, like."

"Will your letter get to him in time, Asa?" Harte said.

"Sure it will. Because the way we'll deal with Shaw, it will be a while afore his stinking carcass is found. By then Billy Blood will have cut up the sister and whoever else was with her and grabbed that damned letter."

"Suppose he can't find it, Asa?" Harte said. "The letter, I mean."

"Billy will find it. He's got a nose like a blood-hound for stuff like that."

Pagg sat back in his chair and sighed. "Ah, good ol' Scarface Billy Blood. He's gold dust, boys, gold dust, and he never forgets them as done him a favor. No, not Billy."

"Good with the blade is Billy," Dean said again. "He can gut a grown man from crotch to chin quicker'n scat. Or a woman, come to that."

"A real talent," Pagg allowed. "Billy's knife hand's got talons as thick as my wrist." He nodded toward the door. "Now you boys go get me that name and address. Time's a-wastin' when there's cuttin' to be done."

CHAPTER TWENTY-NINE

Jack Coffin led the way north, his eyes constantly scanning the foothills of the rugged Carrizo peaks for any suggestion of a hidden cave.

After three hours of riding, he'd found nothing.

The rain had stopped thirty minutes before and now the clouds parted and heat shimmered in the distance.

Around the riders lay the Red Rock Valley, a lost, lonely land of mesas and tall, tormented spires of sandstone that rose from the brush desert floor and echoed with a strange, unearthly silence.

The valley awed a man and made him lower his voice to a whisper, as though he was talking in a cathedral.

"Where did the map say the cave was, Abe?" Flintlock said.

The girl, as silent as the valley, rode behind him, and the Hawken rifle, as had become his custom, lay across the saddle horn.

A black sweat stain banded Roper's hat and dark arcs showed under his armpits.

"Damnit, we should've seen it by now," Roper said.

"We'll find it," Coffin said. "If not today, tomorrow. If not then, the next day, but we'll find it."

Roper removed his hat and rubbed his sweat-beaded forehead with the sleeve of his shirt. "Hell, a man could die of thirst out here first," he said.

"There is water," Coffin said.

"Well, thank God fer that," Roper said. "Lead us to it."

"Later," Coffin said. "Once the danger passes."

Suddenly both Roper and Flintlock were alert.

"What danger, Jack?" Flintlock said. "Speak up, man."

"I don't know," Coffin said. "But I sense it. It is all around us."

Roper's reaction was to slide his Winchester out of the boot under his knee and lever a round into the chamber. He warily looked about him at the rough-hewn rock pillars and smooth-topped mesas and said, "I don't see nothing."

"Me neither," Flintlock said. "And I don't feel any danger."

"It comes, soon," Coffin said. "Best you be prepared."

Behind Flintlock the girl stirred. She turned her face to the blue-denim sky and frowned, fine lines rippling between her eyes.

"Something worrying her?" Roper said. "She's all atremble."

"Maybe," Flintlock said. "I can't figure it."

"Women feel things that men don't," Coffin said. "She senses the danger."

"Then what the hell is the danger?" Roper said. "I hired you to scout for trouble, Coffin. Now, if you've found some, tell us what it is and be done. And be damned to ye fer a conundrum-talking breed."

"I can't stop what's to come." Coffin stared at the sky that had now turned the color of sulfur. A new urgency in his voice, he yelled, "Over there into the arroyo. Now!"

Roper followed the breed's eyes. "Hell, I don't see no arroyo."

"Follow me!" Coffin said.

He swung his horse around and galloped toward the foothills, dust spurting from the hooves of his running horse.

Then Flintlock scanned the distance with far-seeing eyes and saw it.

Less an arroyo and more a slot canyon, it was a narrow V between two rocky hills that looked wide enough to barely allow the passage of a man and his mount.

A breeze fanned Flintlock's cheeks . . . then slapped him hard.

Abe Roper, who'd been sitting his horse watching Coffin's dash for the arroyo, now got the word as the rising wind read to him from the book.

"Sandstorm!" he yelled. "Get the hell out of here, Sammy!"

He followed after Coffin at a gallop.

"Hold on, Ayasha!" Flintlock yelled.

The girl seemed to understand because she threw her arms around his waist and clung tight, her face buried in his back.

The roar of the storm sounded like surf crashing onto a shingle beach and the hornet sting of the sand mercilessly tormented the terrified horses.

The humans, huddled at the bottom of the arroyo amid brush, agave and cat claw cactus, were no better off. Normal speech was impossible because of the deafening din of the wind and the venomous snake hiss of hurtling sand.

Flintlock held his slicker above his head and Ayasha huddled close to him. Her eyes were tight shut and sand powdered her face.

Roper put his mouth against Flintlock's ear and yelled, "Damned wind is as vicious as mortal sin!"

Flintlock nodded; the effort of shouting above the bellow of the storm not worth the effort.

But now and then between gusts he heard a small sound . . . Jack Coffin chanting what he took to be some kind of Apache prayer.

Flintlock fervently hoped the breed was in real good with the Great Spirit.

After fifteen minutes of howling, screeching, hissing violence the storm stopped as suddenly as it had begun and once again the sun shone brightly in a cloudless sky.

Like people rising from bed and throwing off the sheets, sand cascaded from their pummeled bodies as Flintlock and the others rose slowly to their feet.

"What the hell?" Abe Roper said. He looked as though he was wearing a yellow mask. "I never want to go through something like that again."

"Me neither," Flintlock said. "Somebody trying to tell us something?"

He meant it as a joke, but Jack Coffin took

him seriously.

"The guardian of the bell sent the storm as a warning," he said.

Roper, who didn't scare worth a damn even in the worst of times, grinned and said, "Did he now? Well, me and him are gonna have a discussion, but my gun will do the talking for me."

Coffin shook his head. "He cannot be killed. He is the guardian. He dwells in death."

"I ain't seen a man yet who can take a bullet in the belly and not be killed," Roper said. "Did you, Sam'l?"

"Can't say as I have," Flintlock said. He brushed off sand with both hands then palmed Ayasha's gritty hair. Over his shoulder, he said, "Unless you count Lonesome Lon Sanford."

"That story is crap," Roper said. "I was there when Lon got his. In fact I kilt the man who kilt him. But Lon didn't get it in the belly. He got it lower down, blew a chunk out of his thigh an' he bled to death a day later."

Flintlock nodded. "Well, folks tell the stories they want to tell."

"Lonesome Lon wasn't much," Roper said. "He was a miserable sumbitch an' I always figured I'd kill him myself one day."

He nodded to the Hawken rifle that had fallen to the ground during the storm. "See to your guns, Sammy. Sand will foul 'em worse than anything else you can name."

"I was planning on that very thing, Abe," Flintlock said. "But thanks for your concern."

"You will fight the wind with guns?" Coffin said. "You will fight Death itself with Colts and Winchesters?"

"Yup, that's the plan," Roper said. "For two thousand pounds of gold I'd follow Death into hell and gun him at the devil's feet."

Ayasha gave a sudden and sharp little intake of breath.

And Flintlock wondered at that.

"Did you send the storm, Grandfather?" the boy asked.

"To do what, little one?" the old man said.

"Why, to kill the men who come for the bell, of course."

"I don't wish to kill them. I only want them to go away."

"Will they go away now, Grandfather?"

"No. I don't think they will."

"Why?"

"Because their hearts are hard, made of gold."

"Why do you seem so tired, Grandfather?"

"Because you weary me with your questions, little one."

The boy poured some rough red wine into a clay cup and handed it to his grandfather. The Mexican peasants brought the wine as a gift, as their ancestors had once brought gold, and the old man enjoyed it immensely.

"What will you do if the robbers come into the cave?" the boy asked.

The old man took the cup from his lips. "I don't know."

"Will you smite them dead and drag away their souls?"

"No."

"Then what will you do?"

"I don't know."

The old man took another sip from the cup and said, "Men who hunt gold are greedy, and oftentimes they kill each other. Perhaps I will have to do nothing at all."

CHAPTER THIRTY

Charlie Fong had no doubt about the right of the thing.

No matter how crazy it seemed, he had it to do.

He was not normally a man who tilted at windmills, but a respect for his own kind drove him on and he didn't question himself.

His fire was small, built with dry sticks to cut down on smoke, and what little there was rose upward into the soaring cottonwood he sat under, one of many that stood beside the Chaco River.

Fong studied the shard of pottery he'd found close to the tree. He figured it was ancient, made by the Old Ones who'd lived here long before the Spanish men arrived.

This was a harsh, heat-blasted place, the air gasping dry, but pottery suggested a settled way of life. How the Old Ones survived this harsh country was a mystery he could not fathom. Unless the land itself had changed over the centuries, but he didn't know about that either.

He shoved the pot shard in his shirt pocket and chewed on a strip of beef jerky that smelled bad. But he'd left the trading post in such a hurry it was all he'd brought with him.

Months after the spring melt, the Chaco was more dry wash than river, but he'd been able to fill his canteen with the trickle that still survived, and though the water was brackish, it was wet.

Charlie Fong idly watched a cougar prowl the opposite bank. The big cat stopped and stared at him with golden eyes before moving on. . . .

"Couldn't believe it with my own eyes, 'cause I'd never seen the like," the cavalry trooper had told him back at the trading post. "There he was, bold as brass, with them two Chink girls doing his every bidding. Like slaves they was, and maybe a sight worse if the truth be known. He says he bought them girls in Frisco for good American money and they didn't come cheap."

"Pretty?" Fong had said.

"You could say that, if slanty-eyes Celestials are to your taste."

Charlie Fong let that go. The man was talkative, and one thing Charlie Fong had learned in the Tong was that if you let a talking man speak there was no telling what you could learn.

"Feller's name is Silas Garrard and he says he's a retired sea captain," the soldier said. "But I thought to meself, *Aye, slave cap'n is more like.* He's got all kinds of African and Chinese stuff in his cabin, and more'n one picture of black men in chains getting whipped along by fellers wearing long robes and turbans on their heads while a white man watches it all from horseback. You ask me, them little gals ain't long for this world, if that's the way Garrard treated his slaves afore he got them to market."

"Why are you telling me this?" Charlie Fong said.

"Well, beggin' your pardon, you're a Chinaman yourself," the soldier said. "Or haven't you noticed?"

"And you think because I'm a Chinaman I should rescue the girls?"

"If'n they was white women, that's what I'd do."

"They mean nothing to me."

"Suit yourself. But, hell, they might be kin o' yourn."

The soldier, short and thin like most

238

cavalry troopers, leaned forward in his mess hall chair and whispered, "Here's a puzzler, a real humdinger. He said a real strange thing, that Garrard feller. Asked me if I'd heard anything about a golden bell hidden somewhere in the Carrizo Mountains. I said that I hadn't, and he said, 'Well, I might get rid of the two women and go look for it.' I swear that's what he said, so you can make of that what you will."

"A most singular statement," Fong said, pretending to have only a passing interest.

"As to what the cap'n meant about getting rid of the women, well, your guess is as good as mine," the trooper said. "But by the look of that feller, I'd say throat cuttin' is what he had in mind, unless he can find a buyer for them gals."

The soldier rose, adjusted his canvas gun belt and butt-forward Colt, and said, "As to them women, Chinaman, if you're going to do something, better do it quick. I'd say time is running out on them."

Charlie Fong told himself that it was Garrard talking about the golden bell that tipped the scales, but he knew in his heart he'd have gone after the Chinese girls no matter what.

When he came right down to it, blood is

thicker than water, and more than that, it was the way of the Tong to help others of their race.

The cavalry trooper told him where the Garrard cabin was situated. He said it lay on the eastern base of the Hogback, a sharply pointed ridge of raw sandstone and shale that looked like the dorsal fin of a submerged sea monster.

"It's the only cabin along that stretch of the Chaco, so just follow the river north and you'll find it," the man said. "An' if you do venture thataway, then good luck to you."

Charlie Fong added a few sticks to his fire. He calculated that he was about five miles from the Garrard cabin and from there it would be a two-day ride back to the Red Rock Valley. With the women in tow, probably three.

He'd left without telling Roper and Flint-lock, because he knew they'd try to talk him out of it. By now they must be wondering where he was, and Abe, by his very nature, would suspect treachery.

Fong smiled to himself. That was the trouble with outlaws like Abe Roper. They figured everybody was as crooked as themselves.

CHAPTER THIRTY-ONE

It was in Charlie Fong's mind to bed down early under the cottonwoods and strike out at first light for the Garrard cabin.

But the arrival of Pleasant Tyrell riding through the pale twilight put that plan on hold.

The old man, riding a mouse-colored mustang, leading another with a pack on its back, drew rein a ways off and hollered, "Hello, the camp."

Fong rose to his feet. His hand went to the leather-lined front pocket of his pants where he carried his .38 and he yelled, "Come on in."

Later Fong would recount that Pleasant Tyrell was a sight to see.

He looked to be in his late seventies, maybe older. He wore buckskins that had fringes on the shirtsleeves at least two feet long, a yellow bandana sagging low on his chest and a beautiful silk top hat perched precariously on his completely bald head.

Pinned to the crown on the hat two inches above the brim was a deputy United States marshal's star.

Tyrell, a man with humor in his faded blue eyes, wore two ivory-handled Smith & Wesson Russians, butt forward in fine black holsters.

He drew rein again but made no motion to dismount.

"I'd say I smelled your coffee, sonny," he said. "But you ain't got no coffee."

Charlie Fong held up a chunk of the reeking jerky. "Have this, if you've got a taste for it."

"Hell, no. Ate too much of that during the War for Southern Rights."

Tyrell gave his name, then said, "What's a Chinaman from China doing all the way out here in these United States?"

Fong smiled. "I could ask that same question about a lawman who seems to be a fer piece off his home range."

"I never seen a Chinaman out here," Tyrell said, leaning back in the saddle. "Seen plenty of Celestials afore, mind, but never out here."

"There's a first time for everything, Marshal," Fong said.

"What you got in your pocket, sonny? You

seem mighty interested in it."

Fong decided to call it. "A Smith & Wesson sneaky gun."

"You on the scout?"

"Not recent. I might be wanted in Texas, though."

"Hell, boy, everybody's wanted in Texas. What do they call you?"

"Charlie Fong."

"Charlie ain't much of a name for a Chinaman."

"It serves."

The old lawman nodded. "All right, Charlie, are you going to ask me to light an' set?"

"Of course, Marshal, but it pains me to say that I've nothing to offer. My hospitality will be thin, to say the least."

"Well, I got coffee an' I got grub an' I'm in a mind to share. That lay all right with you, Charlie?"

"Light and set," Charlie Fong said.

"Man can't find better camp grub than salt pork and pan bread," Pleasant Tyrell said, wiping off his mouth with his sleeve. "Greases his innards, like, an' guards agin the rheumatisms."

Charlie Fong was hungry and was in a mood to agree. "Yup, it's a sandwich that settles in the belly like a snowflake, all right."

Suddenly Tyrell looked shrewd, his eyes narrowing. "Who you runnin' with, Charlie?"

Fong said, "Do I have to be running with anybody?"

"No, you could be on a high lonesome, I guess, but you don't seem the type. Chinamen ain't the kind to be lone riders, if you catch my drift. Usually when you see one, there's a score of others close by."

"Why do you want to know?"

"I'm a lawman. Is that reason enough?"

"How fast are you with them pistols?"

"Fast enough on the shuck'n'shoot to drill you square afore you pull that belly gun outta your poke."

Charlie Fong grinned. For a moment he listened to the wind talk in the cottonwoods and the coyotes yip in the bone-white hills under the waxing moon. Finally he said, "You're a blunt-speaking man, Marshal."

"And I'm a listening man, Charlie," Tyrell said. "So talk to me."

"Abe Roper and Sam Flintlock."

If Tyrell was surprised he didn't let it show. "A few years back, when he got out of Yuma, Roper took up the train-robbing profession," he said. "I know fer a fact he robbed the *Katy Flier* not a twelve-month gone and that Wells Fargo would dearly love to see him caught and hung."

"And Sam Flintlock? Is he on your wanted list?" Fong said.

"He's a bounty hunter, so you could say we're in the same line o' work. He still carry that ol' Hawken everywhere he goes?"

"Seems like."

"He's fast with the iron, is Sam. Got that big bird tattooed acrost his throat, I recollect."

"It brings him luck. Or so he says."

"Lucky fer him, Charlie, maybe unlucky fer you. There ain't no trains to rob around these parts, so what are you doin' here?"

"You ain't gonna believe me, Marshal."

"Try me, boy. You want that last slice o' salt pork?"

"No. I've had enough."

"Then I'll eat it." Talking through a chewing mouth, Tyrell said, "So, try me."

Charlie Fong told the marshal about Silas Garrard and the two Chinese girls and how he suspected they were being abused. He didn't mention the golden bell.

After listening intently and nodding now and then, Tyrell doffed his top hat, displaying a shockingly bald scalp, then resettled it on his head again, as though it had been threatening to tip over.

"Seems to me that this man Garrard

hasn't broken any laws," he said. "If he bought and paid for them China girls, then they're his to do with as he pleases."

"Marshal, slavery ended with the War Between the States," Fong said. "You can't buy people anymore and do with them as you please."

"Well, maybe you got a point there, sonny. But Celestials ain't real people like white folks, beggin' your pardon. So as I said, I don't see that any laws have been broken. But I'll study on it some."

Prejudice is the bastard child of ignorance, and Marshal Tyrell wasn't about to change his mind about races, so Charlie Fong didn't try to educate him.

"Are you here after Abe Roper?" he said.

"Nope. I got bigger fish to fry, an outlaw and killer by the name of Asa Pagg."

"He's around," Fong said.

"You seen him?"

"Yeah, at Fort Defiance."

"He got Logan Dean and Joe Harte with him? Two real bad 'uns."

Fong nodded. "Sure thing. I'd say you got your work cut out for you, Marshal."

The news obviously didn't sit well with Tyrell. He frowned as though his thoughts were troubling him. Then he sighed deeply and said, "Well, I wear the badge and draw the wages, so I got it to do."

"You can get the soldiers at the fort to help," Fong said.

"It ain't really their concern and men going up against Pagg and them can die real easy."

"Including you, Marshal."

"I ain't been kilt yet, sonny, so we'll see, huh?" Tyrell rose to his feet, worked a kink out of his back, then rummaged in his pack. He came up with a pint of whiskey and a Jew's harp that he held up for Charlie Fong to see.

When the lawman sat again, he said, "Gimme your cup."

Tyrell poured a generous shot into Fong's coffee and did the same for himself.

He wriggled to get comfortable, then grinned at Fong, and with considerable skill, began to twang out "Skip to My Lou," then a great frontier favorite.

Charlie Fong, who knew and liked the song, grinned as he chimed in with the words. . . .

"Fly's in the buttermilk, shoo, fly, shoo,
Fly's in the buttermilk, shoo, fly, shoo,
Fly's in the buttermilk, shoo, fly, shoo,
Skip to my Lou, my darlin'."

Tyrell took the harp from his mouth and sang in a gruff baritone, his right boot thumping out the beat. . . .

"Lost my partner, what'll I do?
Lost my partner, what'll I do?
Lost my partner, what'll I do?
Skip to my Lou, my darlin'."

As the verses went back and forth between the two men, an owl, attracted by the sound, flew silently over the camp. For an instant the flames of the campfire glowed red under its wings and then the bird vanished like a ghost into the darkness.

When Charlie Fong stirred in his blankets at daybreak, Marshal Pleasant Tyrell had already loaded his packhorse and coffee bubbled on the fire.

"You snored all night," the lawman said. "I thought Chinamen didn't snore, thinking it ain't polite, like."

"Sorry," Fong said. He threw his blanket aside and got to his feet. "First time anybody ever told me I snore."

"Don't make no never mind," Tyrell said. "I don't sleep anyway. Feather mattresses have done spoiled me for beddin' down on limestone rock."

His brain still cobwebbed with sleep, Fong squatted by the fire and poured himself coffee.

"How is it?" the marshal said. "Bile long enough?"

"It's just fine. You going after Asa Pagg?"

"Not yet. I have a mind to go with you and see this Garrard feller."

"You don't have to deal yourself a hand in my game, Marshal," Charlie Fong said.

"I said I'd study on it, and I did," Tyrell said. "If Garrard is abusing them little gals like you say he is, then it's a matter for the law."

Fong smiled. "Changed your tune since last night."

"Yeah, well, what I said last night about Celestials not being real people don't go. I was feelin' mean and I guess it showed on me." Tyrell grinned. "Besides, Charlie, you got a real nice singing voice and I wouldn't want anything to happen to it."

Fong spoke over the rim of his tin cup. "And if you ride with me, you can delay going after Asa Pagg and his boys for a spell."

The marshal seemed to think that over, then he slapped his holstered Colts and said, "Charlie, I've been in a score of gunfights and I've killed seven men in the line of duty. You know why I'm still here to talk about it?"

"You were lucky, I guess."

"Nope, that ain't it. Well, it ain't all of it. No, I'm still here because I never went toe to toe with the fast ones, like your pal Sam Flintlock fer instance."

"So what did you do?"

"Got me a sworn posse to back my play, and if I didn't have one o' them, then, why, I'd set up on a ridge somewhere with my ol' Henry and plug the gunslick as he rode past. Either that or I'd shoot him when he was kneeling beside his bed sayin' his prayers or bouncing a young 'un on his knee. I killed Matt Rowe, the Santa Rita gunfighter, as he was a-sittin' in his outhouse reading a store catalog. Two barrels o' buckshot tore a hole right through the ladies' corsets page an' done fer him."

Pleasant Tyrell poured himself coffee. "Know what that's called, Charlie?"

"*Murder* might be a name for it."

"Hell, it ain't murder. It's called gettin' the drop on a man." The marshal smiled. "So you see, I ain't as scared of Asa Pagg as you think. I'll bide my time until I get the drop and then cut him in half with my Greener."

"You might be a handy man to have around at that, Marshal," Fong said.

"Well, one more thing, Charlie. I don't know how this thing with Garrard will pan out, but if there's killin' to be done, I'll do it. We got to stay within the law. Catch my drift?"

"I'll let you call it," Charlie Fong said.

"Then drink your coffee and we'll hit the trail and find what we find," Tyrell said.

Only then did Charlie Fong remember that in his saddlebags he had the map to the cave of the golden bell.

Ol' Abe must be having conniptions by now.

CHAPTER THIRTY-TWO

"Three days. Three lousy, stinking days and we ain't seen hide nor hair of the damned cave," Abe Roper said. "Coffin, you ain't much of an Injun."

"I'll find it," Coffin said. "I don't have the map."

"I know you don't have the map. Charlie Fong took it and damn him fer a Chinaman. So when will we find the cave?"

"When the time is right."

"Hell, that ain't an answer," Roper said. "That's an excuse. Now give a real answer and tell me when."

Sam Flintlock tuned out the argument between the two men and carried his morning coffee into a stand of juniper and piñon and fetched his back against a gnarled trunk.

As he built a cigarette he wondered at the dream that had wakened him from sleep in the darkest hour of the night.

He saw Charlie Fong sitting by a campfire,

singing, and opposite him an old man in a top hat played "Skip to My Lou" on a twanging mouth harp.

But what made it stranger was that old Barnabas hovered in the shadows, doing some kind of mountain man jig to the music.

Then an owl swooped out of the sky and a great wind rose and swept everyone away.

Flintlock lit his cigarette. What did the dream mean? Or did it mean anything?

When old Barnabas invaded his dreams it usually meant there was mischief afoot. Something to do with Charlie, maybe?

Flintlock watched the blue smoke curl from his cigarette and decided he was asking himself questions that had no answers.

But for some reason, the dream still troubled him.

Roper's angry voice cut Flintlock's reverie short. "We'd better find the cave and damned soon, Coffin," he said. "And, hell, look at the sky. It's gonna rain soon and we'll be searching in a damned storm." Roper shook his head. "I declare, around here things are goin' from bad to worse."

But things were about to get even worse than Roper feared. . . .

Eight riders came on at a canter through a

misting rain.

Flintlock rose to his feet as soon as he saw them, especially the man in front, tall, big gutted, dressed in the embroidered finery of a prosperous hacienda owner.

But the only time Carlos Hernandez had set foot in a hacienda was as a raider, rapist and murderer.

The Mexican bandit rode up to the smoking campfire that was fighting a losing battle against the fine but persistent rain.

Hernandez's quick, black eyes swept the camp and registered what he saw.

Abe Roper was on his feet, his thumb hooked onto his gun belt near his Colt. Jack Coffin, slender and dangerous, was five paces to Roper's left and Flintlock stood near the trees, the big revolver in his waistband in sight and significant.

After Hernandez's men fanned out behind him, the big man tipped back his white sombrero and grinned, revealing a mouthful of dazzling white teeth, a diamond set into each of the two front ones.

"Abe Roper, my friend, it's been a long time. Too long, I think," the Mexican said. "How many years?"

Roper nodded. "Howdy, Carlos. Too many years, I reckon. How are things?"

"Oh, very bad, my friend," Hernandez

said. "Very, very bad. As a great patron, I exact tribute from my peons, but they grow poorer every year and as they grow poor, so do I." He raised a meaty left hand and pinched the skin on the back with the forefinger and thumb of his right. "Look, my good friend, look at the slack. Carlos is wasting away from hunger."

"If bacon and beans are to your taste, you can share what we have," Roper said.

Hernandez shook his great anvil of a head. "No, my friend, such a peon's meal is not to my taste. But you know what is?"

"Tell me," Roper said.

"Gold. Much gold is to my taste."

"You came to the wrong camp, Carlos," Roper said. "If I found a ten dollar bill in my pocket, I'd be wearing somebody else's pants."

"Hah! You made a good joke, Abe, my friend," Hernandez said. He turned to his silent, hard-faced riders. "He made a good joke, compadres. Say ha-has."

The men did as they were told, then Hernandez cut off the laughter with a chop of his hand.

"So, I was riding past, deep in devout prayer, when I saw my friend Abe Roper and my friend Sam Flintlock and I said to the Good Lord above, 'Now why would

255

those two fine gentlemen be here where there are no banks to rob or trains to plunder?' And the Good Lord said, 'I dunno, Carlos. Why don't you ask them?' "

Hernandez made a show of moving his pearl-handed Colt into a more accessible position and said, "Now I am asking. Why are you here and with a woman?"

"Hunting," Roper said. "As for the woman, we found her, but she's tetched in the head."

"Ah . . . then that's the explanation," Hernandez said. His face was suddenly shrewd. "What are you hunting?"

"Deer," Roper said. "Bear, maybe, if we can find one."

"There's good hunting around here, my friend. Yet you eat only bacon and beans. No deer steak?"

"We haven't seen a deer yet," Roper said.

"You could hunt deer where you came from, Abe." Hernandez waggled a forefinger. "I think you are here for something else."

"Like what, for instance?"

"Like a golden bell, my friend. If you have come all this way north, with the Apaches out, you must have a pretty good notion where the bell is. No?"

"I don't know what you're talking about,"

Roper said. "This is only a hunting trip, Carlos."

The Mexican sighed. "Ah, dear me, to show you how serious I am, perhaps I must make an example. The Indian maybe? Or my good friend Sam Flintlock."

"Don't even think about it, Carlos," Flintlock said. He moved away from the trees, stopped, then said, "You couldn't shade me on your best day."

"Perhaps. Perhaps not. But now I must have you meet a very, very good friend." Hernandez called out, "Johnny, come and introduce yourself."

A man rode forward and Hernandez said, "This is my good friend Johnny Joslin. Look how eager he is to meet you, Sam."

The man called Joslin swung out of the saddle and Flintlock pegged him for a gun with some killings along his back trail. He wore a Stetson with a curled-up brim, a bolero jacket and the pants stretched across his narrow hips were embroidered at the top of the thighs. He was young, in his early twenties, and wore his twin Colts as confidently as the sneer on his razor-gash of a mouth.

Johnny Joslin seemed slightly bemused, as though this whole thing was beneath his dignity.

"Abe, do you want to say something?" Hernandez said.

The morning was dull, rainy and gray, but nevertheless the diamonds in the bandit's teeth gathered enough light to glitter.

"I never heard of a damned golden bell, and if it's around here, we sure as hell haven't found it," Roper said. "Do we look like we're prospering?"

"But you know where the bell is, my friend," Hernandez said. "That is why the Indian is here, to lead you to it. I have just figured that out."

"Go to hell," Roper said. "I done told you what we're doing here."

Roper looked slightly worried. He knew the odds he and the others faced and they were not in his favor, to say the least.

"Then if you won't tell me, Mr. Joslin will kill Sam. Do you really want your friend's death on your conscience?"

"Flintlock ain't my friend."

"Thanks, Abe," Flintlock said.

"Well, I always tell the truth," Roper said.

"Not this time, I think," Hernandez said. "Ah well, so it has come to this. My heart is so sad I fear it may break. Johnny, kill Mr. Flintlock."

Johnny Joslin couldn't believe he was the

one doing the dying.

Even when Flintlock's second bullet crashed into his chest and his own, unfired guns fell from his hands, he still couldn't believe it.

He rode those two bullets into hell with a look of horror and disbelief on his face, unwilling to believe that for the first time since he'd buckled on his guns and became a somebody, he'd met a real gunfighter.

Sam Flintlock had no time for such thoughts.

Hernandez was drawing.

Flintlock fired. Too fast. The bullet, intended for the Mexican's chest, tracked left and smashed into the man's right wrist as he brought up his Colt.

But in that instant of bone-shattered pain, Hernandez knew he was done.

"My God, don't shoot anymore!" he yelled.

His men, looking to their leader for guidance, sat their saddles, uncertain about what to do next. But they did know that if they ignored Hernandez and pulled guns, half of them would die right there.

They'd heard about Abe Roper, a fast man with the Colt, but Flintlock's speed with the iron was beyond anything they'd ever seen or imagined and they'd no desire to push their luck.

Hernandez settled it.

"No shooting! He'll kill me!" the bandit yelled, his voice ragged with pain.

"Don't call it different or you're a dead man, Carlos," Flintlock said, a haze of gray gunsmoke drifting around him.

Hernandez grabbed his gun arm with his left and stared at the stark red mouth that pulsed blood in the center of his wrist.

"Damn you, Sam Flintlock, you've done for me," Hernandez said. "I'll never be able to use this hand again."

"Too bad, Carlos," Abe Roper said. "Now you and your boys get the hell out of here afore Sam'l gets real mad and reads to you from the book."

"This was ill done," Hernandez said. "I will not forget it."

"I could kill you right now, Carlos," Flintlock said. He was standing very still and tense. Then the moment went out of his eyes and he said, "Go away, and take your dead man with you. Whatever you were paying him, it was too much."

The Mexican spat into the dirt. "You killed him, Sam Flintlock. You bury him."

Hernandez swung his horse away and his men followed.

Flintlock waited until they disappeared

into rain and distance and then stepped to Roper.

He took three cartridges from the man's gun belt and as he punched out the empties from his Colt and fed the fresh rounds into the cylinder, he said, "So I'm not your friend, huh?"

"Sam, Sam, I was joshing," Roper said. "I mean, I figured if I said you weren't my friend, the gunfighter wouldn't kill you." He smiled. "You see how it was with me, huh? I had your own good at heart."

Flintlock nodded. "And I sure believe you, Abe."

He shoved the muzzle of his revolver into Roper's belly and at the same time jerked the man's Colt from the holster.

Roper's eyes got big. Scared big. "Sam . . . what the hell?"

"Bury him, Abe," Flintlock said.

"I ain't —"

Flintlock pushed the gun harder. "Bury him."

Roper looked into Flintlock's eyes and what he saw unnerved him.

"All right, all right, Sam. I'll bury him, but I don't have a shovel."

"Then do the best you can, Abe. And get his guns. He was wearing them under false pretenses."

Roper took a couple of steps in the dead man's direction, then turned and said, "You killed a man and now you're beating yourself up, ain't you?"

"Yes," Flintlock said. "I'm beating myself up."

"Sammy, you got to get over that," Roper said. "It's a fault with you I seen before."

"I know, Abe, but I never will," Flintlock said. "Now get him the hell out of here."

After Roper dragged the body into the trees, Jack Coffin stepped beside Flintlock. "I saw it and he didn't come close, Samuel."

"I reckon not," Flintlock said.

"Only one man is faster than you. The one who calls himself Asa Pagg."

"Pagg is good with a gun," Flintlock said. "Real fast on the draw and shoot."

"Better than good," Coffin said. "If you meet him, walk softly around him."

"I don't think I can do that, Jack."

"Then he'll kill you, as surely as he will kill me," Coffin said.

CHAPTER THIRTY-THREE

"Mr. Pagg, I would consider it a most singular favor if you would walk me around the perimeter of the fort," Winnifred Grove said.

Asa Pagg, who'd been smoking a cigar at the far corner of the porch outside the headquarters building, smiled and said, "Surely a task, and a pleasant one, for your husband, ma'am."

"Alas, the colonel is busy inside with army affairs," Winnifred said. "And I fear he can't be disturbed." She flounced off the wicker chair and pouted. "Oh dear, what a pity to waste such an exquisite moon."

Pagg glanced at the night sky where the waxing moon haloed a few clouds with pink and white light. "It is indeed," he said. He flicked his cigar away and watched it land on the parade ground, showering sparks.

"I'd be delighted to take a promenade with you, dear lady," Pagg said. He stepped beside the woman and crooked his arm for her to take. "Shall we be on our way?"

Winnifred frowned. "You must forgive me, Mr. Pagg, but I find the touch of animal fur most distressing," she said. "Perhaps you could leave your coat on the porch and reclaim it when we return."

"Certainly," Pagg said. "If it distresses you so."

He shed his coat, revealing the big revolvers on each side of his chest.

Winnifred smiled. "I know I'll be safe in your strong hands, Mr. Pagg."

Again Pagg offered the woman his arm. "Then shall we?"

The night air was soft and cool and a gentle breeze from the south carried the scent of sage and pine. The moon bathed the fort and the outlying brush and piñon country with fragile light and gleamed on Winnifred's severely scraped-back hair.

The woman lifted her face to Pagg and said, with an obviously mirror-practiced, coquettish smile, "I would not have wished to ask any other gentlemen to walk with me, Mr. Pagg, because I know that you're the very soul of propriety."

"Indeed I am, ma'am," Pagg said. "You're safe with me."

"But not too safe, I trust," Winnifred said,

smiling again.

She'd laid it on the line and Pagg wondered if he should do her. She was scrawny and didn't get her full helping of looks, but what was it the sailors said? Yeah, any port in a storm.

"Have you enjoyed many women in your life, Mr. Pagg?"

"Hundreds . . . white, black, yellow and red and I liked 'em all."

"And who were the ones that pleased you most, may I enquire?"

"They all pleased me, dear lady."

"Then I must be careful ere that sweet treasure that women guard most diligently might be in danger of a determined assault."

Winnifred smiled again and Pagg thought that a plain-faced woman with horsey teeth doesn't do the hussy well. "Are my fears unfounded?"

"Quite unfounded, ma'am," Pagg said. "I am a gentleman to the core and I will ne'er scale the ramparts of your virtue."

Winnifred looked disappointed.

Their walk had taken them past the parade ground and into a wooded area that was mostly scrub juniper and wild oak.

Pagg grabbed the woman and pushed her against a tree.

"Yes, you know what I want," Winnifred

said. "You're an animal, Asa Pagg, and I want you so badly."

Pagg grinned. "My, my, Mrs. Grove, what will the colonel say?"

"Nothing, because he won't find out." Winnifred's hands became busy. "Quickly," she said.

Looking back, Pagg decided that he'd no way of knowing that Mrs. Grove was a screamer. But indeed she was. Her ecstatic shrieks and squeals carried far in the darkness . . . and alerted the pickets her husband had posted around the perimeter.

Over Pagg's heaving shoulder, Winnifred saw two troopers run toward them, rifles across their chests.

She sidestepped away from Pagg and screamed, "Help! Help! Rape!"

Stunned, it took some time for Pagg to react. He pulled up his pants and turned and then froze when a bayonet pushed against his belly, a hard-eyed cavalryman on the other end of it.

Winnifred pointed at Pagg, her face a mask of terror. "He . . . he dragged me from the porch and tried . . . he tried . . ."

"Calm yourself, Mrs. Grove," a soldier said. "The rogue can't harm you now."

Pagg thought about drawing and shooting it out. But other soldiers were running toward him and he caught a glimpse of an officer's shoulder straps. He was a long way from his horse and the gray-haired trooper with the bayonet would surely stick him before he could clear his guns.

Then things happened fast.

Captain Owen Shaw's baffled face swam into his line of vision. Then the half-drunk First Lieutenant Frank Hedley pushed the trooper's bayonet aside and stuck the muzzle of his revolver under Pagg's chin.

"Damn you, I'll blow your filthy head right off your shoulders."

"No, Lieutenant," Shaw said. "Let the colonel decide this man's fate."

Colonel Grove arrived with a dozen men, and his wife screamed even louder and more urgently than she had as Pagg pleasured her.

"Andrew," she called out, her arms reaching to him, "hold me, for I am undone."

Shaw reckoned only Mrs. Grove's buttons were undone, but he glared at Pagg and said nothing.

"Andrew, he tried to . . . to . . . ravish me," Winnifred shrieked as she fell into her husband's arms.

The colonel's face was black with rage. "Take that foul beast to the guardhouse," he said. "I'll deal with him later."

Pagg knew resistance was futile. He moved

to surrender his guns to Shaw, but the gray-haired trooper saw the movement and he slammed his rifle butt into the side of Pagg's head. The outlaw dropped like a sack of rocks.

Captain Shaw stared down at the unconscious Pagg and he badly wanted to kill him, kick his face in for being so stupid — and with Winnifred Grove of all people.

Damn Pagg's eyes. Now the plan to steal the payroll was well and truly scuppered.

Asa Pagg woke to a pounding headache and the taste of blood in his mouth. He tried to move but his entire body hurt and he sank back onto the prickly discomfort of the filthy straw mattress and groaned.

The damned blue bellies had pounded on him with fists, boots and rifle butts all the way to the guardhouse. To the soldiers, a rapist, even an unsuccessful one, as Mrs. Grove claimed, was the lowest form of life on the frontier.

The thought of what had transpired last night and the treachery of Mrs. Grove made Pagg's anger flare and he forced himself to rise from the bunk and stretch the kinks out of his aching body.

The guardhouse was a low, narrow log cabin, the rusty iron cot its only furnishing.

A single barred window, about the size of an unopened book, looked out onto a stretch of sandy ground dominated by an X-shaped wooden frame where soldiers guilty of desertion or insubordination were strung up by their thumbs.

Pagg was staring out at this melancholy scene when Captain Shaw's face filled the window and blocked his view.

"Damnit, Pagg, why did you do it?" Shaw said. "And the colonel's wife of all people?"

"I didn't rape her," Pagg said. "She was willing. She asked me to do her."

"That's not what Mrs. Grove says. She's taken to her bed in a faint and the colonel vows he'll punish you like he's never punished a man before."

"I told you, Shaw, she was more than willing. But now I'm trapped like a rat in a trap for trying to rape an ugly woman an' all I wanted was to do her a favor. I gave her what she wants but never gets."

"Hell, Pagg, she's a horse. She's even got the whinny."

"I know. A loud whinny. That's the reason I'm here."

"Geronimo attacks in three days, Pagg," Shaw said. "Our time is running out."

"Don't you think I'm well aware o' that?"

"When he finds out you can't help him

like you promised he'll skin you alive like he did Lieutenant Howard."

"Geronimo didn't do the skinnin'."

"His Apaches did."

Pagg thought about that, then said, "Tell Joe and Logan I want to talk to them. They'll bust me out of here."

"The guardhouse is surrounded by a dozen sentries with orders to shoot to kill. That's how mad at you Colonel Grove is. Your boys won't get near the place."

"Then you'll have to do it, Shaw. You're an officer. You must be able to get the key to the door."

"Maybe, once Geronimo starts his attack. But it won't be easy. Now I'm not even sure I want to go through with this thing. I mean with you locked up and facing a possible firing squad."

"Nothing is easy, Shaw. Stealing the money won't be easy. Getting out of this fort with our hair intact after Geronimo attacks won't be easy. Getting the wagon to Mexico won't be easy. The only thing that's gonna be easy is spending it."

Shaw said, "All right, Pagg, you sit tight and I'll see what I can do."

"Captain, don't count on the letter you sent to your kinfolk in Boston," Pagg said.

"What do you mean by that?" Shaw said.

"Just what I say. Don't count on it."

"You mean if I back out, you'll kill me anyway?"

"Yeah, something like that."

"I told you I'll see what I can do. You can trust me, Asa."

Pagg ignored that and said, "What does the colonel have in mind for me? You said something about a firing squad."

"I don't know," Shaw said. "The firing squad is a real possibility, but I can assure you, whatever your punishment is, it won't be pleasant."

CHAPTER THIRTY-FOUR

"Unless I'm much mistaken, that there's the Hogback," Marshal Pleasant Tyrell said. "Ain't it a wonder to behold, Charlie?"

Charlie Fong nodded. "Rises out of nothing, like God set it down there for a spell and then forgot about it."

"He works in mysterious ways, kind o' like your kinfolk," Tyrell said. "You see the cabin? My far seeing ain't so good anymore."

"Damn rain is like a mist," Fong said. "I guess we'll have to ride closer."

A cloud of doubt passed across Tyrell's eyes.

"You reckon this feller Garrard could be a-settin' at a window with a Sharps big fifty sighted in at a hundred yards?" the marshal said. "I mean with the Apaches out an' all."

"Maybe so. But I take consolation in the fact that you're a bigger target than me," Fong said.

"Boy, you jes' went down a couple o' pegs in my estimation," Tyrell said. "An' me havin' just took to liking Chinee fellers."

They rode off a shallow rise onto the sandy flat that gave way to a wide depression thick with brush, cactus and bulging sandstone boulders. The rain didn't quit, still falling steadily from a bruised sky.

When they rode out of the hollow, about half a mile of flat brush country stretched ahead of them.

For a moment the rain parted like a ragged gray curtain and Charlie Fong caught a glimpse of a log cabin huddled close to the foot of the Hogback. Smoke from its chimney rose into the air straight as a string, but there was no sign of the occupants.

"See something?" Tyrell said.

"Yeah, there's a cabin right ahead of us," Fong said. "Now we'll find out if that big fifty notion of yours has any merit."

"Hell of a way to find out, Charlie. Ride into a damned bullet."

Marshal Tyrell glanced at the black and mustard sky and scowled. "Be good to set in a cabin out of this rain and drink coffee." He turned his head and a question framed in his eyes. "How do you want to play it, Charlie?"

"We just ride up, friendly as you please, and let Garrard invite us inside. If the Chinese women are being abused, we'll know it."

"Stick this in your head, Charlie," Tyrell said. "Like I already told you, if there's killin' to be done, I'll do it. I'm the law."

"Sets fine by me, Marshal. But if Garrard draws down on me, all bets are off. You *comprende*?"

"All right, you can't say fairer than that. But there's one more thing, Charlie, I'm the white man here, so I'll make the call on whether or not the women are being abused."

"Call it as you see it, Marshal."

"Then let's go get it done."

Silas Garrard's welcome was a few degrees less than warm.

As Charlie Fong and Pleasant Tyrell rode up to the cabin, Garrard opened the door, a Sharps fifty in his hands and a scowl on his bearded face.

"Big fifty. I told ya, Charlie," Tyrell whispered.

"What the hell do you want?" Garrard said.

He was a short, stocky man with quick, mean eyes and muttonchop sideburns that, untrimmed, grew down to his shoulders and were braided with red ribbon. He wore a sailor's peaked cap with an anchor on the front, a seaman's short jacket and baggy gray pants.

Tyrell answered before Fong could get a word out. "We were passin' by, seen your smoke and figured we'd stop for a cup of coffee an' a friendly chinwag."

"You figgered wrong," Garrard said. "Now be off with you. I don't want you here."

"I'm an officer of the law," Tyrell said. "I got a right to be here, or any place else in this here territory."

"I don't give a damn who you are, mister. And this here cannon I'm holding feels the same way."

"That's a mite unfriendly, Garrard," Charlie Fong said. "You maybe got something to hide?"

"How the hell do you know my name?"

Fong caught a brief glimpse of a small, pale face at the window and then it was gone. "The army told me who you was and where you was," he said. "They don't think very highly of you."

"Well, there's nothing here for you, Chinaman, so light a shuck," Garrard said. "I got faith in this here rifle."

Then Tyrell exerted himself. "We have

reason to believe a couple of Chinese gals are being abused at this residence. Before we ride on, we want to check on their welfare."

"Lawman or no, you won't enter this cabin, and be damned to ye," Garrard said. "By God, make a trial of it and I'll kill you both. You can lay to that."

There was no step-back in Pleasant Tyrell that day. He'd been through it before and he didn't like to be pushed. He swept back his slicker and cleared his guns.

"Mister, make a move to swing that Sharps in my direction and I'll drop you right where you stand," he said. His voice was low, flat, like an undertaker at a wake.

Garrard's face worked as he considered those tough, matter-of-fact words from a strange old man wearing a top hat, rain falling around him, a hundred different kinds of hell in his eyes.

The sailor had been around hardcases before, but now he decided that he wanted no part of the lawman astride the seedy, eight-hundred-pound mustang.

Garrard let the muzzle of the Sharps lower until it was pointed at the ground. "Come in and make your inspection of my women, damn ye," he said. "And don't ask for a taste, for they'll be none forthcoming, lay to that."

"That's very civil of you, Garrard," Charlie Fong said. "Ain't that civil of him, Marshal Tyrell?"

"Civil as ever was," Tyrell said. "And, Garrard, you have coffee in the pot, I hope."

The man's only answer was a sullen silence as he opened the door and held it for Tyrell and Fong to step inside.

The interior of the cabin was as neat and clean as two women could make it. As the soldier had described to Charlie Fong, the walls were covered in prints and artifacts, most of them related to the African slave trade.

But what troubled Fong and then Tyrell when he drew his attention to it, was a cat-o'-nine-tails hanging from a hook on the wall.

Garrard followed Fong's stare and said, "Women are like dogs and horses, they need discipline from time to time." He clapped his hands and the door to the adjoining bedroom opened and the two Chinese girls stepped inside.

They were dressed in calico dresses and both were small, slender and quite pretty. They kept their eyes downcast.

Tyrell couldn't tell one from the other,

but Charlie Fong pegged the slightly taller of the two as the older. He guessed she was about seventeen, the other maybe three years younger.

"There, nothing wrong with them gals," Garrard said. "That's where discipline comes in." He grinned, showing bad teeth. "Listen to this." He roughly grabbed the older girl by the arm — too roughly Fong thought — and said, "Who lives here?"

The girl's brown, almond-shaped eyes lifted for a moment. "Only you, master," she said.

"See what I mean?" Garrard said. "Hell, they consider themselves worthless, not even human beings."

"You did that to them with the whip?" Fong said.

"Sure I did. That's the way I enforced discipline at sea, and, by God, it's the way I enforce it in my own home, lay to that." He pushed the girl away from him and held her out at arm's length. "Not a mark on her, and not a mark on t'other one either. These gals ain't bein' abused. They like the discipline o' the cat, keeps them on an even keel, like."

Fong stepped to the older girl. "Show me your back," he said.

Garrard roared, "I'm damned if she will!"

278

"She will," Tyrell said quietly, relaxed, but with his hands close to his guns.

Garrard had propped his rifle in a corner but didn't seem inclined to go for it and confront the grim old marshal in a close-up gunfight.

Her eyes averted from Fong's gaze, the girl unbuttoned the back of her dress while Garrard stood by and fumed.

"Not a mark, huh?" Charlie Fong said.

The girl's slender back was crisscrossed with whip scars, some red, raw and recent, others stark white and older.

Then the girl surprised him. She pointed at the younger girl and said, "My sister the same. Worse I think."

"So they're marked up a little," Garrard said. "It's none of your damned business. They're mine and I can do what I want with them."

"Charlie, did I see a barn behind the house when we rode in?" Tyrell said.

"Yeah, you did."

"Go see if Garrard has horses. If he has, saddle them up and bring 'em here."

"You leave my damned horses alone or I'll take the whip to you, Chinaman," Garrard said.

He made a move toward the cat, but stopped when he found himself looking into

279

the muzzle of Charlie Fong's .38.

"Give me an excuse to kill you, Garrard," Fong said. "Say something or make a fancy move."

"Charlie, remember what I told you about the killin'," Tyrell said. "That's my baili-wick."

"I remember." Fong glared at Garrard, then pushed his revolver back in his pocket and stepped out the door into the rain.

Chapter Thirty-Five

"What the hell are you doing?" Silas Garrard said.

Pleasant Tyrell smiled without humor. "I'm confiscating your women."

"And my horses." Garrard's voice pitched into a whine. "You can't leave me afoot in this wilderness."

"I can and I will," Tyrell said. "It's the luck of the draw, my man."

The older Chinese girl wore a slicker that Charlie Fong had found in the barn. The younger was lost inside a seaman's oilskin coat and the sleeves drooped over her hands.

Despite their limited English, both girls realized what was happening and Fong decided they seemed more than eager to leave.

He didn't yet know just how eager.

"I paid for those women and I have a bill of sale to prove it," Garrard said to Tyrell. "I'll see you lose your star over this, you damned old fool."

The marshal smiled. "Garrard, this may come as a surprise to you, but it shouldn't — I'm looking for an excuse to gun you myself. So I advise you to back off, stay quiet and lay low."

Frightened now, Garrard let it go like a man dropping a hot brick. "I can die out here without a horse," he said.

"Hell, you're within walking distance of a dozen settlements," Charlie Fong said.

"The Apaches are out, damn you," Garrard said.

"Yeah, so they are," Fong said. "That's bad luck for you."

"Maybe you should try using your whip on ol' Geronimo," Tyrell said. "It worked with . . ." Tyrell sought the right word, then settled for "children."

During this exchange, no one noticed that the older girl had disappeared.

But when she stepped out of the cabin door, everybody took notice, especially Silas Garrard. His eyes as round as coins, he said, "What the hell are you going to do with that?"

The Sharps rifle's twelve-pound weight was a load for a small, slender girl, but somehow she wrestled the gun to waist level. And fired.

Up close, the roar of a Sharps fifty was thunderous, loud enough to cover Garrard's agonized scream.

The recoil knocked the Chinese girl on her back — but the bullet in his groin slammed Garrard to his knees, then his butt.

He looked at the scarlet stain that covered his crotch and he screamed, "She shot it off!"

"My God," Charlie Fong whispered. "Is it true?"

Garrard screeched the words, "Yes, it's true! Look at me! The bitch shot off everything I got!"

Marshal Pleasant Tyrell helped the girl to her feet and said, "Young lady, you sure got a direct way of making a statement."

"Kill her!" Garrard screamed. "Shoot her, you damned idiot!"

Charlie Fong looked at the girl. It looked like the enormity of what she'd done had finally sunk in. Tears ran down her cheeks as her sister put her arms around her and whispered words in Chinese that Fong, an orphan raised by whites, didn't understand.

Garrard rocked back and forth and moaned, his eyes fixed on his ruined groin. Then he glared at Tyrell again and squealed, "She shot a white man. Kill her. Hang her right now."

"Well, I'll need to investigate this and make a report," Tyrell said. "That takes time. By the way, seein' what's happened an' all, can I still call you *Mister* Garrard?"

"Give me a gun!" Garrard pleaded. "Let me kill the bitch. She's ruined me."

Charlie Fong bent from the waist and stared at the man's crotch. "She's done for you, all right," he said. He straightened. "It's a sad thing to say, Cap'n, but your screwin' days are over."

This brought another wail from Garrard, and Fong said to the marshal, "Do you plan to arrest her?"

"Yeah, he's gonna arrest and then hang her, lay to that," Garrard shrilled.

"I reckon not," Tyrell said. "It was an unfortunate accident. Damned gun went off by itself, anybody could see that."

"You crazy old coot, she tried to kill me," Garrard said.

"I don't see it that way . . . ah . . . Mr. Garrard."

Charlie Fong told the girls to mount up, then said to Tyrell, "They'd better come with me."

"Where are you taking them, Charlie?" Tyrell said.

"I'd rather not answer that, Marshal," Fong said.

"You're going to meet up with Abe Roper and Sam Flintlock. Ain't you?"

"Like I said, Marshal, I'd —"

"Rather not talk about it, I know. Well, I reckon them two little gals will eat their weight in groceries on the trail to wherever the hell you're headed. I suggest you go into the cabin and sack up some supplies."

Garrard rocked back and forth and groaned. Bound up in a tight cocoon of pain, he said nothing.

After Fong left, Tyrell said, "Garrard, seein' as how you got a real bad misery an' all, if you want I can scatter your brains, and you won't hurt no more. It's a tough thing, expecting a man to live without a pecker."

Garrard, his mouth all screwed up in a snarl, said, "I hope you die of cancer, old man. You've lived too long."

Tyrell shook his head. "That's the last time I try to do you a favor. You're just not an appreciating man." He smiled. "How you gonna piss? You thought about that?"

"Leave me the hell alone."

Tyrell's eyes hardened until they were steel blue. "Like you left the two little Chinee girls alone? Their lives must have been a hell."

The older girl spat, then said, "He is . . ."

to Tyrell. The next word was Chinese and sounded like *mawguay.*

"What does that mean, little gal?" the marshal said.

"Devil," the girl said. "He is a devil."

Garrard stared at the girl with such a look of demonic hatred that even Tyrell felt its venom.

"He's the devil, all right," he said. He made a tut-tut sound with his tongue and shook his head. "And him without a pecker. Don't that beat all."

"I got the groceries," Charlie Fong said. He smiled at Garrard. "Just about cleaned you out, Silas, but I'm sure you don't mind."

"Let's get out of here," Tyrell said. "I want to feel clean again."

"You're leaving me alone here to die?" Garrard said as the marshal swung into the saddle.

"Seems like," Tyrell said. "And I can't say it was real nice meeting you."

Garrard had lost a lot of blood and he looked as though he was barely holding on to consciousness. But he gritted his teeth, then rolled up his left sleeve and revealed a grinning skull branded with a red-hot iron into the inside of his forearm.

"Gaze on that, old man? It was burned there in Haiti by hellfire. A witch done that, a hag who'd been dead for years and then came back to life. She was what the natives call a zombie woman. Understand?"

"I don't know what you're talking about," Tyrell said.

Garrard's eyes were wild, and as though he hadn't heard, he said, "The skull gives me the power to know if a person will die soon, and God curse you, you'll be dead and rotten before this week is out."

Garrard raised his arm. Blood from his hand ran down his wrist and it looked as though the skull was shedding scarlet tears.

"God curse you," he said again. "God curse you to damnation."

Silas Garrard died with that last, vile blasphemy on his lips.

Pushed to his limit and then beyond, Tyrell drew both his guns and pumped ten bullets into the man, the last eight jerking his already dead body like a rag doll.

Through a drift of smoke, he looked at Charlie Fong and said, "I told him I was looking for an excuse to plug him. He gave me one."

Marshal Pleasant Tyrell tried valiantly to smile, but his lips were bloodless and all at once he looked old . . . and very, very tired.

CHAPTER THIRTY-SIX

"You scared the hell out of me, Jack," Charlie Fong said. "I took you for an Apache."

"Well, you were half right," Jack Coffin said. His eyes flicked to the girls. "Where have you been? China?"

"It's a long story," Fong said, "and I only want to tell it once. Where are Sam Flintlock and Abe Roper?"

Coffin turned in the saddle and pointed toward the Carrizo foothills. "Close. That's their smoke," he said. "Only a bank robber and a gunfighter would make smoke like that in Apache country."

Fong scanned the distance and said, "I see it, south of the big mesa."

"Yes. But tomorrow I'll lead them north to Pastora Peak and we'll search there. It's high, timbered country that could easily hide a cave."

"So you haven't found the bell yet?"

"No, not yet, but I will." He stared closely

at the girls, then said, "We already have a woman in camp. Now we'll have three, and Roper isn't going to like it much."

"Who's the woman?" Fong said. "Anybody I know?"

"A white woman who is not right in her mind. Sam Flintlock calls her Ayasha."

"How did —"

"It's a long story, Charlie," Coffin said. "I'll let Samuel tell it." He glanced at the sky. "The rain is following you."

"Jack, I reckon I've got grief following me," Fong said. "What am I going to do with two young Chinese girls?"

"When you sell the gold from the bell, send them back to China," Coffin said.

"Well, it's a thought," Fong said. "But China is a big place. Where would I send them and to who?"

"Well, you could raise them like your own."

"Do I look like a pa to you?"

"Yes. I think you'd do just fine as a pa."

Charlie Fong smiled. "Jack, that just ain't going to happen."

"Then ask Sam Flintlock for advice."

"Hell, Sammy never had a pa except for old Barnabas and he was part grizzly. What does he know about raising two young girls?"

"That's why he will give you good advice," Coffin said. "Because he knows nothing about raising children."

Charlie Fong couldn't figure that one and didn't try.

And then the rain started.

"I rescued them, Abe, like I told you," Charlie Fong said. "What do you want me to do? Chase them away and let them get eaten by bears?"

Abe Roper scowled. "Get this, Charlie, them gals don't get a share of the golden bell. Same thing I told Sam'l when he rescued the crazy white woman. She don't get a share either." He spat into the fire. "And another thing, we don't collect any more females on this trip. We're overrun with them as it is."

"I got to agree with you there, Abe," Flintlock said.

"Well, I'm glad you do, Sammy, since you're one o' the collectors," Roper said.

Flintlock smiled at that, then said, "This Pleasant Tyrell feller, Charlie, he a tall, skinny old man who wears a top hat and carries two guns? Kinda looks like the pictures of Wild Bill in the dime novels, except older, huh?"

"That's him, all right. Killed that Garrard

feller like I told you, which was probably just as well since he'd no pecker left. Why do you ask?"

Flintlock and the others sat under a canopy of stretched-out slickers and pine branches that ticked rainwater into the hissing fire. Ayasha, still silent, sat between the Chinese girls who fussed with her hair, spoke to her in a language she couldn't understand and made her smile.

"Why do you ask, Sam?" Fong repeated.

"Oh, three years ago, maybe four, I was in the Nations hunting a black farmhand who'd taken up an ax and chopped his employer, his wife and a visiting neighbor into a hundred little pieces."

"Did the farmhand count them?" Roper said.

"Hell, yeah, he sure did. And I meant the old man and the two women were each chopped into a hundred pieces."

"Making three hundred pieces in total, like," Roper said.

Flintlock nodded and Roper said, "I just want to get the story straight."

"Well, anyway, I tracked the feller, as I recollect his name was Hamp Wade, to a sod cabin on the bank of a place called Dead Beaver Creek, on account of how he now had a thousand-dollar bounty on his head, dead or alive. Besides hisself, he had a kept woman in there, a Choctaw, who had an ass so big she couldn't have sat down in a number three washtub."

"Interesting that, about the ass I mean," Roper said as he poured coffee into his cup.

"Yeah, I guess it is at that," Flintlock said.

"Where does Marshal Tyrell come in?" Charlie Fong said.

"I'm getting to that," Flintlock said. "How it come up, I saw smoke rising from the cabin chimney and there was a sow and a litter of piglets rooting around out front. So I reckoned ol' Hamp was to home."

"Them pigs was a dead giveaway, rootin' around like that," Roper said. "And the smoke."

"Yeah, Abe, that's exactly how I had it figured," Flintlock said.

"Then what happened?" Roper said.

"What happened was, I left my horse in some wild oaks and cat-footed it toward the cabin."

"Your gun was drawed, I hope," Roper said.

"It most certainly was, Abe."

"Just makin' sure."

"Well, I figured to kick in the door of the cabin and —"

"What kind of door?" Roper said.

292

"Just an ordinary planed timber door on leather hinges, Abe."

"Gettin' things straight in my mind, Sammy," Roper said, his gaze concentrating on the cigarette he was building.

"Anyhoo" — Flintlock shook his head — "wait a minute, why the hell did I decide to tell this story? It's like it goes on forever."

Thunder rumbled in the distance and lightning briefly turned the pines into slender columns of steel. Rain hissed around them and rattled on the slickers like a snare drum.

"You're tellin' it good, Sammy," Roper said. "And now I guess we're gettin' to the exciting part, the killin' an' the cuttin'. Though I did cotton to the bit about the pigs. I've took to likin' pigs real recent."

"To make a long story short," Flintlock said, with a sidelong glance at Roper, "I was about to step in front of the door —"

"To kick it in, like," Roper said.

"Yes, indeed, Abe," Flintlock said. "To kick it in."

He sighed and said, "Just as I stepped in front of the door a voice behind me yelled, 'Shotgun!' I dived for the dirt and a moment later a scattergun blast blasted a hole in the door that you could've driven a team of mules and a Studebaker wagon through."

"To make a hole that big, it was a ten gauge," Roper said. "Had to be."

"That's what it turned out to be, Abe," Flintlock said. "Well, a minute later out comes ol' Hamp with the Greener in his hands and a killin' light in his eyes."

"An' you plugged him square, huh, Sammy?"

"Nope. This old feller comes up and cuts loose with two .44-40 Russians. Hamp drops, dead when he hits the ground. Then the Choctaw comes out with a knife in her hand and the old coot shoots her down. Time passes, about as long as a slow-talking man would take to count to five —"

"How slow would he talk, Sammy?" Roper said.

"And then" — ignoring Roper — "this towheaded kid charges through the door, blasting away with a Colt's self-cocker, screaming like a wild Comanche."

"An' then what happened?" Roper said. "This is gettin' real good."

"The old man gunned him. Three dead on the ground in less than a minute."

"And the old feller was Pleasant Tyrell?" Charlie Fong said.

"As ever was, I reckon. Seemed he had a warrant for Hamp Wade for murder, and me and him happened to arrive at the cabin at the same time."

"And then what?" Roper said.

"Well, I'd taken some buckshot in my right shoulder and ol' Tyrell patched me up and later we split the thousand-dollar bounty on Hamp. I always reckoned that was real white of him, seeing as how I almost got my head blowed off and never fired a shot."

Flintlock poured himself coffee and said, "After that I never seen or heard from him again until you mentioned his name, Charlie. He's a tough, hard old man is Pleasant Tyrell. And mighty fast on the draw and shoot."

"He won't take any sass," Fong said. "I can tell you that."

CHAPTER THIRTY-SEVEN

"We're getting close," Jack Coffin said.

"How close?" Abe Roper said.

"Close enough that I can sense a presence . . . something young and something very ancient, the one the Mexican peons call the *Angel de la Muerte.*"

Roper turned in the saddle. "Sam'l, have you any idea what the hell he's talkin' about?"

Sam Flintlock shook his head. "We're not catching your drift, Jack."

The breed stared ahead of him at the gently rising ridge of Pastora Peak and its mantle of pine, juniper and winter oak.

"I don't know the reason for my feelings or what they mean," Coffin said. "But by and by, we will all find out." He looked at Roper. "The golden bell is guarded by the Angel of Death. To see and touch the bell is to die."

"And you'll lead us right to it, huh?"

Roper said. His eyes were greedy.

"Yes. I'll lead you to the bell, and to the one who protects it."

"Don't bother yourself about no damned angel of death," Roper said. "He gives us any trouble an' I'll gun him."

Flintlock's attention was caught by the Chinese girls. Usually they chattered to each other in their own tongue, but now they were strangely quiet and had been since the peak came into view.

The older girl felt Flintlock's eyes on her and she stared at him with frightened black eyes. Then she said, *"Si shen."*

"What does that mean?" Flintlock asked her.

The girl answered in her own tongue, and Charlie Fong, his face troubled, translated. "I don't speak much Chinese, but the gist of what she said is that we are entering the realm of *Si shen,* the Grim Reaper."

Abe Roper overheard and he said to the girl, smiling, "Don't you worry your pretty little head about that, honey. I'll gun that *Si shen* sumbitch as well."

Then the Mexican woman stepped into their path. She held a gray horse by a lead-rope.

Abe Roper drew rein and looked around

him, his head moving fast from side to side. He slid his Winchester from the boot and said, "Look sharp, boys. This could be an ambush."

The peasant woman was very old, her face wrinkled, eyes milky white.

She held the horse by a halter and said nothing.

Flintlock helped Ayasha to the ground and propped the Hawken upright on his thigh. He rode beside Roper and said, "You're thinking Carlos Hernandez, huh?"

"Damn right I am," Roper said. "Just like that Mex to use an old woman as bait and then bushwhack us. He's a sneaky one, is Carlos."

"I don't think so, Abe," Flintlock said. "The Mexican would bushwhack us all right, but sending an old woman as bait isn't his style."

Coffin rode up and said, "There is only the old woman and the horse."

"You sure?" Roper said.

But then the woman spoke and expelled all doubt.

In passable English, she said, "You will take the *caballo* as a gift and go away from here."

Roper sat erect in the saddle, and said, "Who are you, old woman? Speak now. Be up-front, mind. We're white men here."

"I am nobody," the woman said. "The gray horse is for you."

"Woman, who gives us this fine horse?" Coffin said.

The younger Chinese girl gave a little yelp of fear and Flintlock turned and looked at her.

"A great lord," the woman said. "You must take his gift and go back from whence you came. Go home and never return here again."

"Woman, who is this feller?" Roper said. "This great lord ranny?"

The old peasant's face showed no emotion.

"He is the one all of us fear," the woman said. "He is a great lord, but his heart is as cold as ice and there is no pity in him."

"*Si shen!*" the older Chinese girl called out.

Suddenly Roper was angry. "Well, lady, you go back and tell Carlos Hernandez that the first time I see him I'll put a bullet into him. Great lord my ass. He's a damned, low-down, thieving outlaw."

"Pot calling the kettle black, huh, Abe?" Flintlock said, grinning.

"I'm a professional, Sammy, a gentleman highwayman who robs banks and trains. I don't steal frijoles out of the mouths of

299

Mexican children."

Without waiting to hear what Flintlock had to say, Roper said, "Charlie, grab the gray. That's one good-lookin' hoss."

"No, Charlie, leave it be," Flintlock said.

"What the hell, Sam'l?" Roper said.

"Look on the left shoulder, Abe. See the red handprint?"

"Yeah, I see it. So what?"

"It's the mark of death, made in blood. Let the horse go back."

Roper shook his head. "Damnit, Sam'l, you're as bad as the Chinese gals. Charlie, go grab the horse."

"After what Sam just said, not me, Abe."

"The horse has been ridden by demons," Jack Coffin said. "That is why it bears the mark of death."

Roper cursed loud and long, then said, "What a bunch of women! I'll get the damned hoss my ownself."

He kneed his own mount forward. . . .

And then the wind came.

And the rain.

As Sam Flintlock would recall later, the tempest originated at the top of Pastora Peak and drove downward. Shrieking its fury, the wind shredded leaves and branches from the pines and oaks and drove a hammering rain before it.

Abe Roper's horse reared, frightened arcs of white showing in its eyes, and the outlaw was thrown. He hit the ground with a thud and lay there stunned as his mount galloped past him.

The rain was torrential, coming off the mountain in raking sheets, and the noise of the storm was tremendous, like the rumbling roar inside a railroad tunnel as a deadheading express rackets past.

"Into the trees!" Flintlock yelled. The wind snatched the words from his mouth and tossed them away with the blowing leaves.

Charlie Fong herded the Chinese girls deeper into a pine thicket and Flintlock jumped out of the saddle, grabbed Ayasha around the waist and followed.

A series of splintering crashes sounded from higher up the mountainside as the wind freed a rain-loosened boulder and set it rolling down the slope. Above the peak, lightning scrawled across the tumbling sky.

Flintlock heard a woman scream, then realized it was Ayasha. He pulled her close to him and she buried her face in his chest, tree branches and fluttering leaves cartwheeling around them. A few feet away the Chinese sisters huddled against the base of a pine, Charlie Fong, with outstretched arms, doing his best to protect them.

The storm climaxed in a bellowing, clashing uproar that Fong would later describe as sounding like the finale of a Russian overture he'd once heard in a San Francisco concert hall.

Then, as suddenly as it had begun, it was over.

The clouds parted, the sun came out and a few random raindrops ticked from the trees.

There was no sign of the old woman or the gray horse.

Abe Roper groaned and got to his feet slowly and painfully.

He saw Sam Flintlock step toward him and said, "What the hell happened?"

"Storm," Flintlock said.

Roper put his hands on his hips and arched his back, working out the kinks. "Where's my damned hoss?" he said.

"He's around somewhere," Flintlock said. "He won't have gone far in all that wind and rain."

"Just sprung up, didn't it?" Roper said. "It just came out of nowhere."

"Yeah," Flintlock said. "Strange, that."

"Big storms happen all the time in the

mountains," Roper said. "Squalls hit out of the blue. Damn, I'm soaked to the skin."

"Me too," Flintlock said. "And I guess everybody else. I'll get a fire started and we can dry out our duds."

"And keep a watch for Hernandez. He didn't fool us this time, but he'll try again."

"Don't you think that storm was a little odd, Abe?" Flintlock said.

"In what way?" Roper had taken off his shirt and was wringing water out of it.

"I mean, just blowing up like that."

"I told you, Sammy, sudden storms happen in the high country all the time." Roper flapped his shirt, trying to get it dry. It made a slapping noise. "They last for a few minutes then move on."

He looked over to where Charlie Fong stood with the women. "Everybody all right, Charlie?"

"Seems like," Fong said. "But we're soaked."

"Yeah, we're all soaked. Where is the Injun?"

"Right here, Abe." Jack Coffin stepped out of the trees, his wet hair hanging lank over his shoulders.

"The squall's got Sammy spooked," Roper said. "Thinks maybe it was sent by boogermen, I reckon."

"You should have taken the horse," Coffin said. "You should've gone home."

"Hell, now don't you start," Roper said. "Listening to Sammy is bad enough."

"You should have taken the old man's gift."

"I tried to take it, but then the storm came down."

"The storm was sent by the old man who guards the bell," Coffin said.

Roper's face lit up. "Then we're close, huh?"

"Too close," Coffin said.

CHAPTER THIRTY-EIGHT

"Asa, I have news and it's bad," Captain Owen Shaw said.

"A hanging?" Asa Pagg said. He looked anxious. "Don't tell me it's hanging. I'd rather be shot."

Shaw hesitated as though he was trying to soften the blow, then said, "It's the Rogue's March, I'm afraid."

"What the hell is that?"

"It's a punishment the army reserves for scoundrels of every stripe, thieves, deserters, slackers and all the rest. You'll be drummed out of the post."

Pagg smiled. "Is that all? Hell, I've been thrown out of better places than this."

"It could be bad, Asa," Shaw said. "Depending on what Colonel Grove has in mind, it could be real bad."

Now Pagg was suspicious. "What are you telling me, Captain?"

A shrill bugle call razored through the

quiet of the morning.

"Assembly," Shaw said. "I have to go."

"Wait! Damn you, wait!" Pagg called. "How bad?"

But Shaw was already gone, walking under a lemon-colored sky to where the troops, mounted and foot, were already falling into line.

Now Asa Pagg was a worried man.

Getting thrown out of the fort didn't trouble him in the least, but would they give him his horse and guns? And a few dollars in his pocket?

Pagg took some comfort from the fact that Shaw would see to all these things. He gritted his teeth. He'd better. Or he was a dead man.

The guardhouse door swung open and a huge cavalry sergeant stepped inside, a squad of riflemen behind him.

"All right, sonny Jim, it's time," the soldier said, in a strong English accent.

"What's going on, damnit?" Pagg said. "I've got a right to know."

"You'll get thirty, and then be drummed out," the sergeant said.

"Thirty what?"

"Lashes, man," the sergeant said. His smile did nothing to soften his coarse, cruel mouth. "Think yourself lucky, you could've got a hundred, and after that little lot, I'd have to scrape up what was left of you with a manure shovel."

Asa Pagg was a big man and he wasn't going anywhere without a fight.

He swung at the sergeant's chin, but the Englishman was no bargain. A veteran of the French Foreign Legion he'd later served three years as a first mate on the New York hell ships. He'd learned his skull-and-knuckle fighting in a hard school and now he proved it.

The sergeant slipped Pagg's wild swing, then brought up his own right in a vicious uppercut that landed square on the outlaw's chin. Pagg crashed onto his back. He was hit hard but still conscious and cursing and he kicked out at the soldiers who rolled him on his belly and tied his hands behind him.

But for Asa Pagg worse indignities were to come.

His boots were removed and then the soldiers used their bayonets to cut his clothes from his body. He was hauled, naked and bleeding, to his feet and bundled out the door.

The timber punishment frame had been removed from outside the guardhouse and now stood in the middle of the parade ground. X marked the spot of Asa Pagg's coming degradation.

As he was dragged toward the whipping post sand burrs tormented Pagg's bare feet and as he got closer he saw affixed to one of the uprights a painted sign that read:

I am a
RAPIST

Pagg cursed and struggled as his wrists were lashed to the frame, then the soldiers stepped back and a silence descended on Fort Defiance.

Close by, Pagg heard a bird singing and he craned his head to see what was going on behind him. Out of the corner of his eye he saw a group of civilians, McCarty the sutler, a couple of men he didn't know, and a fainting Winnifred Grove supported by the widowed Maude Ashton.

There was no sign of Dean and Harte. All Asa Pagg saw that morning were scores of enemies and no friends. Even Shaw was nowhere to be seen.

The big sergeant stepped beside Pagg, a coiled, braided leather whip in his right hand. His face set and grim, the man looked expectantly in the direction of the headquarters building.

Pagg heard Colonel Grove yell the command, "Music to the front!"

Then, "Thirty, Sergeant Fuller! Carry out the sentence!"

A snare drum rattled into life and Fuller shoved a chunk of wood between Pagg's teeth. Then a moment passed as the whip uncoiled and . . .

Crack!

The plaited leather cut deep and Pagg flinched as pain bladed across his naked back.

Now a single fife accompanied the drum, piping out the jaunty air of the "Rogue's March."

As the whip cracked and tore into flesh, some of the older soldiers, who'd seen this many times before, chanted the words to the tune, unchanged since the colonists had borrowed them from the British during the Revolutionary War.

"I left my home and left my job,
Went and joined the army.
If I knew then what I know now,
I wouldn't have been so barmy."

The whip ravaged Pagg's back and he shut his eyes and bit hard into the wood, his breath coming in short, agonized gasps.

"Poor old soldier, poor old soldier.
If I knew then what I know now,
I wouldn't have been so barmy."

Pagg turned his head and through a
scarlet haze of pain he saw Winnifred Grove
watching him intently, her thin lips wet. The
woman shuddered . . . smiled . . . shuddered again . . . and Maude Ashton looked
at Winnifred, her face taking on a look of
dawning horror.

"Twenty," Sergeant Fuller said, loud
enough for Pagg to hear.

Pagg groaned, pain and humiliation now
the entire focus of his being.

"Gave me a gun and a big red coat,
Gave me lots of drilling.
If I knew then what I know now,
I wouldn't have took the shilling."

The soldiers had no sympathy for Pagg
since he was only a civilian and not one of
their own, but a few of the younger recruits
seemed glad when the last lash was delivered
by Sergeant Fuller, every bit as vicious as
the twenty-nine that had gone before.

For the moment the fife and drum lapsed
into silence, as did the chanting of the soldiers.

"Water, Sergeant Fuller, if you please," Colonel Grove said.

The big noncom threw a bucket of water mixed with salt and vinegar on Pagg's back and the outlaw gasped as another kind of pain burned him like fire.

"Cut down the prisoner!" Grove ordered.

Pagg's bonds were cut and he collapsed to his knees. But Fuller and a couple of soldiers dragged him to his feet.

Trying desperately to hang on to consciousness, his back aflame, Pagg watched Grove ride closer. The colonel drew rein and said, "Bind him."

Pagg's wrists were again tied behind his back, then Fuller took the sign from the top of the frame and hung it around the outlaw's neck.

"Drum him out, the rogue!" Grove yelled.

The fife and drum took up the march again as soldiers with fixed bayonets prodded Pagg toward the perimeter of the fort. He staggered forward to the chants and jeers of the troops.

"Sent me off on a real old boat,
By Christ she was no beauty.
So far across the sea we went,
Afore to do my duty."

311

"Youngest soldier forward!" Grove roared above the rattle of the snare drum and the tinny fluting of the fife.

As was traditional, when Pagg reached the perimeter of Fort Defiance, the youngest soldier present, a beardless but booted cavalry trooper, kicked him hard in the ass.

Pagg staggered forward and fell . . . and the derisive laughter of the soldiers followed him as he struggled to his feet and stumbled into the uncaring wilderness.

That fine summer morning, the whipping and humiliation changed Asa Pagg forever.

Before he had been a badman, a killer and robber . . . now he was a monster.

CHAPTER THIRTY-NINE

"They did not take the gray horse, lord," the old woman said. She bowed low. "I have failed you."

The old man smiled and put his hand on the woman's white head.

Once she had been a great beauty, but that was more years ago than she or the old man could remember.

"The fault was mine," he said. "When men lust for a great fortune in gold, a horse is not much of a prize."

"Then you do not blame me, lord," the woman said.

"No. I do not blame you."

"But you will come for me."

"Three nights ago when the moon rose, did I not come for you then, child?"

"Is that why I walk in mist?"

"Yes, since I visited you."

"Then what do I do, lord?"

"You must go now."

The old woman did not argue. The great lord's icy heart would not be moved. She walked down the slope from the cave and disappeared into the haze of the morning.

The boy was puzzled. "Grandfather, are you really the lord of death?"

"I am what people believe I am."

"I believe you are just an old man who guards the golden bell," the boy said. "The last of your kind."

"Then that's what I am, and that's all that I am," the old man said. "Come, I will show you something. You will be the guardian one day soon, and it is time you saw the bell that never rang and the bird that never sang."

The boy bowed. "Grandfather, you do me great honor."

"It will only be a fleeting glimpse and at a distance," the old man said. "To approach the bell too closely is to die."

"I will remember," the boy said.

"Good, my days are numbered short," the old man said. "Soon you will be the guardian."

"Will I be a great lord like you?"

"If you wish it."

"I do not wish it, Grandfather."

"Then be the guardian, little one, and nothing more."

Jack Coffin watched the old woman walk down the hill and vanish like smoke into the pines.

The day was growing hot and sweat beaded his forehead. The knot in his belly tightened, a tension that was close kin to fear.

Coffin felt the time of his death approaching, but now or later, he had no way of telling.

It was best that he prepared.

Hidden from the cave mouth by trees, Coffin tethered his horse then kneeled and took a round mirror from around his neck and with it a small buckskin bag, beaded in the blue and white Apache style.

Coffin drew his knife and cut deep into his forearm. He mixed his blood into the powder he'd taken from the bag then smeared two lines of yellow war paint across his cheeks and the bridge of his nose.

He checked himself in the mirror and nodded. It was good.

Yellow was the color of death. But it also meant that the wearer was a heroic warrior who had led a good life and was therefore eligible to follow the buffalo in the next world.

Coffin sang his death song then mounted his horse.

It was time to find the golden bell . . . and fulfill his destiny.

CHAPTER FORTY

"Did you enjoy seeing justice done, my dear?" Colonel Andrew Grove said.

"Perhaps, Andrew," Winnifred Grove said. "But I keep having the most singular thought that a hundred lashes would have been more appropriate."

"A hundred might have killed him, especially laid on by Sergeant Fuller."

"He's a brute, a savage beast, and I am sure he could have survived a hundred of the best."

Grove shrugged. "Fuller would have torn him to ribbons. But it's a thought." The colonel rose to his feet. "Now, my dear, if you will excuse me. Duty calls."

"Of course, Andrew. I'm sure Mrs. Ashton will take excellent care of me."

After the colonel left, Maude Ashton, plump and motherly, stepped to the decanters on the parlor table. "A sherry, Winnifred?"

"Please. I must confess, I'm a bit used up after the excitement of the morning."

"Is that the word you choose to use, Winnifred — *excitement*?"

"Is there another?" Winnifred Grove's thin eyebrows arched.

"To see a man whipped to an inch of his life and then publically humiliated is hardly exciting."

"It was droll then." She flashed her huge teeth. "Positively droll, I should've said."

Maude handed Winnifred her glass and sat opposite her by the cold fireplace.

"Tragic," she said.

"I beg your pardon?" Winnifred said.

The sherry was a leftover from Colonel Ashton's stock and after Winnifred sipped, she made sure Maude saw her make a face.

"It was tragic, not exciting. It was a tragic thing to see, a strong man broken that way. It reminded me of how the Roman soldiers whipped our blessed Savior."

"Asa Pagg is hardly Jesus," Winnifred said. "He did try to rape me, you know."

"Is that what he did?"

"Do you doubt my word?"

"I watched you on the parade ground as the naked man was being lashed, Winnifred," Maude said. "I have always believed that such paroxysms you displayed were

318

confined to the male of the species."

"I don't understand," Winnifred said. "And I certainly didn't understand the word you used."

"Paroxysm? Why, it means convulsion, spasm, throe . . . I'm sure now you understand."

Winnifred's cheekbones reddened. She searched for something to say, but the words eluded her.

Maude Ashton filled in the blanks.

"Mrs. Grove, you're a cheap slut," she said. "And this morning you took pleasure in seeing the man you seduced cut to ribbons with a whip."

Winnifred rose to her feet. "So what if I did? What are you going to do about it?"

Maude laid down her glass, got to her feet and said, "Get out of my house, madam."

Then, reciting the words of what would be her death warrant, "I'll talk to your husband later. But first I'll read my Bible and pray for your immortal soul, for surely you are damned, like the whore Salome who demanded the head of John the Baptist."

The open window in Maude Ashton's tiny parlor pleased Winnifred Grove greatly. She smiled to herself. It was made for murder.

Unfortunately, the only weapon to hand

was her husband's .41 caliber Colt Clover-leaf revolver, a gift from some general or other, and it held only four rounds.

Winnifred frowned. Well, it would just have to do. And after all, she was a good markswoman, as the colonel had often told her.

She removed four extra rounds from the box in the drawer and slipped those and the little revolver into the pocket of her gray day dress. Winnifred stepped to the rear of her quarters, opened the back door just wide enough for her head, and she looked around.

Jolly good. There was no one in sight.

A sandy, cactus-studded area lay beyond the headquarters building and stretched all the way to officers' row where Maude Ashton's quarters were located. Here and there a few spruce and piñon cast dark circles of thin shade and Winnifred watched a jackrabbit run into a jumble of rocks and vanish from sight.

The woman scowled. The sand was not good since it would hold her footprints, but there was no other choice. She could hardly march right up to Maude's front door and demand entry. She'd attract too much attention that way.

No matter, the old bitch had to be silenced. She was a troublemaker.

Winnifred stepped outside, the heat hitting her like a fist. The sun burned white hot in a colorless sky and there was no breeze.

She walked past the rear of the headquarters building at a fast pace and was glad to see that in most of the windows shades had been pulled down against the glaring sunlight. Winnifred was sure she'd passed unnoticed.

Her breath coming in little gasps, she hurried to the officers' quarters. There she felt safe from prying eyes, since all the officers and noncoms were attending one of the colonel's interminable meetings.

The Apache prisoners were due soon and Andrew was beside himself with worry, fretting about supplying the savages with food and water before escorting them to Fort Grant.

As though anyone cared!

But her husband's worries worked in Winnifred Grove's favor. There had been no one around to see her and now she walked on cat feet to the open window, crouched low and raised her head just high enough to see inside.

Relief flooded through Winnifred. It looked as though she'd made it just in time.

Maude Ashton had laid her Bible on the dresser and now, her broad back turned to the window, she settled her shawl around her shoulders.

Winnifred grimaced. She was going to speak to Andrew, the vicious old biddy.

Slowly, carefully, Winnifred brought up the Colt, laid the short barrel on the windowsill, aimed and fired.

The impact of the bullet staggered Maude Ashton for a moment and then she tried to turn. But Winnifred was already shooting again. Two more bullets slammed into the woman's back and left side and she slowly sank to the floor, dragging the Bible with her.

The Good Book fell on top of the woman and fluttered open. As to what chapter and verse was revealed, Winnifred did not know or care. She had other things on her mind.

Hurry! Hurry! Reload!

Her hands trembling, Winnifred fumbled out the empty shells, shoved them into her pocket and grabbed the fresh rounds.

From somewhere she heard shouts and running feet, and tears sprang into her eyes.

Oh my God, she was going to be too late!

A groan rattled in Maude Ashton's throat as Winnifred finally loaded the three empty chambers of the Cloverleaf and thumbed the cylinder shut. Praying that she was still in time she bolted for her own rooms in the administration building, and immediately cut loose with her revolver, shooting wildly into the air. As she ran, firing her remaining three shots, she methodically retraced her own footsteps.

Finally Winnifred reached the rear door of her quarters . . . and swooned expertly in a faint.

"Oh, my dearest, my darling, what more horror can befall you?" Colonel Andrew Grove said as he patted the back of his wife's hand.

Winnifred's eyelids fluttered open. The first person she saw was Captain Owen Shaw standing across the room, a cynical smile on his lips, his brown eyes slightly amused.

So you know, Winnifred thought. *Damn you, you know!*

It was time to pile it on. The only man that mattered here was her husband.

"Oh, Andrew, it was terrible. I saw poor Maude die before my eyes."

"You've had an awful experience, my love, but there is good news. Maude Ashton is still clinging to life."

"She's what?" Winnifred said. It was more

323

exclamation than question.

Grove smiled. "Yes, my dear, it's true. She was a soldier's wife and she's a tough lady." His smile widened. "There, does that make you feel better?"

Winnifred avoided looking at Shaw's grin and she said, "That is the most singular good news, Andrew, and of the greatest moment. I feel my womanly spirit soar."

She closed her eyes. The bitch was still alive! What rotten luck!

Her husband was talking again. "Now, if you feel up to it, can you" — he waved a hand toward his officers — "tell us what happened?"

"Andrew, it's most painful to relate."

"I know, my brave love. But please try."

The story Winnifred told was that Maude Ashton was reading to her from the Bible when she was so terribly wounded.

"I recall that she just finished reading that blessed passage from Mark 5:34 where Jesus says, 'Daughter, your faith has made you well. Go in peace and be healed of your suffering.' "

Winnifred looked as though she was about to swoon again, but Colonel Grove said, "Bear up, my love. Tell us . . . tell us all . . ."

"I will, my dear. I will do my very best." Winnifred took a deep, shuddering breath and said, "Maude got up from her chair to pour me a glass of sherry, ere I fainted from the sheer emotion I felt in my breast."

"My poor love!" the colonel exclaimed, apparently in the deepest despair.

"And it was then that a rifle rang out, again and again. Oh sweet Jesus! Poor Maude fell, shot through and through, weltering in her blood."

Winnifred was careful not to let her eyes linger on Captain Shaw.

Why did he keep smiling like that?

After her husband urged her to tell more, Winnifred told him that after her "narrow escape from a fate worse than death," she'd taken to carrying the small revolver she'd found in her husband's desk to protect her "greatest treasure."

"And I'm glad you did, my poor darling," the colonel said.

"Thus armed, I sprang to my feet and ascertained that the shots had come through the open window," she said. "I rushed outside, only to see the shadowy figure of a murderous savage among the trees."

"An Apache, my dear?" her husband said. "Was it an Apache?"

"One would suppose," Winnifred said. "Oh, I was so afraid, but I shot at the animal in human form. And then, still firing, I ran to seek you, Andrew, but fainted ere I found you."

"My brave, stalwart love!" the colonel said, tears welling in his eyes.

He'd gotten down on one knee beside his wife, but he sprang to his feet.

"Captain Shaw, organize a search of the country around the fort. Bring me that damned Apache," he said.

"I doubt if we'll find him, sir," Shaw said. He looked directly at Winnifred. "Such Apaches are phantoms."

Shaw continued to stare directly at Winnifred, but her eyes slid from his like lizards off a hot rock.

"I don't want your doubts, Captain," Grove said. "I want results. Bring me the Apache's head."

"Sir," Shaw said, saluting sharply.

He cast a last, lingering look at Winnifred and stepped outside, calling for Sergeant Fuller.

CHAPTER FORTY-ONE

The black bear was interested but wary, the sight and smell of a naked human beyond anything in his experience.

But he was hungry and hunger can make a bear bold.

Asa Pagg, his back against an arrowhead of sandstone rock that jutted from the bed of the dry wash, knew he was in a heap of trouble.

Weak from the whipping he'd taken and unarmed, he was in no shape to tackle an aggressive bear one-on-one.

Pagg's wrists and the palms of his swollen hands were scraped raw and he felt blood trickle down his fingertips. He'd worked his bonds against the sandstone for an hour, but felt no loosening or even a suggestion that the rope was fraying.

The bear shambled toward Pagg, its soulless eyes, like black beads, never leaving his face.

Pagg filled his chest with air and yelled at the top of his lungs, "Get the hell away from here, Ephraim!"

Momentarily puzzled, the bear stopped, then reared onto its hind legs as though to get a better look at the human.

Then it came on again. Its coat was muddy and stuck all over with dead leaves and one ear was notched, a V-shaped chunk bitten off in some old mating tussle.

If a man says his prayers at night and is real lucky, he can sometimes holler a loud yell that will frighten off a brown bear or even a grizzly.

But not the black bear.

If he has his heart set on killing a man, he'll keep on coming and with fang and claw he'll always finish the job he started. It's harsh and cruel, but it's his way.

And nobody knew that better than Asa Pagg.

"Damn you, Ephraim, get it over with," he yelled, his face stiff with fear.

The bear trotted forward and now only a dozen yards separated Pagg from a horrific and lingering death.

Then six . . .

Then three . . .

Then . . .

Pagg saw the animal drop a split second

before he heard the shot.

He looked around him and saw a drift of smoke in the pines that topped a rock ridge to the north of the draw.

The outlaw kept his eyes on the smoke that finally faded away, to be replaced by a man riding a mustang and leading another.

As the man rode off the ridge, Asa Pagg recognized Deputy Marshal Pleasant Tyrell by his top hat and lanky frame.

He sighed. Out of the frying pan into the fire, damnit.

Tyrell drew rein about ten feet from Pagg and let his eyes roam over the dead bear.

"Lucky I happened along, Asa," he said.

"Not for the bear," Pagg said. "His luck ran out."

"You seem to be prospering, Asa," Tyrell said.

"Yeah, I took to walking around the high country nekkid."

He squinted at the lawman, who had his back to the glare of the sun. Pleasant was always a careful man.

"What brings you to these parts?" Pagg said.

"You."

"So I figgered. You got a warrant?"

"Sure do. Dead or alive, the choice is yours."

"Where are you taking me, Pleasant?"

"Fort Defiance, I reckon, Asa. I'll lock you up there until I can arrange for your transportation to Santa Fe."

"Hell, they just kicked me out of Fort Defiance and I've got the scars on my back to prove it," Pagg said.

"When I tell them what a nice, wholesome feller you are, Asa, they'll welcome you with open arms," Tyrell said.

"You'll see I get hung in Santa Fe, huh?"

"Sure I will, Asa, but only after you get a fair trial."

"You're gold dust, Marshal."

"Hell, I know that," Tyrell said.

He stepped out of the saddle.

"Get to your feet, Asa," he said.

Pagg smiled. "I can't do that without help, Marshal. I'm as weak as a baby and you'll have to lift me."

The expression on Tyrell's face didn't change. "Asa, get to your feet or I'll kill you," he said.

"Be damn to ye fer a hard-hearted old rogue," Pagg said.

But he scrambled to his feet.

"Turn around, Asa," Tyrell said. He stared at Pagg's back, then said, "That's a hell of a thing to do to a man, even a lowlife like you."

"Thirty of the best, Tyrell," Pagg said. "Laid on by a sergeant I mean to kill one day."

"That day will never come, Asa," Tyrell said. He was silent for a while, then said, "Your hands are swelled up to twice their size." Then, after another pause, as though he'd been studying on the ramifications, "I'm going to have to cut that rope off'n you, Asa, and let you work your fingers awhile."

"You're a white man, Pleasant," Pagg said.

"Well, I'll take pleasure in seeing you hang, Asa, but I won't torture a man for no good reason."

Tyrell used a folding knife to cut the rope. "Your hands and wrists are a mess," he said. "And your back is even worse. I got something in my saddlebags that will ease them wounds. You ever hear of Dr. Wilson's Miracle Balm?"

Pagg flexed his fingers and the pain of returning circulation made him wince. "No, I never have," he said.

"It says right on the bottle in printed letters that it cures the croup, rashes, cancer, ague, toothache and the rheumatisms. So it'll cure your back and wrists, I reckon."

Pagg's eyes slid to a spot farther up the dry wash where a chunk of ancient driftwood stuck out of the sand.

He hatched his plan.

Pleasant Tyrell had survived so long in a dangerous profession because he was a careful man. Normally he would've stepped warily around Asa Pagg and watched for any fancy moves because the man was a killer and he was almighty sudden.

But Tyrell let his guard down a little, thinking that a naked man, weak from a terrible whipping, exposure and loss of blood, presented no great danger.

It was the kind of mistake that kills a man.

As Pleasant Tyrell rummaged in his saddlebags for the balm, Pagg, barefooted and silent on sand, stepped to the chunk of wood. It was part of a hardwood branch, bleached and hard as iron, a sharp, splintered spike at one end.

Pagg advanced on the lawman, making no sound.

"Got it!" Tyrell said, turning his head.

Pagg swung, a roar of triumph escaping from his open mouth.

The wooden spike, shaped like a claw, crashed into Tyrell's left ear and drove deep. Tyrell fell against his horse, the side of his head scarlet with sudden blood. Stunned, his eyes glazed, he made no move toward his guns.

Pagg, growling like an animal, had to work the spike to free it from muscle and bone. Tyrell dropped to his knees and Pagg swung the club again, this time aiming for the marshal's head.

Tyrell's skull shattered like an eggshell and he groaned then fell, his head and shoulders covered in blood, brain and bone.

Pagg threw the club on top of Tyrell's body. "Damn you, you'll never come after me again with an alive or dead warrant," he said. "May you rot in hell, old man."

Tyrell's fancy buckskin shirt was too small to stretch across Pagg's great beer barrel of a chest and enormous shoulders, but the old man's pants and boots, though snug, fit him. He found a slicker behind the marshal's saddle and donned it in place of a shirt.

Like Tyrell, Pagg favored butt-forward shoulder holsters, but the old marshal's gun rig felt awkward to him. No matter, he'd trade gun belts with the next man he killed and try them for fit.

He went through the old man's pockets and found a nickel railroad watch that he kept and a mouth harp he tossed away. He'd already found eight dollars stuffed in Tyrell's pocket.

Pagg kicked the old man's body. "Damned pauper," he said. "You were hardly worth killing."

He stepped to the marshal's horse, then stopped where he was, his back stiff.

His instincts honed to a sharp edge by a lifetime of outlawry, Pagg knew when he was being watched.

He turned and saw at least two score of Apaches sitting their ponies not twenty yards away, Geronimo among them.

Asa Pagg raised his open hand in a gesture of peace and friendship.

But, judging by the ferocious scowl on Geronimo's face, he'd some sweet talking to do . . . and fast.

CHAPTER FORTY-TWO

Sam Flintlock woke to a hand shaking his shoulder.

When Jack Coffin felt the muzzle of the Colt pushing into his belly, he smiled and whispered, "Come. Quietly."

Not by nature a questioning man at times like these, Flintlock got to his feet and shoved the revolver back into his waistband. He looked around him. Everyone else was asleep, though Ayasha stirred and muttered something, her dreams full of demons.

Flintlock picked up the Hawken and followed Coffin into the trees.

Old Barnabas, his face streaked with yellow paint, sat at the base of a juniper braiding ribbons of the same color into his beard.

He stared at Flintlock, shook his head and sighed.

Then the old mountain man was gone and Flintlock heard the wind sigh through the pines.

"What delays you?" Coffin said, appearing out of the gloom.

"Nothing," Flintlock said. "I thought I heard a voice."

Coffin stepped to the juniper and picked up something. He came back and held the yellow ribbon high for Flintlock to see. "Yours?" he said.

"No, it's not mine," Flintlock said.

"Then I'll keep it," Coffin said.

Flintlock let that go, then said, "Why do you wear death paint?"

"My time is close."

"Is it because of the bell?"

"I don't know."

"I think the bell is cursed."

"Bad old Barnabas told you so?"

"I saw him. He was wearing yellow paint and he sighed. But I think it was the wind in the trees I heard."

Coffin nodded. "Yes, you saw only the brightness of the ribbon and heard the wind. That was all."

"I reckon that was the case."

"Good, now let us go from here."

Flintlock followed Coffin through the trees but looked back at the juniper.

He saw nothing but darkness and the bony light of the moon.

From a clump of pines near the bottom of the slope that rose to meet the ridge, Sam Flintlock's eyes tried to penetrate the gloom.

"I don't see a cave," he said. "I don't see anything."

"Nonetheless, it's there," Coffin said. "The cave of the golden bell is there. I saw it."

"I wasn't even sure the cave existed," Flintlock said.

"Well, now you know."

"Yeah, but I still don't know if there's two thousand pounds of golden bell."

"I don't know that either."

"Well, should we go take a look-see?" Flintlock said.

Coffin answered that question with silence. But after a while he said, "We'll go closer, Samuel. I want to show you something."

The breed crouched low and made his way carefully toward the base of the slope. Flintlock, following, wondered at that. The trees and brush hid all movement, yet Coffin was wary, afraid to be seen.

The man was scared . . . of what?

Crouching on his heels, Coffin stared

through pines and pointed out a massive outcropping of sandstone rock that ran the whole length of the ridge.

"Do you see it?" he said.

Flintlock nodded. "I see it. The damned thing's big enough." He craned his head forward, searching into the distance. "Where's the cave?"

"Below the rock shelf," Coffin said.

Flintlock figured that, during the passage of ages, the tremendous weight of the towering mountain that loomed behind the ridge had pushed a great slab of rock over the rim. The shelf had come to rest about fifty feet above the cave mouth and hung there, brooding and threatening.

"The whole rock shelf could come down, Samuel," Coffin said.

Flintlock said, "Hell, it's hung up there for thousands of years. It'll stay for thousands more."

"No. The sandstone is rotten," Coffin said. "It wouldn't take much to bring it tumbling."

The outcropping projected about twenty feet from the ridge and it was webbed with deep cracks. But how long it had been like that, Flintlock had no way of knowing. The fractures could've happened yesterday or ten thousand years ago.

He grinned at Coffin. "We'll have to step careful, huh?"

"If there is a bell in the cave as large as you say, you'll need a heavy wagon and mules to get it out and carry it down the slope."

"Not if we break it up first," Flintlock said.

"And then the noise and vibration of sledgehammers could bring a whole mountain down on top of you."

"So what do you suggest, Jack?" Flintlock said, remembering that he disliked this man.

"I suggest nothing. My task was to bring you to the cave, and that's what I've done."

"Not until we're sure this is the right cave," Flintlock said. "There could be dozens, hundreds in the Carrizo Mountains."

"This is the cave, Samuel. I'm sure of it."

"I'm going to take a look," Flintlock said. He checked the action of the Hawken, then smiled. "I'm loaded for bear."

Coffin shook his head. "You leave the Winchester behind and carry the old Hawken, Samuel. You are a strange man."

"It brings me luck," Flintlock said.

Coffin stared at the ridge, his eyes pensive. "Something tells me you're going to need it."

CHAPTER FORTY-THREE

Sam Flintlock got to his feet and angled across the bottom of the slope until he reached a well-worn ribbon of path that led upward, only to lose itself in a patch of brush. Where the trail went after that was not visible.

The Hawken at the slant across his chest, Flintlock took to the path and made his way up the incline.

Beyond the ridge the mountain peaks were black against the sky, blotting out the stars. The wind tugged at Flintlock as though to slow his progress and his booted feet slipped now and then and dislodged small showers of shale.

He followed the path into the brush and stepped around stands of cholla and prickly pear that threatened to invade the path.

After Flintlock cleared the scrub the slope grew steeper, but rose straight as an arrow before disappearing into darkness.

Breathing hard, he stopped and looked behind him. There was no sign of Jack Coffin. The shy moon had pulled a cloud in front of its face and the land around him was everywhere deep in gloom and silence. Only the moaning wind made a sound.

Despite the coolness of the night, sweat beaded Flintlock's forehead and dampened his shirt between his shoulder blades.

He had the urge to yell, "Hello, the cave!" if only to shatter the smothering quiet.

But he decided that would be foolish and resumed his climb.

The cave came in sight a few minutes later, Flintlock's view of the opening aided by the no longer bashful moon.

He planted his feet, raised the old Hawken and made a scan of the opening, about the width of a tall man with his arms outstretched and maybe twice as high.

Nothing moved within the line of his vision. The cave was deserted, unless the entity that guarded the place was asleep. Flintlock smiled to himself. Did Death ever take a nap? No, he was way too busy for that.

He was wary enough to study the cliff face for a couple of minutes until he climbed the last few yards to the opening.

The Hawken still at the ready, Flintlock

said, "Anybody to home?"

He was greeted by the echoes of silence. This close, the cave entrance looked like a great open mouth, ready to devour him. The wind whispered a secret into Flintlock's ear, but who can understand the wind?

He stepped into the cave and total darkness shut down his vision.

For a moment Flintlock stood still, listening. There was no sound. The air smelled stale and old, like opening an old clothes trunk that had lain undisturbed in an attic for years.

In moments of stress a smoking man will turn to tobacco. Flintlock propped the Hawken against his leg, then, his movements skilled and practiced, he built a cigarette and thumbed a match into flame. There were things to look at in the cave, but he had eyes for only the oil lamp that stood just inside the entrance.

The unlit cigarette dangling from his mouth, he lit the lamp and flooded the cave with thin, yellow light. The match burned his fingers and he shook his hand and let it drop. He lit his smoke from the lamp and only then did he look around him.

An old, ornate armchair dominated the small space. A footstool and a natural rock shelf made up the other furnishings. The shelf held a loaf of round, peasant bread, standing beside it an earthenware jug and two clay cups.

But what caught Flintlock's attention was a hanging Navajo blanket, its top pinned in place by a series of iron nails driven into the sandstone. He decided that the blanket must partition off another part of the cave.

And he figured that the golden bell must be behind the curtain.

The damp, gloomy and smelly cave was an improbable place to hold such a fabulous treasure, like a diamond in a pack rat's nest.

Suddenly Flintlock was anxious to see what two thousand pounds of gold looked like.

He jerked back the curtain . . . and stared into a tunnel of darkness.

Disappointed, Flintlock raised the lamp and light splashed on walls about ten feet apart. Here the roof of the cave was so high it was lost from sight. He had no way of knowing how far the cavern tunneled into the ridge and the mountain behind, but he guessed it could be a considerable distance.

He propped the Hawken against the cave wall, ground out his cigarette butt under his heel and then, the oil lamp raised above his head, made his way forward, glad of the solid, reassuring weight of the Colt in his waistband.

Flintlock didn't know what lay ahead of him . . . but he had an odd sense of dread and the feeling that he was being watched.

After counting a hundred paces, Sam Flintlock figured he was well beyond the ridge and somewhere deep under the mountain. The air was fetid and hard to breathe and the oil lamp guttered, casting shifting scarlet and black shadows on the walls.

He stopped two or three times and stood very still, listening for sounds, but heard none. He kept moving through the cave, steadily and quietly.

After another fifty steps or so, the tunnel made a sharp jog to Flintlock's right. He made the turn and kicked something that skittered away from his boot and made an odd, metallic clink!

When he shone the lamp on the spot, light gleamed dully on an old helmet, its steel showing here and there through a patina of green mold and rust. Flintlock had seen pictures of its like, the elegant, crested morion worn by the old Spanish soldiers.

A moment later he found the wearer.

The skeleton lay sprawled on the ground, the position of the bones suggesting that the man had been crawling on all fours when death took him. The yellow skull grinned without humor and the eye sockets were dark with shadow.

Raised by mountain men, a superstitious breed, Sam Flintlock had heard stories of ha'ants and boogermen and the like, and he hurried past the skeleton, wishing that he'd never seen the damned thing.

As it happened, he didn't have far to walk. The cave turned again, this time to the left, and directly in front of him was a huge bell, black as night, squatting on a plinth of rock like a great toad.

Warily, his breath coming fast and hard, Flintlock stepped closer.

The crown of the bell, where the rope attached, had been cast in the shape of a bird, in the act of plucking feathers from its own chest.

Unbidden, words swam into Flintlock's mind . . .

The bell that never rang . . . the bird that never sang.

He shook his head. Where did that come from?

There was no time to consider the question. He had other, more important things to do.

Flintlock's head spun and he felt as though an anvil was crushing his chest. He smelled something he couldn't identify, something vile, something dangerous. . . .

Weakening fast, he opened his pocketknife and stepped to the bell. He placed his hand on its side. It was cold. Cold, impersonal to the touch.

Working carefully, Flintlock scraped the black surface with the Barlow's carbon steel blade and as he'd expected, he uncovered the gleam of gold.

He stepped back, his red-rimmed eyes wide, unbelieving.

The legend had been right. The whole damned bell was made of solid gold.

Gold!

Flintlock's reeling mind immediately built fantasy castles in the air, parapets, ramparts, battlements, towers and spires . . . the stuff of his wildest dreams . . . and all of them made of glittering, solid gold.

Gold!

Gold enough to keep a man in luxury for the rest of his life, penned up in a golden cage and never the need to kowtow to anybody.

But wait! There wasn't enough to share!

No, by God, he had only enough for himself.

Why, to satisfy his ravenous gold hunger he was willing to pour it molten, down his throat until he gagged. But he was not willing to part with an ounce of it.

Flintlock growled like an animal and bared his teeth.

He'd kill to keep his gold. He'd kill everybody — Abe, Charlie, the women, every damned one of them. They were all thieves and they'd get together to plot how they could steal his fortune.

He threw back his head and screamed, "It's mine! The golden bell is all mine!"

His face contorted, the expression of a madman, Flintlock staggered away from the bell that now seemed to have grown bigger and more ominous.

"I'll be back," he said. "You know I'll come back for you, don't you?"

The great bell rang in reply . . . a clashing, clanging, cacophony that clamored through the cave, the echoes reverberating louder and louder . . . deafening Flintlock, threatening to shatter his fragile hold on sanity.

He screamed and ran.

As he bolted through the cave, the oil lamp dropped from his hand. He couldn't breathe, his chest hurt terribly and he tasted raw blood in his mouth.

Finally, unable to run any longer he fell headlong, sprawling onto the hard rock of the cave floor.

Flintlock groaned and turned his head. The yellow skull grinned at him and said, in a voice that sounded like the rustle of dry parchment, "Welcome to your golden death. . . ."

Chapter Forty-Four

Asa Pagg had a feeling that death could be close. Geronimo didn't look like he was in the mood for conversation.

He considered briefly making a dash for Tyrell's horse, but he immediately dismissed the idea. He'd be cut down in a hail of lead before he took a couple of steps.

As it happened, only Geronimo rode forward, but his face was grim. It was a measure of the Apache's anger that he chose to speak English, a language he knew but hated. He called it "bitter poison on his tongue."

"Why are you not at the fort?" the Apache said.

"They kicked me out," Pagg said. "But —"

"Why did they kick you out, Pagg?"

"They said I tried to rape a woman. But I didn't. I swear it."

"Who is the man you just killed?"

"Nobody. I needed his horse."

Pagg figured that was something an Apache would understand, and indeed, the foul expression on Geronimo's face didn't change, as though he accepted the explanation without question.

"We will attack Fort Defiance tonight, by moonlight," he said. "You will not be there."

Geronimo turned his head and said something Pagg didn't understand. But he felt a spike of fear as half a dozen warriors rode forward, none of them young bucks, but older, experienced men. There would be little pity in them.

Thinking fast, Pagg said, "I'll ride with you, Geronimo." He slapped the butts of his revolvers. "I know how to use these."

"This is not what we agreed."

"I know, but they kicked me out. When we attack" — Pagg liked that *we*, making it a foregone conclusion that Geronimo would forgive him — "I've got some killing to do, scores to settle."

Geronimo said words to his warriors and the oldest of them nodded. He was a somber man with a deep scar on his left cheek, an ancient Mexican saber wound.

"They agree with me that I should kill you, Pagg," Geronimo said.

"When you attack the fort, you'll need

350

every gun you've got," Pagg said. "Killing me will only weaken you."

"I am thinking of that," Geronimo said.

Pagg shrugged out of the slicker and let it fall. He showed his back.

"The soldiers know that you and I are friends, Geronimo, so they whipped me."

The Apache didn't react. "I have told you before that you are not my friend, Pagg," he said. "My people have no friends."

Pagg opened his mouth to speak, but Geronimo held up a silencing hand. "Let me think on this," he said. "But be fearful of your life. Make the resolve now that if my decision is death you will die well and not like a woman screaming in childbirth. You have disappointed me, don't disgrace me."

Geronimo closed his eyes and bowed his head and the warriors around him chanted, their voices rising and falling like the song of a gusting wind among pinnacles of rock.

Asa Pagg figured his next move.

If Geronimo's verdict was death, he'd draw and shoot.

He fingered his beard and chose his targets. Four, maybe five Apaches would go down, Geronimo among them, then, in the confusion he'd make a run for his horse.

The mustang was small, but since Pleasant Tyrell owned it, the little horse would be fast and have sand enough that it would run until its heart burst.

The old man's butt-forward guns felt damned awkward, but Pagg was confident he'd shuck them quick enough if bad news came down.

Five long minutes passed and for Pagg it seemed like an eternity.

But suddenly Geronimo's head snapped erect. A mist cleared from his eyes and he said, "The path I must take has been revealed to me, Pagg." He waited a moment, then said, "You will lead the attack on Fort Defiance."

Relief flooded through Pagg. He said, "You do me great honor, Geronimo."

"We will see . . . when you charge at the front of the Apache."

"When do we attack?"

Geronimo pointed to the sky directly above his head.

"When the moon is there."

"I'll be ready," Pagg said.

"We will return for you, Pagg," Geronimo said. "Be here."

"Of course," Pagg said.

The Apache swung his horse away and the warriors with him followed.

Silhouetted against the sky, a hawk that

looked like it had been cut with a razor from a sheet of black paper paused in flight and then dropped like a lightning bolt into the brush.

A squeal and a small death . . . but neither the uncaring land nor Asa Pagg took any notice.

It was Angus McCarty, the dour Scots sutler, who would later get the credit for saving Fort Defiance.

And for dealing a severe defeat to the Apaches.

"They say up in Canada there's still herds of buffalo, herds as big as they was right here in the U.S. a ten-year ago," Cavalry Private Steve Wilkins said. "That's what I heard, all right."

"I doubt it," McCarty said, wiping the bar with a damp cloth. "After Sitting Bull massacred the gallant Custer he led the Sioux into Canada and they damn near starved to death."

"That was then, this is now," Wilkins said, as stubborn as the Scotsman. "Nobody knows what's in Canada."

"Canadians," McCarty said.

He moved down the bar to serve another customer and stopped in his tracks. The windows of the store were open to allow the cool night air to enter and the fog of pipe and cigar smoke to leave.

But it was what McCarty heard, not smelled, that troubled him.

Quail tend to be quiet birds and seldom call out at night. Besides, all the quail around Fort Defiance had been hunted out years before by generations of soldiers.

There should be no quail calls where there are no quail.

Ignoring the impatient protests from his customer, McCarty began to move around the store and quietly close and bolt the window shutters.

"Hey, McCarty, it's hot enough in here," a man yelled. "Keep them shutters open."

"Apaches," McCarty said.

There were eight soldiers in the store and immediately the sutler had their attention. All wore a sidearm, but none had a rifle.

"Wilkins, split ass across to headquarters and warn them," McCarty said. "The rest of you men follow me."

The sutler stepped to the gun rack and began to hand out Winchesters.

"Ammunition in the chest over there," he said. "Load up and be quick about it."

Angus McCarty had been a sergeant in the British Army's 27th Regiment of Foot and had served in India. He had not lost the habit of command and no one questioned his authority.

"Right lads, let's get the lamps out," he said.

As the oil lamps were extinguished a soldier said, "What do we do now?"

"We wait until the time is right," McCarty said.

"When will that be?" the soldier said.

"When I tell you, Kelsey," McCarty said.

Outside a quail called again. Closer this time.

CHAPTER FORTY-FIVE

From somewhere close, Sam Flintlock heard an owl hoot. He opened his eyes and saw the moon directly overhead, bloodred, like a malignant spirit.

He tried to draw a deep breath, but his chest felt painful and raw, as though he was trying to breathe in a smoke-filled room.

Flintlock panicked and struggled to sit upright, fearing that he could suffocate.

"Take it easy, Samuel, just small, quick breaths."

Jack Coffin's voice.

A moment later the man's head blocked out the moon and Flintlock stared into the wide blur of his face.

Unable to talk, he grabbed Coffin's arm, his wild, frightened eyes clamoring a question.

"There is something in the cave that poisons the air," the breed said. "It nearly done for you."

Flintlock's breathing eased a little, but he still didn't trust himself to speak. He tightened his hold on Coffin's arm.

"When you went into the cave and didn't return, I followed you," Coffin said. "I found you hugging a skeleton and dragged you outside." The breed's teeth flashed white. "I thought you wouldn't make it, Samuel. It would've been a great loss to humanity."

"The bell . . ." Flintlock gasped.

"Is there. Yes, I know."

"Gold . . ."

Coffin nodded, but said nothing.

"It . . . it made me raving mad."

"Gold can do that to a man," Coffin said.

Flintlock shook his head. "Evil . . . Jack, it's evil."

"The bell isn't evil. But it's made of gold and gold can bring the evil that lies dormant in every man to the surface."

Flintlock breathed easier, the lethal gas he'd inhaled slowly clearing his lungs. But speaking still came hard.

"Jack," he said, raising his head a little, "I wanted to kill everybody . . . to . . . to keep my gold."

"You were not in your right mind, Samuel, huh?" Coffin said.

"I don't want the damned bell, Jack."

"Then you will not have it," Coffin said.

He helped Flintlock to a sitting position. A small fire burned close by. "There is coffee."

Flintlock nodded. "That would be good." Suddenly he looked around him, his head jerking this way and that.

Coffin smiled. "I have the Hawken."

"It was given to me —"

"By Barnabas. Yes, you told me. I'll get you coffee, Samuel. Breathe easy and don't try to move yet."

As Coffin stepped away, Flintlock saw old Barnabas sitting by the fire, twanging on a mouth harp. The tune was "Skip to My Lou" and the old mountain man played it badly.

Finally Barnabas took the harp from his mouth, stared at it and slipped it into his pants pocket. He looked at Flintlock. "Found your mama yet?"

"No," Flintlock said.

"A man should have his own name," Barnabas said. "In hell, nobody is called by name. Did you know that?"

"No," Flintlock said.

"Well, it's true. Everyone is damned, so their names don't matter. But yours still does."

Barnabas faded gradually, like a mist in a

wind. Only his words lingered. . . .

"Don't let the golden bell be your death, Sam."

Coffin stepped beside Flintlock, a steaming tin cup in his hand.

"You talking to yourself, Samuel?" he said.

"Barnabas."

"Don't play worth a damn, does he?"

"You heard him?"

"And saw him. I see many things with an Indian's eyes, Samuel, and I hear with an Indian's ears."

Flintlock took out the makings and built a cigarette.

Coffin watched him for a while, then said, "Your lungs have been poisoned, yet you smoke tobacco."

"I'm a smoking man, Jack," Flintlock said. "Besides, docs say smoking is real good for the lungs. Clears them out, you know."

"Sometimes the things doctors say are wrong."

"Maybe so, but they wouldn't make that big a mistake."

Flintlock lit his cigarette, drew deep and doubled over as violent coughs wracked him and jerked tears from his eyes.

Abe Roper charged out of the night, a gun in his hand and fire in his eyes.

"What the hell, Sammy?" he said. "I woke up and you were gone. I thought you'd been taken by the Apaches."

Flintlock nodded in Coffin's direction and said, "Only that Apache."

"What's going on?" Roper demanded.

For a moment, Flintlock thought about lying, but Roper deserved the truth. "I saw the bell, Abe."

Astonishment showed on Roper's face. "You saw it?"

"Damn right. Two thousand pounds of gold, if it's an ounce."

Roper squatted on his heels beside the fire. "Don't that beat all, Sam'l, we're rich."

"Abe, the bell is cursed," Flintlock said. "I want nothing to do with it."

"You talkin' about it being guarded by Death an' all that crap? It's nothing but a big story."

"It is guarded by Death," Flintlock said. "There's poisonous gas in the cave and it can kill. I reckon that's how the story that the cave is guarded by Death got started."

"Hell, you survived."

"Only just. If Jack Coffin hadn't pulled me out of there I'd be a dead man."

Roper tilted his head and stared into Flintlock's eyes. "Sammy, you wouldn't be lying to me so you can keep the gold to yourself, would you?"

"Samuel speaks the truth, Roper," Coffin said. "He would've died in there if I hadn't saved him."

Roper wasn't convinced. "You two in cahoots?"

"I don't want your gold, Roper," Coffin said. "It's an evil thing."

"Then all the more for the rest of us," Roper said. He laid a hand on Flintlock's shoulder. "At first light, you'll take me and Charlie into the cave. I want to see the bell."

"I told you, Abe, there's some kind of gas in there and it's deadly," Flintlock said.

"I'll take my chances," Roper said.

"You don't believe me, do you?"

"I know what gold fever does to a man," Roper said. "I've seen it many times before."

"Count me out, Abe. I'm never going back in there."

"Then me and Charlie will go our ownselves," Roper said.

"You'll find the bell, but you'll also find your deaths," Coffin said.

"Says you," Roper said, putting a wealth of meaning into two words.

"Abe, let me explain this to you," Flintlock said. "The only way you can get the bell out of there is to break it up inside the cave. And you can't do that, because the gas will kill you before you even start. Is what I'm telling you too difficult to understand?"

"All right, then we toss a loop on the bell, hitch up the pack mules and drag it out," Roper said.

"For one thing, you won't get mules to go in there, and even if you did, mules can't drag a two-thousand-pound bell through a narrow cave that twists and turns," Flintlock said.

"Hell, Sammy, somebody dragged it in there."

"Yeah, monks and maybe hundreds of Indians," Flintlock said. "And it could be that back then the poison gas hadn't yet seeped into the cave."

Roper bit his lip in frustration. But then his face brightened and he said, "All right, so you're telling me the truth, Sammy. And if that's the case, the only solution is dynamite."

"I sure hope I'm not catching your drift, Abe," Flintlock said.

"Listen to this . . . there's crowbars in the mule packs. Right?"

Flintlock nodded.

"Right. So me an' Charlie run in there with wet cloths over our mouths, crowbar the bell high enough to slip a stick of dynamite underneath, and then we scamper."

"And the whole damned mountain comes down on top of you."

"No. See, that's the beauty of the thing. The explosion blows up the bell, but hurts nothing else. You see what I'm saying? It's just like when you were a boy an' put a firecracker under a cup. The firecracker went off, broke up the cup but didn't blow up maiden aunt Jemima's front porch."

Roper rubbed his hands together. "It's gonna be great! Me and Charlie run inside again, pick up the pieces and carry them away from the gas. Hell, Sammy, we won't have time to get poisoned."

"A two-thousand-pound bell makes for a lot of pieces and a long time in the gas, even if your hare-brained scheme works, which it won't," Flintlock said.

"Samuel, an explosion could bring down the rock shelf," Coffin said.

Irritated, Roper said, "Damnit all, what rock shelf?"

"It hangs over the mouth of the cave, Abe," Flintlock said. "You could bring it down then you and Charlie would be trapped. We could never dig you out of there."

Roper's frustration boiled over. "Then

give me something, Sammy."

"Abe, I've got nothing to give you. Anyway you cut it, the bell is beyond reach."

"I'll get it out of there," Roper said. "As God is my witness, I'll have that damned bell."

CHAPTER FORTY-SIX

Asa Pagg stared into shadowed stillness of Fort Defiance and allowed himself a twinge of concern.

The lamps in the sutler's store had been extinguished at least two hours earlier than they should've been, and the headquarters building and the barracks block were also in darkness.

Damnit, did they know?

He turned in the saddle to the Apache at his side. "Geronimo, I don't like this," he said. "Send a couple of your warriors to scout the place."

"The soldiers are all asleep, Pagg."

"Where are the pickets?"

"White men don't keep good watch," Geronimo said.

"There's something wrong here, something that doesn't set right with me."

"You are afraid to lead the attack?" Geronimo said.

A shooting star blazed a fiery track across the night sky to the west and the Apache and Pagg followed it with their eyes. When the meteor disappeared, Geronimo said, "We have been visited by the omen of death. This is good. The soldiers will fall to us like broken reeds."

Geronimo laid his Springfield across his thighs. "The Apache await you, Pagg."

The outlaw shook his head. "I told you, Geronimo, I don't like this."

The Apache was old, but he was quick.

Geronimo brought up the butt of his rifle and slammed it into the right side of Pagg's jaw. Pagg tumbled out of the saddle backward and he was unconscious when he hit the ground.

The Apache looked down at the stunned man and said without undue emphasis, "Coward. Better you'd died in battle, Pagg, and gone home a hero."

Geronimo raised his rifle high and yelled his war cry. He charged directly at the headquarters building, his young men behind him.

Moments later rifles crashed and scarlet flame seared the starlit darkness of the night.

Angus McCarty ordered half the soldiers to man the gun ports cut into the shutters and they laid down a covering fire as he led the others onto the porch and ordered them to drop to a shooting position and fire at will.

The effect was devastating.

Lead from nine repeating rifles ripped into the Apaches as they galloped across the parade ground toward the headquarters building.

Half a dozen bucks dropped with the first volleys and a couple more bent over on their ponies, one of them coughing up black blood.

Moments later the soldiers posted at the windows of headquarters opened up.

The fire from the sutler's store had shattered the Apache charge. Now blasted by hails of lead from two sides the warriors milled around, taking hits from enemies they couldn't see.

Geronimo, blood on his right arm where a bullet had tagged him, shrieked in rage. He yelled at the young men around him to follow and he charged directly at the sutler's store.

It was a lethal mistake.

The Apaches charged headlong into a withering fire and Geronimo was suddenly surrounded by riderless ponies. The attack faltered, and the younger bucks, new to warfare and not on ground of their choosing, pulled back.

The soldiers from the headquarters building poured out onto the parade ground and their officers and noncoms chivvied them into line.

Within moments controlled volley fire smashed into the Apache rear and more warriors went down. Half Geronimo's original number now lay dead or dying on the ground . . . and the battle for Fort Defiance was lost.

Asa Pagg groggily raised himself to a sitting position and watched the disaster unfold.

He rose, stumbled to his horse and mounted. A pall of gray smoke obscured the slaughter on the parade ground, but Pagg saw a few wounded Apaches drift away into the night. There was no sign of Geronimo.

There were two things on Pagg's mind: Find the pay wagon and steal as much gold as he could carry. Track down Winnifred Grove, the lying bitch, and kill her.

Keeping to the shadows, Pagg rode his horse at a walk and wove among high brush and scattered, disused buildings until he reached the western edge of the parade ground.

Now the wounded Apaches were being

killed and clumps of men gathered to watch, slapping one another on the back, grinning their congratulations for a battle against a hated enemy that had been fought and won.

Pagg doubted that there would be anyone inside the headquarters building and to bolster that thought, he was sure he saw Major Grove talking with Owen Shaw near the sutler's store.

Shaw was also on Pagg's death list. If not tonight, then later.

Thunder rumbled far off, and the sky above the bleak brush country to the east flashed with blue electric light. The rising wind was strong enough to tangle itself in Pagg's beard and blow it across his naked chest.

As he reached the gable of the headquarters building, soldiers yelled and laughed as they hoisted a wounded Apache onto the frame where Pagg had been lashed. The Apache's head hung but he made no sound as whips cracked.

Pagg dismounted in darkness and drew his guns.

For Winnifred Grove, the Apache attack was a heaven-sent opportunity.

As soon as an excited soldier ran into her husband's office to warn of the impending assault, Winnifred had immediately volunteered to stay by dear Mrs. Ashton and protect her, "lest a murderous savage gain entry to her quarters."

Colonel Grove, distracted as he tried to silently assemble his scattered troops, nonetheless was touched by his wife's compassion and devotion to duty and readily agreed.

Winnifred shunned his offer of a revolver, saying that, "The Good Lord will be our protector."

It had all been so laughably easy.

Now she stood beside Maude Ashton's bed and looked down at the sleeping woman. Winnifred smiled. This time she'd finish the job and make sure that Maude wouldn't blab . . . to anyone . . . ever again.

Winnifred pulled the feather pillow out from under the woman's head and in one swift motion pushed it over her face. Gritting her huge teeth, she bore down with all her strength and . . . she had to admit it . . . *enjoyed* poor Maude's feeble struggles.

In fact, she enjoyed it, you know, *that way.*

Breathing hard, Winnifred lifted the pillow and stared at Maude Ashton. She smiled and nodded to herself. Yes, the poor dear was dead . . . dead as . . . what was it her husband always said? Ah yes, dead as a wooden Indian.

What a thrill that had been!

Winnifred was still grinning, the pillow bunched in her hands, when she turned and saw Asa Pagg standing in the bedroom doorway, as grim and silent as a ghost.

"You!" she said. Her eyes widened in fear.

Outside, guns still banged but Pagg had no time to talk pretties. But the stony expression on his face said it all.

He shot Winnifred Grove between her breasts and the woman was dead when she fell onto Maude Ashton's bed. A vase of wildflowers stood on the table. Pagg grabbed the flowers and tossed them over the two women.

He smiled. It was a good joke.

Asa Pagg was fast running out of time.

The shooting and yelling from the parade ground had petered out and he had only a few minutes to find the pay wagon and grab what he could.

He remounted his horse, then made a fast scout of the open land behind the headquarters building, riding in bright moonlight.

Pagg found the wagon — but it was empty.

"The money is gone, Asa, locked up for safekeeping."

Pagg swung his horse around. Captain

Owen Shaw stood behind him, his military cloak blowing in the wind.

He had his service Colt in his hand.

"Damnit, Shaw, I don't have time," Pagg said. "Where is the money?"

"Locked up in the guardhouse, Asa." Shaw smiled. "The colonel insisted on using a couple of Wells Fargo padlocks, huge iron things."

Pagg racked his brain, trying to come up with an answer to this latest problem. But he stopped when he heard the triple click of Shaw's revolver hammer.

"Sorry, Asa, but you have to go," the captain said. He smiled. "All bets are off, and by killing you I'll make myself a hero in Colonel Grove's eyes. Hell, I might even get a medal."

"Damn you, Shaw, I always took you fer a dirty, low, two-timing —"

Pagg drew and fired in one dazzlingly swift movement.

Surprised and caught flatfooted by the outlaw's speed from the leather, Shaw already had a bullet in his chest by the time he triggered his Colt.

He missed, badly.

And Pagg shot him again.

An experienced gunfighter, Pagg knew he'd fired killing shots. There was no need to stick around. As voices rose behind him in the darkness, he swung his horse around and galloped headlong into the brush.

They'd follow him, he knew, figuring him for an escaping Apache.

It was time for Asa Pagg to put a heap of git between him and Fort Defiance.

CHAPTER FORTY-SEVEN

"He was here," the old man said. "The one who wears an animal skin and has the mark of the thunderbird on his throat."

"Did he find the bell, Grandfather?" the boy said.

"Yes, he did. And he found the gold madness that comes with it."

"Will he come again?"

"Perhaps."

The boy was silent for a while, thinking. The old man sat in the great Spanish chair and watched him, wondering what the boy would say next. He didn't have too long to wait.

"You are not Death, Grandfather."

"Did I ever say I was?"

"The poisoned air in the cave is death. It choked me and made my head ache and made me very sick."

"That is so, little one, but it was well that you did not linger long. In the past many

374

people came to steal the bell, and all of them lingered long and all of them died. It was the Mexican peons who said I was *El Muerte* and I was happy to let them think that and spread the word. That was all."

A frown gathered between the boy's eyebrows. "If the poisoned air protects the bell, then why the need for a guardian?"

"There has always been a guardian. Before me, there were many."

"And I will come after you."

"Yes. You will wear the robes of a monk and guard the bell."

"Why, Grandfather?"

"Because the bell once rang in heaven and it is a holy thing."

"You said the bell never rang."

"Well, it did. But only in heaven."

The old man's white eyes went to the small bundle on the cave floor, a shirt, a pair of sandals and a piece of rye bread.

"You are leaving me I think, *mi niño*?"

"Yes, Grandfather."

"Why?" There was sadness in the old man's eyes.

"I do not want to guard the bell until I grow old like you and die."

"When did you decide this thing?"

"After you carried me away from the bell, Barnabas spoke to me."

"And he told you to leave?"

"He said that you will die in this cave, Grandfather, and that I am too young to suffer the same fate. He told me I should heed him better than his own grandson, who is an idiot."

"Barnabas says many things, not all of them wise. He told me to offer the seekers the gray horse, and that did not work."

"Barnabas looks at the bell many times, does he not?" the boy said.

"Yes. That is because he already passed to a dark realm and the bad air cannot harm him."

"He says he follows the buffalo."

"Yes, he does. That is his fate. It is what God ordained for him."

The boy was silent again for a moment. Then he said, "God has not ordained that I guard the bell, Grandfather. Barnabas told me so."

"In those words?"

"No, he said, 'For the love of God, leave here, kid.' "

The old man smiled slightly and nodded. "And that's what you want to do?"

"Yes. I will go and live in a Mexican village. I will be a doctor and heal their ills."

The boy picked up his bundle. "Please don't grieve for me, Grandfather."

"I will pray for you, that you will become a great healer."

The boy leaned over and kissed the old man on the cheek, and then he walked out of the cave and down the slope to the village.

The old man tried to watch him leave, but his eyes were filled with tears and he could not see.

"I just don't see it, Abe," Charlie Fong said. "Dynamite could blow the bell sky high without breaking it."

"Damnit then, Charlie, what do we do?" Abe Roper said.

"I don't know."

Ayasha, still silent but less withdrawn, sat near Sam Flintlock. The Chinese girls chattered to each other, seemingly oblivious to the men's conversation.

"Well I say we try blowing it," Roper said. "What have we got to lose?"

"Only two thousand pounds of gold," Fong said.

The morning was coming in fresh but gray.

Yet another summer thunderstorm threatened and dark clouds piled high in massive ramparts above the Carrizo Mountains. The morning seemed to have passed without a sunrise and a gunmetal light spread across the land like a fog.

"What do you say, Charlie, want to take a look?" Roper said.

"In the cave, you mean?"

"That's what I mean, damnit."

"If what Sam is telling us is true then we're taking a dangerous risk, Abe."

"Ain't a fortune in gold worth a risk, huh?"

Charlie Fong looked at Flintlock. "What do you reckon, Sam?"

"I say don't do it. You could both die in there."

"Hell, Charlie, Sammy's scared. With or without you, I'm gonna take a look at the damned bell and figure a way to get it clear of these damned mountains. Now, are you comin' with me or no?"

Fong turned the question over in his mind, but he was still not convinced. "Sam?" he said.

Flintlock shook his head. "You're a grown man, Charlie. I can't tell you what to do."

He rose to his feet, the Hawken cradled in his arm. "I'm going to shoot us some camp meat. I'll leave the bell to you and Abe."

Ayasha, who never let Flintlock out of her sight, got up and stepped beside him.

"No, you stay here," he said.

The girl shook her head.

"Hell, you can't hunt in a dress," Flintlock said.

Ayasha's only reaction was to draw closer to Flintlock's side.

"The ladies love you, Sammy," Roper said. "Take the little gal hunting."

"What about Sister One and Sister Two?" Flintlock said.

"They'll come with us," Charlie Fong said. He saw the horrified expression on Flintlock's face and added, "As far as the mouth of the cave. They can wait there until we come back out."

"So you're going up there, huh?" Flintlock said. Rain began to fall around him.

"Only for a look-see," Fong said. "We won't stay long."

"If I say don't go there, you won't listen."

"That's how she stacks up, Sam'l," Roper said.

Flintlock shook his head. "Then you boys will learn . . . the hard way."

CHAPTER FORTY-EIGHT

The Navajo say the sandstone Sonsela Buttes that straddle the Arizona and New Mexico border were formed by stars falling to earth, their explanation for a remote, lost land marked by ancient lava beds, petrified forests and the ruined pueblos of the Old Ones who lived there thousands of years before the Navajo themselves.

Asa Pagg rode through brush and sage country a couple of miles west of the buttes. To his left lay the massive rift of the Canyon de Chelly, ahead of him soared White Cone Mountain, a triangular peak that looked as though a great wind had blown a pyramid all the way from the Giza plateau. To the east rose the Chuska Mountains, holding up a blanket of black rain clouds.

Pagg knew he had pursuers on his back trail. He'd watched their dust for the past hour.

The questions were: How many and how

determined were they?

He'd soon find the answers.

Men like Pagg, outlaws who were always on the run, dodging, ducking, going to ground in some stinking prairie dugout or one-horse hell town, had a pathological fear and hatred of being hunted like an animal.

But those who were skilled gunfighters and mankillers could be pushed so far and no farther. Eventually they'd put their back to a wall and let their guns do the negotiating.

Asa Pagg was one of those.

He drew rein and scouted the flat country behind him with care and caution. He knew the manner of men he faced, leather-tough cavalrymen with experience fighting Apaches. They'd be no bargain.

But how many?

Rain now ticking on his slicker, he sat his horse in a patch of piñon and waited, his eyes constantly scanning the badlands.

Pagg reckoned he could let the soldiers come up on him, sudden-like, and he'd take them by surprise.

Again, it all depended on their numbers, probably many, given Colonel Andrew Grove's likely rage.

Well, Pagg wasn't about to take on a cavalry troop. If the army was coming at him in strength, he'd turn and run and trust to his horse.

The rain was settling the dust and Pagg no longer had a rising brown column to help him fix his pursuers.

All he could do now was wait. . . .

A coyote skulked out of the brush then stopped, did a double take when it saw the rider, and trotted quickly away.

The animal rustled into the sage and then the only noise was the steady drum of rain and the jangle of the bit as Pagg's mount impatiently tossed its head.

And then the horse stiffened and stared across distance, its ears pricked forward.

Pagg saw them then.

Four riders, barely visible behind the falling rain. Thunder banged above the mountains, still far off.

Pleasant Tyrell's .44-40 Henry was in the boot under Pagg's left leg, but it didn't enter his thinking to use it. He was no dab hand with a long gun and in a rifle battle with trained soldiers he would surely come out the loser.

He'd rely on surprise . . . and the Smith & Wesson Russians in his holsters.

Aware that the slicker he wore was an encumbrance, Pagg shucked it and the rain fell cold on his naked chest and back. His beard, long untrimmed, hung in an unruly amber bib to his navel and his battered hat shaded his glittering eyes.

Looking more pirate than pistolero, Asa Pagg drew his guns . . . and readied himself. . . .

The four cavalry troopers came on through a pelting rain, the soldier in front bending over from the saddle, scouting for Pagg's rapidly disappearing tracks in the sand.

Pagg grinned. Fifty yards away and they hadn't seen him yet.

Thunder boomed and lightning split the sky. Cloud piled on black cloud and the dark morning became a roaring, flashing bedlam of noise and shimmering light. The wind slapped hard against Pagg and under him his horse grew restive and nervously tossed its head.

Forty yards . . .

Pagg's hands were wet, slick on the smooth ivory of old Tyrell's revolvers. He set his chin. Well, he'd shot guns in rain before and killed his man. He'd manage.

Twenty yards . . .

And they'd spotted him!

The point rider threw up his hand, and the three behind him drew rein.

Asa Pagg charged.

Ten yards . . .

Time to get his work in.

The troopers had been surprised and it slowed them. They ignored their booted carbines and grabbed for sidearms.

It was a big mistake.

Pagg worked his revolvers with amazing skill and rapidity, the result of a lifetime of training.

One . . . two . . . three saddles emptied. The surviving trooper, a man with dark features and eyes, got off a shot then swung his horse away.

Pagg, fighting his own animal, let him go.

The man now had a story to tell and others would listen to what he had to say and decide that maybe chasing a named gunfighter wasn't such a good idea after all.

Three men lay sprawled on the ground, two dead, the other clinging to life.

But not for long.

Pagg shot the man between the eyes, then reloaded his guns.

His cold eyes lifted from the Russian to the fleeing trooper who was flapping his chaps like the devil himself was after him.

Pagg smiled, reckoning that the three dead men would testify in hell that they'd indeed met a demon . . . the evil patron saint of six-guns.

Asa Pagg swung east past White Cone Mountain and at dusk made camp in the Chuska foothills. He managed to light a fire in a grove of juniper and piñon that sheltered him from the worst of the rain and dined on strips of jerky and a stick of peppermint candy he'd plundered from Pleasant Tyrell's pack.

He considered his options and they were limited.

Heading south was out of the question. Grove was still hunting him.

West lay some mighty rough country and heading east across the mountains didn't appeal to him either.

Then he remembered Sam Flintlock and Abe Roper.

Pagg sucked on the candy stick, thinking things through.

Flintlock and Roper were idiots, but it might just be possible that there was a golden bell up in the Red Valley. Call it a hundred-to-one chance.

It was thin, mighty thin. But worth a ride up there to see what was what.

A cold drop of rain dripped from a tree branch, got under the collar of his slicker and hit Pagg in the back of his neck. He hardly noticed.

If there was a bell, a big *if,* he could take it for himself and live like an English lord for the rest of his life.

It was a pleasant thought, a thought a man could build dreams around.

Pagg nodded. Right, it was a plan, not a great one, but a plan nonetheless. He'd move out at first light and head for the Red Valley.

After all, he'd nothing else to do.

CHAPTER FORTY-NINE

Deer hunting in rain washes away human scent and a man with good eyesight can often make a kill in a downpour and put meat on the table.

But rain accompanied by lightning, and all bets are off.

"I never did know mule deer to come out in a thunderstorm," Sam Flintlock said.

Ayasha looked at him blankly, tendrils of wet hair falling over her forehead. Flintlock was struck by how pretty she looked.

He smiled. "Well, anyway, that's a natural fact. We won't see any deer until this passes."

After a glance at the lowering sky, Flintlock said, "Let's make our way back. I could use some coffee."

They stood in the lee of a rock face no higher than a man on a horse, but it was slightly overhung and protected them from the rain and rising wind.

Flintlock took Ayasha's hand and said, "Let's go."

But the girl held back and he said, "What's wrong with you, girl? You don't want to get wet?"

Ayasha turned up her face and stared into Flintlock's eyes. Her fingertips traced the thunderbird on his throat and she smiled. Then her lips parted and her mouth hungrily sought his.

Flintlock shook his head and pushed the girl away.

"No, this ain't right," he said. "You're tetched in the head, Ayasha. You don't rightly know what you're doing."

The girl didn't look hurt. She didn't look anything.

Flintlock, trying to reach her, said, "Why?"

Ayasha mined her brain for words, the habit of speech no longer coming easily to her.

"I . . . wanted . . . to . . . know," she said.

It was the first time Flintlock had heard the girl utter a complete sentence and he was both pleased and concerned. Above their heads thunder rolled and when it was quiet again, he said, "What did you want to know?"

"If . . . I could . . ." Ayasha, unable to find words, gave up on that and started again. "Can I . . . love a man? Can I . . . love you?"

Flintlock had little understanding of women, and finding answers to Ayasha's questions pushed him to the limit. The girl had gone through hell and her thinking was no longer as it should be.

In the end, he smiled and said, "Sure you can love a man. You'll meet a fine, upstanding young feller and get hitched and have kids. Hell, Ayasha, you'll have a house with a picket fence and window boxes and you'll forget that you were ever . . . well, you'll forget all the bad things that happened to you."

The girl smiled. "You can do this . . . Sam?"

Flintlock raised Ayasha's hand and kissed it gently. "No, I can't give you those things. I'm a rough-living man and I lead a desperate, violent life. I'm not the husband for you, but don't worry, the right young feller will come along. I guarantee it. He'll play the geetar an' sing 'Sweet Violets' to you on the garden swing. You bet he will."

"Can that still happen to me, Sam, after . . ."

"Yes, it can. Just have faith, Ayasha. Know that it will happen."

"My name is Prudence, Prudence Walsh."

"Good to know you, Prudence."

"I think I prefer Ayasha."

"There you go. Then that's what I'll keep on calling you."

The hiss of the rain grew louder and Flintlock said, "This isn't going to pass over any time soon. Best we make tracks back to camp."

Ayasha put her tiny hand on his arm. "Sam, you could've taken me."

"Yeah, I know. It would've been a big mistake on both our parts."

"Sam . . . thank you for not being . . . an Apache."

Flintlock smiled. "I reckon that young feller you'll meet will count himself among the luckiest men in the world, Ayasha." He swallowed hard. "Damn right."

"Damn right they was here," Chastity Gauley said. He fussed with the neckline of his peasant blouse. "Picked up a young gal that was undone by Apaches and took her with them." He pulled out the top of the blouse. "Damn loose threads."

"When was that?" Asa Pagg said.

"Oh, 'bout a week ago, maybe more."

"They say where they were goin'?" Pagg said.

"North into the valley. At least that's the

way they was headed."

Pagg nodded. "Got any grub? And I need a shirt."

"Stew in the pot. Men's shirts, at cost, in the store at the back."

"Whiskey?"

"You could call it that."

"Seen anything of two men, call themselves Logan Dean an' Joe Harte? Real desperate-looking characters."

"That's the only kind I get around here, but I can't say I've met them two." Gauley settled the hang of his red skirt, then, without looking up, said, "You're Asa Pagg, ain't you?"

"Why do you want to know?"

"Well, like, I seen your face in the newspaper, a drawing, mind, but a good likeness. So if you are, or if you ain't, you know the grub an' the shirt you want?"

"What about them?"

"I'd wait until Bear Blodwell clears the premises," Gauley said. "He ain't in a sociable mood today an' that's why I'm out here, even though it's raining on my nice new outfit. The skirt and blouse are Mexican, you know."

"You see a foundling swatch on me, like I'm some poor orphan afraid of his shadow?" Pagg said.

391

"Bear ain't a nice man, Mr. Pagg if you are, Mr. Nobody if you ain't. He's drinking an' threatening to drop the hammer on somebody."

"Then wait 'til he gets a load of me," Pagg said.

Gauley shrugged. "Your funeral."

"Come inside and dish me up some o' that stew and a bottle of Bass if you got it," Pagg said.

"I got a bottle somewhere. I also got a shovel and I think I'm gonna need it afore too long."

Asa Pagg was a killer and he recognized Bear Blodwell as a blood brother.

The man was big, as big as Pagg, dressed in the plaid shirt and mule-eared boots of a prospector. He wore a brown canvas coat and a battered railroad hat with a high crown and stingy brim. His Colt was holstered in a cross-draw gun rig. Like Pagg, he had a full, spade-shaped beard, as black as his eyes.

When Pagg bellied up to the bar, Blodwell, bent over a whiskey bottle, glanced at him and said, "What the hell do you want?"

"The proprietor has my order," Pagg said. He smiled. "Rainy out today, but I reckon it might clear up by suppertime."

Blodwell ignored that and said, "Hey, Gauley, don't serve this pilgrim nothin' until you see his money. Hell, he can't even afford to put a shirt on his back."

Gauley laid a bowl of stew and a dusty bottle of Bass ale in front of Pagg. "Man's hungry, Bear," he said.

"Take that grub away, like I told you," Blodwell, said, straightening up.

"Leave it," Pagg said.

Gauley hesitated. "I'll get shot if I do an' shot if I don't."

"Try to lift my meal and you'll very definitely get shot," Pagg said.

Blodwell pushed himself away from the bar. He moved easily for a big man, wide of shoulder, slim of hip, he was well-balanced on his feet.

"I'll lift the damned thing," he said.

Blodwell reached across for Pagg's bowl and gave the outlaw the only chance he needed.

Pagg's massive right fist swung and crashed into Blodwell's face, just under his left eye, splitting skin, drawing blood. Blodwell staggered back, cursing. He went for his gun but Pagg wanted none of that, not when his blood was up and he was fighting mad.

He grabbed Blodwell's wrist before he

could bring up the Colt, twisted hard and spun the big man around. Pagg pushed Blodwell's right arm hard and high up his back until the shoulder locked.

Blodwell screamed and dropped his gun. Pagg kept his grip on the man's arm, grabbed him by the back of his coat and charged him into the cabin wall. Blodwell hit headfirst and dropped, his eyes rolling.

He shook his head to clear his fogging vision and drops of scarlet blood flew from the cut under his eye.

But the big miner was game.

Blodwell staggered to his feet, stepped forward and swung a looping right that hit Pagg on his bearded chin and staggered him. Pagg crashed against the bar, but bounced back swinging. He was grinning for the sheer love of knuckle and skull fighting.

Both were big men and they stood toe to toe exchanging blows with big-knuckled iron-hard fists that battered their faces to bloody pulp.

Gauley yelled at them to "Stop or I'll scream," but they ignored him.

Finally after a minute of moving back and forth over the timber floor, Blodwell broke loose. He feinted a left, then as Pagg slipped the blow, met him with a ripping uppercut that plowed into Pagg's belly. Retching bile, Pagg held on for grim life, hugging Blodwell to him. Then he drove his boot heel onto the miner's instep and Blodwell roared in and pushed Pagg away, breaking the clinch.

Warily now, their faces scarlet masks, the two big men circled each other, fists flicking like snake tongues as they probed for an opening.

Pagg missed with a straight right that unbalanced him and the two men clinched again. Pagg saw his opportunity and took it. He smashed the top of his forehead into the bridge of Blodwell's nose and was overjoyed to hear bone shatter.

Blodwell staggered back, badly hurt, and Pagg went after him.

He jabbed another straight right into the other man's splintered nose and when Blodwell flinched, followed up with a powerful left hook into the miner's ribs. Blodwell gasped like a stranded fish and tried to break. But Pagg wasn't about to let him off the hook.

He stepped forward, swinging, every punch finding its target.

Blodwell was weakening fast. His stamina had never been tested in a long fight and now he knew he needed to end this . . . and quickly.

He swung a right into Pagg's battered face, but the outlaw shrugged it off and counterpunched, another right to Blodwell's ruined nose.

Desperate now, his legs weakening, Blodwell wrapped his powerful arms around Pagg's waist in a bear hug and forced Pagg back, trying to break his spine.

Pagg's thumbs jabbed into Blodwell's eyes and gouged deep. To protect himself, the miner broke his hold and took a step back. He didn't cover up and it was a bad mistake.

Pagg, his fist coming up from his knees, smashed a roundhouse right into Blodwell's chin. The man dropped like a felled ox. He got up on one elbow, raised a surrendering hand to Pagg and gasped, "Enough. I'm done. It's over."

It was a testament to the quality of Pleasant Tyrell's holsters that both Pagg's guns had stayed in place during the rough-and-tumble.

Now he drew and shot Blodwell between his horrified eyes.

"Wrong," Pagg said. "Now it's over."

Gauley stepped to Pagg's side and lifted his skirt to avoid Blodwell's blood. "Mister, you sure hold a grudge," he said.

"My stew still warm and the beer cold?" Pagg said.

"I don't know."

"Then go find out," Pagg said.

"What about him?" Gauley said.

"What about him? He got kin around here?"

"No."

"Then bury him."

"Look at the size of him," Gauley said. "He's going to take a heap o' burying."

"I don't know about that," Pagg said. "There ain't much of him left."

CHAPTER FIFTY

"Where's Charlie?" Sam Flintlock said when he and Ayasha returned to camp.

"Charlie's dead," Abe Roper said. His lips were unnaturally pale. "Leastways, I think he's dead."

"What happened, Abe?" Flintlock said. "Choose your words carefully. I was fond of Charlie."

"I'm half dead my ownself, Sammy. I can scarcely breathe. I'm on fire." Roper put a hand to his chest. "In here. I coughed up blood just afore you arrived."

"What happened?" Flintlock said. "Tell me what happened in the cave."

Roper looked at him and didn't like what he saw in Flintlock's eyes.

"You were right about the gas," he said.

"I know I was," Flintlock said. "Where is Charlie?"

"He's still in the cave," Roper said. His face jumped, like a man about to take a bullet. "I left him in there."

"You left him to die?"

"Sammy, I was too weak to carry him. I barely got out of the cave alive myself."

"Abe," Flintlock said, "I should gun you. Right here and now I should put a bullet in you."

"Please, Sammy, be reasonable," Roper said. His eyes, no longer holding on Flintlock's, cut to the black sky. Then he said, his voice low, "I never want to go back into the cave. It's the door way to hell, Sam."

"Changed your tune real fast, Abe," Flintlock said.

"Had it changed for me, you mean."

"I'm going after Charlie," Flintlock said. "Look after the women until I get back." He turned. "Ayasha, you stay here."

"I want to go with you," the girl said.

"No. It's too dangerous."

Despite his misery, Roper said, "Damnit all, she talks."

"Yeah, maybe too much," Flintlock said.

He turned on his heel and strode away in the direction of the hill.

Behind him, Ayasha called out, "Take me with you, Sam."

But Flintlock pretended he didn't hear. Right then he was scared, and angry at himself for feeling that way.

■ ■ ■ ■

The murmur of a man in prayer reached Sam Flintlock from the cave and he stood still in a swirl of wind and rain and listened.

There was no mistaking it. Somebody in the cave was chanting prayers.

It sure as hell wasn't Charlie Fong, who wasn't exactly on speaking terms with God. Then who?

Flintlock pulled his revolver and made his way up the rain-slick path. Around him the land shimmered white as lightning slashed across the sky, this way and that, as though the wind was blowing in all four directions at once.

He reached the cave entrance and a deep breath caught in his throat.

Charlie lay sprawled just inside, an ancient, white-haired man in a monk's robe on his knees beside him. The man's hands were steepled together and his bloodless lips moved. His hollow cheeks and eye sockets were in shadow, like a death mask.

"Back away from Charlie, mister, or I'll gun you," Flintlock said.

The old man lapsed into silence and slowly turned his head to look at the intruder.

"He came for the bell, like you did," he said.

"What did you do to him?" Flintlock said.

"Nothing. I found him in the cave and carried him here." Then, as though that needed explanation, "He is a small man."

"Is he —"

"Dead? No. But he is very sick. He will recover, I think."

Suddenly angry, Flintlock said, "Why the hell didn't you tell us that there's gas in the cave?"

"Would you have believed me?" the old man said. His eyes, as white as buttermilk, lifted to Flintlock. "Would you?"

Flintlock shoved his gun back in his waistband. "No. I wouldn't."

He kneeled beside Charlie and lifted the little man by the shoulders until he was in a sitting position. "Charlie, can you hear me?" Flintlock said. "Come back from China or wherever the hell you are."

Fong made no answer, but the old man said, "I think he is breathing easier. I don't think he was in the cave long enough to damage his lungs permanently. But let him sleep awhile."

Flintlock eased Charlie Fong onto his back again, and then stood. Beside him the old man struggled to rise. Flintlock put his hand on his elbow and helped him to his feet.

"Who are you?" he said.

"I am the guardian of the bell," the old man said.

"They say you are Death itself. Any truth in that?"

"The cave is death. Not me."

Charlie Fong muttered something, his head moving back and forth, and Flintlock took a knee beside him. "Can you hear me, Charlie?" he said.

But Fong had again retreated to a dark place and was still.

"Who appointed you guardian," Flintlock said, his anger flaring again. "Or did you just take it on yourself?"

The old man took the earthenware jug from the shelf and the two cups. He poured wine into both, as red as blood.

"Drink, it will do you good," he said, extending the cup.

Flintlock took it and sniffed the wine suspiciously.

The old man smiled. "It is not poisoned. See" — he took a sip — "it did me no harm."

The wine was rough, but Flintlock drank, for politeness's sake. Or so he told himself.

In fact he wished to calm his clamoring nerves.

The old man had an unearthliness about him that set Flintlock on edge.

"Before me there were fifty guardians," he said. "I am the fifty-first and I will be the last."

"Why all the guardians?" Flintlock said.

"To warn greedy men away from the cave and the gas that kills."

"You're a monk, huh?"

"No, not a monk."

"Then what?"

"A guardian."

"Well, that's a lot of help," Flintlock said.

Then, out of the blue, the old man said, "Do you smoke tobacco?"

Surprised, Flintlock said, "Yeah, I do. I was taught to roll cigarettes by Texans who are much addicted to them."

"Ah," the old man said. "I don't know these cigarettes, but perhaps you will roll one for me?"

"Sure," Flintlock said. He got out his tobacco sack and papers and said, "When did you last have a smoke, pops?"

The old man counted on his fingers. "Sixty years. Before I was made guardian. I had a pipe once, a beautiful pipe. It was a Spanish clay pipe and I enjoyed it immensely."

Flintlock stuck the cigarette between the old man's pale lips and lit it.

"Well, enjoy it," he said.

The old man drew deep, smiled and behind a cloud of blue smoke, said, "Ahh . . . it's even better than I remembered."

Then he surprised Flintlock again.

The old man again struggled onto his creaking knees beside Charlie Fong. He drew deep on the cigarette, and then gently blew the smoke into the unconscious man's nose.

He did it a second time.

And then a third.

Long moments passed. Rain slanted across the mouth of the cave and lightning flashed, searing the hillside. Thunder roared and Flintlock felt the cave floor tremble under his feet. Dust drifted from cracks in the roof and he thought he heard the growl of grinding rock from . . .

Outside!

It had to be!

Flintlock's hair stood on end. My God, the hanging rock shelf above the cave entrance was shifting. . . .

But then the ground under his feet stilled and the only threatening sounds were made by the storm.

Flintlock blinked. Had he imagined the whole thing?

Maybe. Or maybe not.

Charlie Fong made a small noise in his throat and his eyes fluttered open.

"He has come back," the old man said. "He will live."

Flintlock kneeled beside Fong and said, "Charlie, are you all right?"

"Where am I?" Fong said.

"In the cave of the golden bell," Flintlock said. "The poison gas got to you."

"It didn't kill me?"

"No. You're alive, Charlie, I promise."

Charlie Fong looked into Flintlock's face and grinned. "Sam, old Barnabas says you're an idiot."

CHAPTER FIFTY-ONE

Asa Pagg was fifteen miles north of Buffalo Pass in the rugged red butte country when he experienced the familiar, uneasy feeling that he was being watched.

Horse Mesa was two miles ahead of him when he drew rein.

The instincts of a dangerous, hunted animal warned Pagg that there was someone on his back trail, close enough to have sight of him.

He swung his horse around, and as he expected, two riders were heading toward him through rain and wind.

Pagg grinned. There was no mistaking Logan Dean's flashy paint and beside him, hunched in the saddle reading a poetry book the way he always rode, Joe Harte on his big American stud. He'd made a tent of the front of his slicker to protect the book and had no eyes for the trail.

But Logan Dean was aware. And when he

spotted Pagg he punched Harte on the shoulder to get his attention.

Harte looked up, blinked, and said, "It's Asa, as ever was."

"Yeah, and we got some explaining to do," Dean said.

"You boys got some explaining to do," Pagg said. "I'm trying to decide if I should listen, or shoot you off'n them ponies."

"Over there, Asa," Dean said. He nodded toward a natural sandstone arch that promised shelter. "Let's get the hell out of the rain."

"You two ride ahead of me," Pagg said. "I got a bounty on my head and maybe you got a mind to collect it."

"You can trust us, Asa," Dean said. "Me an' Joe are true-blue."

"Maybe. But all the same, ride in front of me," Pagg said.

The span of the arch was only about twenty feet and about ten wide, but it was enough to keep off the worst of the rain and the cutting wind.

When the lightning played on Pagg's face it looked like glistening stone. "All right, why did you run out on me?" he said.

Harte looked at Dean and his eyes pleaded with him to do the talking.

"It was like this, Asa," Dean said. "After

407

you done the colonel's wife —"

"She wanted it," Pagg said.

"— and was tossed in the brig, some hard talk was thrown in our direction, on account of you an' us bein' almost like kin, Asa," Dean said.

"So you skedaddled and left me to face the music, huh?" Pagg said.

"When I heard what had happened to you, Asa," Harte said, "I thought my heart was going to break. Poor 'trampled man with smarting wounds.' " The gunman smiled. "The poet Samuel Taylor Coleridge wrote them words."

Pagg ignored that and stared at Dean. "You didn't try to spring me, Logan."

"Asa, there were too many soldiers and you were padlocked in tight," Dean said. "We'd no chance to help you make a break."

"You heard about the Apache attack?" Pagg said.

He looked as though he was weighing something in his mind, and that set Dean on edge.

"Heard about that and we was right sorry, ain't that the truth, Joe," he said.

"True as ever was, Logan," Harte said. "But by the time we heard, it was all over and you were a hounded fugitive, Asa."

Dean, fearing Pagg's volcanic temper,

tried to steer the conversation into safer waters.

"Heard something else, Asa. There's a heap of talk goin' on around these parts."

"About what?" Pagg said.

"Do you recollect Abe Roper talking about a golden bell somewhere up in the Red Valley? Well, it turns out it could be true."

"How come that?" Pagg said.

"It seems a prospector started jawing about the bell and showed a map to the place where he said it's hid," Dean said. "We heard a bunch of tinpans already headed up that way to take a look, but were wiped out by Apaches before they even got close to the valley."

"Who told you all this?" Pagg said. He felt a little twinge of worry.

"We got it from miners at a trading post over to the Tohatchi Flats country," Joe Harte said. "There's talk of a gold rush. It's like all of a sudden folks are saying that the bell is real and it's there for the taking by anyone lucky enough to find it."

"Two thousand pounds of gold is hidden in a cave, Asa," Dean said. "That's what they're sayin'."

"So why are you telling me this, Logan?" Pagg said. "Because it makes a good story, maybe?"

"You know what it took for me and Joe to find you, Asa?"

"Tell me."

"Three dead cavalry troopers. The one that got away said they'd been bushwhacked up near White Cone Mountain by bandits led by a man that matched your description. We figured it was you, Asa, then a man-woman at the trading post north of Buffalo Pass said he'd seen you, that you'd killed a man and then headed north toward the valley."

"And here we are," Harte said.

"The man I killed gave me this," Pagg said as he touched his battered face. "It was his mistake. Now you've told me how you found me, now tell me why."

"The why is easy, Asa. So we can go get the golden bell afore an army of tinpans is crawlin' all over them mountains up there," Dean said.

Pagg decided to be affable. He'd kill Harte and Dean after they helped him get the bell, not before.

"You've bested me, boys," he said, smiling. "That's the very thing I was plannin' on doing my ownself."

Harte echoed Pagg's smile. "Then we're well met," he said.

"If the bell exists, and that's a big *if,* there's always the chance that Abe Roper and Sam Flintlock already have it," Pagg said.

"So we put the crawl on them two and take it," Dean said. He shrugged. "Or gun them if we have to."

"Joe, that set all right with you?" Pagg said.

"Suits me just fine, Asa. We split the gold three ways, right?"

"Of course. We're partners, ain't we?" Pagg said.

"Then let's go get that damned bell and make ourselves rich," Logan Dean said.

CHAPTER FIFTY-TWO

A bullet *spaaang*ed off the inside wall of the cave and then bounced around like an angry hornet in a box.

"What the hell!" Sam Flintlock said. "Charlie, you stay right where you're at."

"I'm not going anyplace, Sam," Charlie Fong said to Flintlock's retreating back.

Flintlock ran to the cave mouth, his Colt hammerback and ready in his hand. He hit the ground, rolled to his right and then came up on one knee, his eyes on the slope.

"Halloo," Abe Roper yelled. "Can you hear me, Sammy?"

"Damn you, Abe!" Flintlock called. "You could've killed us."

"I had to get your attention, Sammy," Roper said. "I can't walk up the rise, me feeling as bad as I do."

He was leaning on his rifle, using it like a cane, and his head was bent as though breathing came hard to him.

"I'm bringing Charlie down," Flintlock said.

"Is he still alive?"

"Yeah, he is. Lucky for you, Abe. You must be saying your prayers at night."

Flintlock stepped into the cave. There was no sign of the old man.

"I'm taking you out of here, Charlie," he said.

"Hell, Sam, I can't walk."

"I know. I'll carry you."

"I'm too heavy for you," Fong said. "You could fall real easy."

"You're a little Chinaman. How heavy can you be?" Flintlock said.

He lifted Fong effortlessly and carried him like a man would carry a child, toward the entrance of the cave.

"Grab my Hawken from the wall there, Charlie," he said. "Can you hold it?"

Fong nodded, reached out and picked up the rifle. He laid it across his belly and said, "Got it, Sam. Let us proceed."

"Abe!" Flintlock yelled when he walked out of the cave. "Shoot at us again and I swear I'll gun you right where you stand."

Roper said nothing, but he waved and stepped away, leaning heavily on the Winchester. He looked like a man carrying a burden on his shoulders.

"What do you mean they just lit out?" Flintlock said.

"Sammy, I don't know rightly what happened," Abe Roper said. He hesitated a moment, then said, "Well, I do know. After you left to get Charlie I must've passed out. When I woke, they were gone and so were their horses."

Flintlock said to Ayasha, "You didn't try to stop them?"

"They're afraid of the thing in the cave," the girl said. "They wanted me to go with them, but I wouldn't. No, I couldn't stop them, Sam."

Flintlock again turned his attention to Roper. "So we got two little Chinese girls wandering out there in the wilderness somewhere?"

Roper nodded, his face a mask of misery. "I reckon that's how it stacks up, Sam'l."

"Damn you, Abe," Flintlock said. "I should've shot you years ago."

Charlie Fong was lying beside the fire, fat raindrops filtering through the pines splashing on his blanket. Now he got up on an elbow and said, "Sam, I'll help you find them."

414

"Not a chance, Charlie," Flintlock said. "You're still too sick. I'll go after them."

"The ground's soft, Sammy," Roper said. "They'll be easy to track."

"I figured that out for my ownself, Abe," Flintlock said. He was still angry at Roper and it showed.

The girls' tracks headed due east into the high desert country.

The only settlement of any size was at least fifty miles away and the chances of two young girls getting there alive were slim.

It consoled Flintlock to recall that the army was scouting the area, rounding up bronco Apaches. Maybe the girls would bump into a cavalry patrol.

But this was a country of vast, lonely distances, of scarred, somber peaks, shadowed canyons and long winds. The land was harsh and unforgiving and could kill a grown man a hundred different ways.

The odds were not in the girls' favor, and Flintlock knew it.

One thing he had going for him was that they were not far ahead of him, and, despite the downpour, their tracks were fresh.

Buttoned up into his slicker, rainwater running off the brim of his hat, Flintlock stuck doggedly to the trail east, even though the devil of impatience rode him.

And a slow-burning anger.

Roper and Charlie Fong had ignored his warning about the cave and both were now sick and would probably take at least a couple of days to recover. Right then they were in no shape to defend themselves . . . and the Apaches were still out. Ayasha clung to him, mentally fragile and vulnerable, and he needed to be with her, now more than ever.

What he didn't need was to chase two hysterical young girls across a rain-lashed, broken land where humans, white or Indian, rarely ventured.

Sam Flintlock clenched his teeth. Damnit, it seemed problems had piled up on him.

But what he didn't know then was that were more to come. . . .

Flintlock was ten miles east of the Red Valley when it dawned on him that he wasn't closing the distance between himself and the fleeing Chinese girls.

Their horses bore a lighter burden than his and they were putting a heap of distance between him and the sisters.

He was reluctant to tire out his mount and kept the sorrel reined to a distance-eating walk. But his progress was slow and he reckoned there were only about four hours of daylight left. It was little enough time.

When Flintlock reached Shiprock Wash he saw a cabin on the east bank, its pine log structure almost invisible behind the relentless march of the rain.

It was an obvious place for the girls to hole up for the night.

Habits of a lifetime die hard, and Flintlock unbuttoned his slicker to clear the way to his Colt. He kneed his horse forward.

No smoke came from the cabin's chimney and the door was hanging aslant on one hinge. The glass in the only window was bullet pocked and a dead hog lay in the mud outside. A screeching windmill still turned at the back and nearby a dead cottonwood raised skeletal fingers to the sky.

Wary now, Flintlock swung out of the saddle and advanced the remaining fifty yards to the cabin on foot, taking advantage of the little cover available.

The smell hit him when he was still a dozen yards away.

Flintlock drew his gun. Was it the hog? Or dead men?

He stepped to the door, jerked it wide and looked inside.

The two dead men lay sprawled on the

floor, one gray, the other a young towhead. Their faces were distorted in death, but the men looked remarkably alike. Father and son miners, Flintlock told himself, and they'd both been shot multiple times.

Flintlock's immediate reaction was to pin the killings on the Apaches.

He'd thought Geronimo would be in the Sierra Madres by now, content to raid into Mexico, until the U.S. Army gave up the chase and returned to barracks.

But had he in fact swung north?

Apaches were the most notional people on God's earth, and there was no guessing what a man like Geronimo would do.

Then Flintlock studied the cabin more closely.

The place had been ransacked; something young Apache bucks would do as they searched for guns, ammunition and trinkets.

But the floorboards had been pulled up and the sod roof had been probed with a broom handle. No Apache would've done that. But white men on the hunt for gold certainly would.

The dead men were tinpans and they'd been murdered because their killers suspected they'd a stash of dust hidden somewhere in the cabin.

The rank, sweet stench of decay sickened

Flintlock and he backed out of the door . . .
into the hard, impersonal muzzle of a rifle.

CHAPTER FIFTY-THREE

"Sam Flintlock, my friend," Carlos Hernandez said. "How good it is to see you again." He held up his right hand, the fingers curled into a claw. "See, my wrist is getting better, but — this is very sad — my hand, he is withering."

The Mexican had eight men with him — and two girls.

The Chinese sisters sat miserable and soaking wet on their horses, guarded by a huge bandit with a scarred face and a bad attitude. When the man turned his nail keg of a head and stared at Flintlock his black eyes glowed with murder.

Flintlock had no cards to play. He knew he was already a dead man.

"Carlos, let the girls go," he said. "Your business is with me."

Hernandez smiled, the diamonds in his teeth catching the thin light of the gloomy day. "You are so right, my friend, my business is with you . . . and it is a business that will take a long, long time."

The Mexican shrugged. "As for the girls, I want them for myself." He tapped himself on the chest. "They will amuse Carlos Hernandez the great bandit chief for a while and they will consider it a great honor. Then, when I am finished with them, I will give the señoritas to my men. Because" — Hernandez opened his arms wide, threw back his head, and yelled — "I am a flowing river to my people!"

This last drew cheers from the bandits and one of them fired his rifle into the air in celebration.

After the commotion died down, Hernandez said, "Flintlock, my friend, an eye for an eye, so what do I take for a hand that has withered to a twisted hook?"

Flintlock answered that question with one of his own. "Why did you kill the miners, you damned savage?"

"Gold," Hernandez said. "But they had none and that was unlucky for them."

Flintlock tried again. "Let the girls go and we'll talk."

Suddenly Hernandez was angry. "I don't wish to talk about the women. They are nothing. We will talk about what you will give me for my good right hand."

The Mexican stood, grim-faced, waiting for Flintlock's answer.

Rain ticked on the shoulders of his oilskin army cloak as thunder roared and lightning clashed. To the north, above the distant mountains, a streak of light gray showed among the black clouds, a promise that the storm had reached its climax and would not last much longer.

"When I get back to Texas, I'll send you a couple of bucks," Flintlock said. "How does that set with you?"

Hernandez made no reply, but his unspoken answer was obviously "not well," because he used his left hand, heavy with rings, to deliver a smashing backhand to Flintlock's face.

The blow came out of nowhere, caught Flintlock flatfooted and he staggered and fell. His gun jerked out of his waistband and the Mexican kicked it away.

Hernandez didn't give him a chance to rise. His boots thudded again and again into Flintlock's ribs, vicious kicks that hurt and robbed him of breath.

Finally the bandit stepped back and said, "Get him to his feet."

A couple of men dragged Flintlock erect. Hernandez smiled at him and said, "A hand for a hand, my friend. How does that set with you?"

The taste of blood in his mouth, Flintlock said, "You go to hell."

"Ah, then you agree with my judgment," Hernandez said. "But you will be the one in hell, my friend."

He turned to his men and said, "Juan, bring your ax. And a block."

The man called Juan had the eyes of a lizard. He pulled a tomahawk from his belt and stepped in front of Flintlock who swayed on his feet, weak from the kicking he'd taken.

Juan pointed out an upright, blade-scarred log near the cabin. "Bring me that," he said. When a couple of men laid the cutting block at his feet, he looked to Hernandez for guidance.

"I will cut off his hand, his gun hand," the bandit chief said. "Prepare him for my justice, Juan."

Several grinning Mexicans manhandled Flintlock onto his back. After a rope was looped around his right wrist, a man sat on the wet mud and pulled, forcing the hand onto the block.

Hernandez took the tomahawk from Juan and said, "Flintlock, my very good friend, this may take more than one . . . how do you say? . . . chop. But I will do my best."

"Hernandez, you're a damned, filthy animal," Flintlock said, between gritted teeth.

"Perhaps." The Mexican grinned. "But I am the one with the ax, I think."

Hernandez stooped a little, stared at Flintlock's hand for a few moments . . . and then raised the tomahawk.

The blow never fell.

A .45-70 bullet drilled through the crown of Carlos Hernandez's sombrero, smashed into the top of his bowed head and exited at the base of his skull in a gory eruption of blood, bone and brain.

The Apaches struck with incredible swiftness and violence.

Smarting from their defeat at Fort Defiance, they fell on the Mexicans like ravening wolves.

Within a couple of minutes, the ground was littered with dead bandits. Those were the lucky ones.

The man called Juan was taken alive . . . and so was Sam Flintlock.

The ten Apache women who emerged from Shiprock Wash in the wake of the warriors were wild with grief for the sons, husbands and lovers killed at Fort Defiance.

Knives drawn, they sprang on the bodies of the dead Mexicans and soon their hands and arms to the elbows were scarlet with blood, as they cut, stabbed and mutilated.

The bandits were not soldiers, but they were still the hated enemy of a people without friends.

Juan, shrieking in pain and terror, was hacked to death and his decapitated head was kicked along the rain-soaked ground like a football.

Throughout this terrifying, crimson-splashed nightmare, Flintlock was left alone. No one came near him, even when he brushed past a warrior and stepped beside the Chinese girls who were still mounted and like him, unharmed.

Numbed by the horror around him, the human intestines curled on the ground like pink snakes, Flintlock tried to say something to the girls, but the words stuck in his throat as though he'd swallowed a dry chicken bone.

Why was he being ignored?

Flintlock felt a twinge of fear. As the only white man among the bandits, was he being singled out for special treatment by the Apache women?

Their anger finally slaked, the women stood in a bloodstained group, consoling each other amid tears and wails.

Flintlock counted only eight warriors, all of them young bucks, who now stood in silence, rifles in their arms, and stared at him, their black eyes revealing nothing.

Then he saw Geronimo.

Mounted on a small mustang pony, the Apache seemed heedless of the rain as he rode toward Flintlock. He looked old and tired and the lines on his face had deepened. Geronimo was a man who'd ridden one trail too many and knew it.

His shoulders stooped, he stopped a few yards from Flintlock and said, "There is a mountain to the east of here the white men call Shiprock. The peak was once the nesting place of a giant bird of prey, like the one you bear on your throat. It is a sacred place."

Flintlock nodded as though he understood the Apache's drift. He didn't.

Geronimo said, "I had a vision at the mountain. I saw the great bird of prey swoop down and gather up all the Apaches, men, women and children, in its talons. Then it flew away with my people into the setting sun. This caused me great sadness."

"What does it mean, Geronimo?" Flintlock said. He figured his life was hanging by a thread and he was determined to be affable.

"It means that soon the Apache will be no more. Their day is done."

"Sorry to hear that," Flintlock said. "The Apache are a brave people."

Geronimo nodded. "It is good to be brave, but the white men are more in number than the stars in the night sky, and they have guns and cannon."

He shook his head, his face drawn. "I will lay down the heavy load I have carried since boyhood. I will follow the white man's trail and make him my friend, but I will not bend my back to his burdens."

"You will surrender, Geronimo?"

"When the great bird took my people, I saw a few fall from its claws. Those that are left I will save. Yes, I will surrender."

The Apache said something to his warriors and they gathered the Mexican horses and their guns and ammunition.

"Sam Flintlock, you are under my protection," Geronimo said. "I give you your life." He looked at the Chinese girls. "Yours?"

Flintlock said, "Yes, they are mine."

"Then you may have them."

"You saved me, Geronimo," Flintlock said. "I would have no hands if you hadn't showed up when you did. I would've bled to death."

"Let me see the tomahawk," Geronimo said. "I may keep it to remind me of this day."

Flintlock picked up the weapon and handed it to the Apache. Geronimo stared at the tomahawk for a while, then threw it away. "*Faugh,* it is Pima and a filthy thing."

He swung his horse away and his warriors and the women followed.*

*Sam Flintlock would see Geronimo again, at the 1904 World's Fair in St. Louis. They did not speak.

CHAPTER FIFTY-FOUR

"You little gals have caused me nothing but grief," Sam Flintlock said. "I swear, if you run away again I'll leave you to get eaten by bears."

"We were afraid of the mountain and the cave," the older sister said.

"Yeah, well, we're pulling out as soon as I get back to camp," Flintlock said. "We'll take you somewhere safe."

"Where will that be?" the girl said.

"I don't know. But we'll find a place."

Then the girl surprised him. "We will go where Charlie goes," she said.

Flintlock smiled. "I'm not sure about that."

"We are," the girl said.

"You ran away from Charlie," Flintlock said.

"Yes, we did, but he would have found us."

There was some female logic in there

somewhere, but Flintlock couldn't find it, nor did he try.

"Let's ride," he said, kneeing his horse forward.

Behind him the naked, bloody bodies of Carlos Hernandez and his men stared at the sky with eyes that could no longer see.

His choice of profession had made Abe Roper a cautious man and Flintlock made a point of hailing the camp before he and the Chinese girls rode into sight.

It was a wise precaution because Roper and Charlie Fong stood away from the firelight in darkness, rifles in their hands.

"Halt. Who goes there?" Roper yelled.

"Hell, Abe, it's me. Don't you recognize my voice?" Flintlock called out. "And who in blazes taught you to say, 'Halt. Who goes there?' "

"The army teached me that at Fort Defiance, Sammy," Roper said. "I took a liking to it, on account of how it sounds official an' that." The outlaw deepened his voice. "Halt. Who goes there? That'll stop a man in his tracks all right."

"Stopped me in mine, that's fer sure," Flintlock said. "We're coming in."

When he rode into camp, Charlie Fong said, "The wanderers return."

"You seem to be doing better, Charlie," Flintlock said.

"I wasn't in the gas for too long, I guess," Fong said. "The old man dragged me out of there."

Flintlock nodded. "I know."

He swung out of the saddle and Charlie helped the girls dismount. Then he took them aside and with much finger jabbing chided them. They didn't look too penitent, Flintlock decided.

"Where did you find them, Sam'l?" Roper said.

"Out by Shiprock Mountain," Flintlock said. Then, anticipating Roper's question, "It's about twenty miles due east."

"Them little gals rode a fer piece," Roper said.

"They're afraid of the cave," Flintlock said. "And so am I. Come morning, I'm pulling my freight, Abe."

"Sets fine by me," Roper said. "Though it sure hurts to leave the golden bell behind."

"I don't see that we have any choice," Flintlock said. "Maybe wait twenty, thirty years and try it again."

Ayasha ran to Flintlock and threw her arms around his neck. "I was so worried about you, Sam," she said.

Flintlock smiled. "And with good reason."

He said to Roper, "I got a story to tell, Abe, after I unsaddle the horses. Put the coffee back on to bile, huh?"

After he returned to the fire and poured himself coffee, Flintlock built a cigarette, ignored Roper's growing impatience, and said to Ayasha, "You look much better. The smile is coming back to your eyes."

The girl nodded. "Maybe it's thinking so much about the house with the white picket fence."

"Keep thinking that way, Ayasha. It will happen one day," Flintlock said.

"Damnit all, Sammy, what's your story?" Roper said. "You know I love stories, so tell it."

So Flintlock did.

"Ol' Carlos Hernandez is dead, huh?" Roper said when Flintlock had finished.

"You sound almost sorry, Abe," Flintlock said.

"I guess I am," Abe said. "He was a good bandit, an uncivilized man in a country that's closing in on us, Sam'l, slowly makin' us all civilized." He shook his head. "Even the train-robbing profession has gone to hell and Jesse ain't around anymore to bring it back."

"Good ol' Carlos was about to cut off my gun hand," Flintlock said.

Roper nodded. "Yeah, I know, I know. But he was always gettin' up to pranks like that. He didn't mean nothin' by them."

Flintlock was about to jump down Roper's throat for the "pranks" remark, but he let it go and allowed Abe's eulogy for a brother outlaw stand.

It was Geronimo, not civilization, that had killed Carlos Hernandez, but Roper was so down in the mouth, Flintlock decided not to mention it.

During the night the rock shelf above the cave entrance groaned and slid a foot lower, stone grinding on stone.

The old man, who'd been asleep in the Spanish chair, woke when he heard the rock grumble.

He stepped outside. The rain had stopped, the sky had cleared and the moon was bright.

His eyesight was not good, but his ears were keen and he listened. The rock shelf was now still, but a few pieces of stone the size of river pebbles had been shaken loose and they fell and hit the rain-soaked ground with soft thuds.

The shelf seemed more threatening and loomed above the cave entrance like a massive, clenched fist.

The old man was very afraid. The shelf was ready to come down and bury the cave entrance behind tons of rock. It was only a matter of time, he thought. Today, tomorrow, a year from now?

He had no way of knowing.

But right then he made the decision that he would no longer leave the cave. If the mountain buried him forever then let it be his tomb.

The old man stepped back inside and sat in the Spanish chair.

He sensed that his death was very close, coming from the south, riding through rain.

The prayer he whispered was not an appeal for his life, rather it was an expression of his gratitude for the great honor of guarding the bell that fell from heaven.

He heard the rock shelf shift again, just a few inches, but enough to grate and grind a warning.

The old man smiled, and then slept without dreams.

CHAPTER FIFTY-FIVE

"Does it rain all summer long in this part of the territory?" Asa Pagg said.

"Seems like," Logan Dean said.

Irritated, Pagg said, "Where the hell is Joe? He should be back by now."

"Maybe he met up with Abe Roper an' them," Dean said.

"A meeting of idiots," Pagg said. "It's what that would be."

Ahead of him rose the peaks and mesas of the high country. The tall mountains, green trees growing here and there on their slopes, looked like mildewed bronze in the morning light.

"You really reckon they found the bell, Asa?" Dean said.

"They're idiots. How the hell should I know?" Pagg said.

"Abe Roper is a gun," Dean said. "And so is Flintlock."

"So?"

"I'm just sayin'."

"You sceered, Logan?" Pagg said.

"Nope."

"You leave Roper and Flintlock to me," Pagg said.

Dean smiled. "You can shade 'em, Asa. I got no doubt about that."

"Damn right I can," Pagg said. "There ain't a man born of woman that I can't shade."

Joe Harte showed up fifteen minutes later.

"Well?" Pagg said before the man could talk.

"I found them, Asa. About two miles ahead. They got three women with them," Harte said.

"All the comforts of home, huh?" Pagg said.

"Two little Chinese gals and a white women, and she's a looker," Harte said.

"Good. After we have the bell, if Roper's found it, we'll take their women. They'll be a comfort to us when we're riding down to Old Mexico."

"Take 'em even if we don't get the bell," Harte said.

"That goes without sayin'," Pagg said. As Harte kneed his horse beside his, Pagg said, "Did you go into their camp? Tell them we're on our way?"

Harte shook his head. "No, sir, I scouted them at a distance." He looked at Pagg. "Roper's all right. He can be affable by times, but not Flintlock. He's good with a gun and he's a killer. I reckoned it was time enough to ride into their camp when I had you backing me, Asa."

Pagg nodded. "Probably a wise decision. If Flintlock drew down on you, he'd kill you."

"Maybe he would, maybe he wouldn't," Harte said. "But I don't want to put it to the test. It's way too close. Know what I mean?"

"I know what you mean, but he ain't close to me or even near," Pagg said.

"An' that's a natural fact, Asa," Dean said.

"Hello, the camp," Asa Pagg hollered from the pines.

"Who goes there?" Roper said, drawing a hard look from Flintlock.

"Asa Pagg, Logan Dean an' Joe Harte," Pagg yelled. "All respectable, friendly folks."

"Come on in, Asa," Roper said. "Coffee's on the bile."

His slicker glistening, Pagg rode close to the fire that was reasonably well protected under trees.

"Is this all it does in this here country?

437

Rain?" he said.

"Summer storms is all, Asa," Roper said. "You boys light an' set."

Pagg and the others swung out of the saddle and the outlaw's eyes ranged over the women who were huddled near the fire.

He turned his attention to Flintlock, who had opened his slicker.

"Howdy, Sam," he said. "Good to see you again."

"What brings you to this neck of the woods, Asa?" Flintlock said.

Pagg made no answer. He squatted by the fire, lifted the lid of the coffeepot and glanced inside. After finding a tin cup, Pagg poured himself coffee and told Dean and Harte to do the same.

After a few moments of silence, Pagg said, "You make good coffee, Abe."

"Thankee," Roper said. "A fistful of Arbuckle and the bile does the rest. Eggshells are good because they settle the grounds, like. But I don't have none o' them."

Flintlock stepped to the fire. "Why are you here, Asa?"

"You asked me that afore," Pagg said.

"I'm still waiting for an answer."

"All right, did you find the golden bell?"

"We surely did. It's in a cave up there in the rock cliff."

Now Pagg's eyes lit up. "Is it as big as they say it is?"

"Two thousand pounds of pure gold, Asa," Flintlock said. "And it's there for the taking."

"You can't move it, huh?" Pagg said. "And you can't break it up."

"We haven't tried."

Pagg thought about that, then said, "You wouldn't be lying to me, would you, Sam?"

"Don't call me a liar, Asa," Flintlock said. He was ice cold.

It entered Pagg's mind that now was as good a time as any for a gun showdown. But he quickly dismissed the thought. If Flintlock was telling the truth, he would need help to break up the bell and tote the pieces down from the cave. Gold was heavy and Pagg was not a man overly fond of manual labor.

He made a show of backing down. "No offense intended, Sam, but you took me by surprise about the bell an' I spoke out of turn."

"Hell, Asa, Sam'l knows that. He doesn't want trouble," Roper said. "Do you, Sammy?"

"No," Flintlock said. "No trouble."

"Glad to hear it, Sam," Pagg said. "I always said you was true-blue."

But trouble came . . . and from a direction no one expected or could have foreseen.

Jack Coffin came from behind Pagg's horse, carrying a black bundle he'd taken from the saddle horn. He stepped to the fire opposite Pagg and held it high.

"What is this, Pagg?"

"What the hell does it look like? It's scalps."

"Where did you get them?" Coffin said. His face was the color of death.

"They're Apache, and a few Mex. You know what they're worth down in Old Mexico? Last I heard the bounty on a buck was runnin' about a hundred dollars." Pagg grinned. "I never turn down a business opportunity."

Coffin studied the scalps. "Women, children and old men," he said.

Pagg shrugged. "We gathered what we could find. Any of them kin o' yourn, breed?"

Coffin threw the scalps at Pagg. They landed on the outlaw's lap and he brushed them away.

"Get on your feet, Pagg," Coffin said.

The breed's hand was close to his gun. He never wore a slicker and he was soaked to the skin, his long black hair falling in wet, tangled strands over his shoulders.

"You plan on taking my scalp an' trigger finger, breed?" Pagg said. He laid his cup aside and stood. "Any time you want to try is fine with me."

"Jack, let it go," Flintlock said. "He'll kill you."

"Not this time, Samuel," Coffin said.

He drew.

And died right where he stood.

Suddenly Flintlock's gun was in his hand and Dean and Harte had also skinned iron.

"No!" Roper yelled. "I don't want that!" He charged between the tense, ready men. "Sam, it was Jack's fight, not yours."

Pagg's smoking revolvers were pointed at Flintlock. "Listen to Abe, Sam. The breed drew down on me. Put the revolver away or too many men will die here this morning."

Ayasha cried out and ran to Flintlock, shielding him with her body. "No, Sam, don't fight him," she said.

"It's done, Sam," Pagg said. "Do as the little lady says."

"Sam'l!" Roper said, his voice rising to an urgent shout. "Jack told me he'd sung his death song and was ready to die. He said Asa would kill him and fulfill his destiny, whatever the hell that meant."

Roper did a little jig of agitation. "He

committed suicide, Sam. He drew on Asa to kill himself."

"Abe's tellin' it like it was, Sam," Pagg said. "A man draws down on me, he's lookin' to die." Pagg's face hardened. "Take my advice and don't push it any further."

"Do what he says, Sam'l," Roper said. "We don't need another killing here."

Ayasha was in the line of fire, and Flintlock had other plans for Asa Pagg. He pushed his gun back into the waistband.

"You're riding a lawman's horse and carrying his guns, Asa," he said.

"Yeah, the Apaches done fer him. Too bad."

Only now did Pagg holster the Smith & Wesson Russians. He told Harte and Dean to do the same, then sat at the fire again and poured himself more coffee.

"Sooo," he said, "tell me about the bell."

"I'll tell him, Abe," Flintlock said. He was in a killing rage. "Right after I bury Jack."

CHAPTER FIFTY-SIX

"The way I figure it, the bell weighs two thousand pounds," Flintlock said. "And gold is worth twenty-one dollars an ounce."

"That makes the bell worth six hundred and seventy-two thousand dollars," Asa Pagg said.

"We split it five ways and each of us gets a hundred and thirty-four thousand, near enough," Flintlock said. He pretended a camaraderie he didn't feel. "Enough to keep you in whiskey and whores for the rest of your life, Asa."

"Can't beat that," Joe Harte said, smiling.

"An' American money goes further down in Old Mexico, don't forget," Logan Dean said. "We'll live like kings, I reckon."

"Then it's done and done," Pagg said. He extended his hand to Abe Roper who looked puzzled. "Let's shake on it, Abe. And you too, Sam."

Flintlock felt a sickening revulsion as he

took Pagg's hand. But he had to play the game to its end.

"But, the cave —" Roper said.

Flintlock fixed him with a glare, and Roper lapsed into silence.

"What about the cave?" Pagg said.

"We have to get the bell out of there is what Abe was about to say," Flintlock said. Another dagger of a look, then, "Ain't that so, Abe?"

Roper wasn't stupid and he caught on quick.

"Yeah, that's the problem, all right," he said.

"It's only a problem for idiots, not for me," Pagg said. "I want to take a look at the bell and then I'll figure what's to be done."

Again Flintlock silenced Roper, a talking man, with a glower.

"I'll take you up there, Asa," Flintlock said. Then, to keep the outlaw off guard, "If anyone can come up with a solution, it's you."

"Damn right, I can," Pagg said. He rose to his feet. "Later we'll talk about sharing the women, but the gold comes first."

"You're the boss, Asa," Flintlock said.

"Just so you know it, Sam," Pagg said. "Now show me the damned bell." He turned to Dean and Harte. "You two come with me."

Later Flintlock wondered if the tragedy that followed could've been averted if he'd gone into the cave with Pagg. But logic told him that he'd no way of knowing how much of a mad-dog killer Asa Pagg had become.

Evil was right in front of his face, but Flintlock didn't recognize it as such, a fact that would haunt him for the rest of his life.

"Ain't you coming in out of the rain, Sam?" Pagg said.

"No. I've seen the bell enough times already, Asa. I'll wait for you here."

Pagg shrugged. "Suit yourself. How do I get to it?"

"Just follow the cave."

"Let's go, boys," Pagg said. "Time to see how we're gonna get rich."

Harte and Dean gave a little cheer, then followed Pagg up the slope.

Flintlock watched them go . . . and saw the old man step into Pagg's path, his arms outstretched in a fragile barrier.

Pagg hesitated, but only for a moment.

Then he drew and shot the old man in the belly.

It happened so fast, Flintlock had no time to react.

By the time the enormity of what Pagg had done hit him, the outlaw had already stepped over the murdered man's body and disappeared into the cave.

Flintlock climbed the remainder of the hill at a run, then took a knee beside the old man.

A man gut-shot by a large-caliber firearm suffers tremendous shock. When Flintlock lifted the old man's head in his arms, the guardian was beyond speech. But his milky eyes spoke volumes, wide open, staring up at Flintlock with a mix of fear, surprise . . . and relief.

The old man died without making a sound and probably with no pain. At least Flintlock hoped that was the case.

He laid the old man gently on the floor of the cave. Then he stepped outside.

He'd meet Asa Pagg in the rain. And kill him.

A gusting wind sprang up and drove sheets of rain into the mountains. Above the cloud-capped peaks, lightning scrawled and thunder crashed.

Flintlock was tempted to enter the cave and meet Pagg there. But he realized that it would be too confining and claustrophobic. If he didn't shade Pagg on the draw and shoot he'd need space to move and try to best him in a running gunfight.

The downpour drummed on Flintlock's hat and the shoulders of his slicker and he kept his gun hand inside where it would stay dry.

Drawing down on Asa Pagg was a mighty uncertain thing and there was a knot of fear in Flintlock's belly. The man was fast, maybe the fastest there ever was.

It was not a comforting thought.

Then old Barnabas sat beside him in the grass. It was raining hard but the old mountain man was as dry as Moses in the middle of the Red Sea.

"Why did I have such an idiot for a grandson?" Barnabas said.

"Go away," Flintlock said.

"You can't shade Asa Pagg. You won't even be close," Barnabas said.

He smelled of buffalo dung.

"I'll take my hits and outlast him," Flint-lock said.

"Idiot," Barnabas said. "Remember this: falling rocks can kill a man like Pagg."

"What falling rocks?" Flintlock said.

But the old man dissolved in the rain and only the smell of dung lingered.

Falling rocks . . .

Flintlock stared at the ledge above the

cave. It looked as though it had moved since the last time he saw it, and it seemed there was now a foot-wide space between the top of the ledge and the cliff.

Was it ready to come down?

Old Barnabas thought it would. But what did he know?

Ten minutes later Asa Pagg staggered to the cave entrance and roared his rage.

"The air is poisoned," he yelled. "Logan and Joe are dead."

"They'll be greatly missed, Asa," Flintlock said.

He opened his slicker.

"You knew!" Pagg said.

"Of course I knew," Flintlock said.

"You hoped the gas would kill me."

"Ain't that the truth, Asa."

The Smith & Wesson Russians on each side of Pagg's chest gleamed as lightning flashed. The man himself shimmered, as though he was made of crystal.

"You failed, Sam. Damn you, you failed," Pagg hollered. "I didn't die and I'll come back for the bell after you and Abe Roper are dead."

Pagg laughed, a strange, animal bellow. "I'm gonna gut-shoot you, Sammy. You'll lie on this hillside for a long time, screaming in pain and you'll curse me and the mother who bore you."

"Asa, you talk too damned much," Flintlock said.

He drew as he dived for the ground.

Pagg, taken by surprise, fired from both guns. One shot was a clean miss, the other bullet-holed Flintlock's hat and burned across the top of his skull, drawing blood.

Flintlock fired. A hit.

A scarlet flower of blood blossomed on Pagg's right thigh, but the man stood his ground, his guns hammering.

Mud spurted around Flintlock as he rolled to his right. He yelped in sudden pain as a bullet slammed into the top of his left shoulder and broke the collarbone.

He was losing this fight!

A glance at Pagg revealed that the man was steadying himself for a killing shot.

Desperate now, Flintlock rolled the dice.

He ignored Pagg and fanned his remaining four shots into the rock shelf.

Nothing . . .

Pagg lifted both his guns. The man grinned like a death's-head.

Flintlock rose, prepared to die on his feet instead of groveling on the ground.

"So long, Sam," Pagg yelled.

He fired.

Or Flintlock thought he did.

But it was not the roar of a gunshot he heard, but the sharp crack of splitting stone. The entire rock ledge fell with a horrifying crash. Instantly the cave entrance was lost behind tons of shattered rock.

Flintlock thought he heard Pagg scream, but he wasn't sure.

Despite the rain, dust rose and a terrible hush descended on the hillside.

Asa Pagg was entombed as surely as any ancient Egyptian pharaoh.

A terrible man, he now faced a terrible death . . . and he'd die alone . . . in darkness.

Epilogue

The Chinese girls, with considerable skill, rigged a sling for Sam Flintlock's left arm. But he needed Abe Roper to help him saddle his horse.

The rain had stopped during the night and the morning was coming in bright and sunny.

"Hell, Sammy, you wouldn't know a cave was ever there," Roper said.

Flintlock looked up the slope to the rock fall. It looked as though part of the mountain had come down with it.

"It's just as well," Flintlock said. "I reckon the golden bell is buried forever."

"And Asa Pagg with it," Roper said. "He was good with a gun, was Asa."

"Best I ever saw," Flintlock said.

He stepped into the saddle. "Charlie, take care of them," he said.

"Me and Abe will see them all right, Sam," Fong said. "No harm will come to

451

them as long as we're alive."

"Then quit the train-robbing profession," Flintlock said. "You'll live longer."

"I was thinking that very thing," Roper said. "I figure Charlie an' me will get into some line of business, so long as it's basically dishonest."

"We thought we might prosper in the saloon trade," Fong said.

"Never was truer words spoke," Roper said. "I got some rich kinfolk down Laredo way who might bankroll a venture like that."

"The Tong would advance me money, Abe," Charlie Fong said.

"Then one way or t'other, we can give our three gals a good life, Sam'l," Roper said. "Don't worry yourself about that."

Ayasha stood beside Flintlock's horse, looking up at him, her eyes moist.

"Take me with you, Sam," she said.

"I got to ride alone, Ayasha," Flintlock said. "I already told you that." He smiled. "Just set your heart on the house with the white picket fence and never lose sight of it."

"I'll find her a good husband, Sam'l, a man kinda like myself," Roper said.

"She could do worse," Flintlock said.

"And what will you do, Sam?" Charlie Fong said.

"Find my mother and claim my rightful name," Flintlock said.

"You still got to make a living, Sammy," Roper said.

"I'm a manhunter. That's all I ever was and all I'll ever be," Flintlock said. "And it's all I ever want to be."

He kneed his horse into motion and said, "We'll all meet again. I know it."

"Sam, come back," Ayasha said. "Come back to me."

But Flintlock didn't answer.

He rode into the golden heart of the day . . . the old Hawken rifle across his saddle horn.

ABOUT THE AUTHOR

J. A. JOHNSTONE ON
WILLIAM W. JOHNSTONE
"WHEN THE TRUTH BECOMES LEGEND"

William W. Johnstone was born in southern Missouri, the youngest of four children. He was raised with strong moral and family values by his minister father, and tutored by his schoolteacher mother. Despite this, he quit school at age fifteen.

"I have the highest respect for education," he says, "but such is the folly of youth, and wanting to see the world beyond the four walls and the blackboard."

True to this vow, Bill attempted to enlist in the French Foreign Legion ("I saw Gary Cooper in *Beau Geste* when I was a kid and I thought the French Foreign Legion would be fun") but was rejected, thankfully, for being underage. Instead, he joined a traveling carnival and did all kinds of odd jobs. It was listening to the veteran carny folk, some of whom had been on the circuit since the late 1800s, telling amazing tales about their experiences, which planted the storytelling seed in Bill's imagination.

"They were mostly honest people, despite the bad reputation traveling carny shows had back then," Bill remembers. "Of course, there were exceptions. There was one guy named Picky, who got that name because he was a master pickpocket. He could steal a man's socks right off his feet without him knowing. Believe me, Picky got us chased out of more than a few towns."

After a few months of this grueling existence, Bill returned home and finished high school. Next came stints as a deputy sheriff in the Tallulah, Louisiana, Sheriff's Department, followed by a hitch in the U.S. Army. Then he began a career in radio broadcasting at KTLD in Tallulah, Louisiana, which would last sixteen years. It was there that he fine-tuned his storytelling skills. He turned to writing in 1970, but it wouldn't be until 1979 that his first novel, *The Devil's Kiss,* was published. Thus began the full-time writing career of William W. Johnstone. He wrote horror (*The Uninvited*), thrillers (*The Last of the Dog Team*), even a romance novel or two. Then, in February 1983, *Out of the Ashes* was published. Searching for his missing family in the aftermath of a post-apocalyptic America, rebel mercenary and patriot Ben Raines is united with the civilians of the Resistance forces and moves to the forefront of a revolution for the nation's future.

Out of the Ashes was a smash. The series would continue for the next twenty years, winning Bill three generations of fans all over the world. The series was often imitated but never duplicated. "We all tried to copy *The Ashes* series," said one publishing executive, "but Bill's uncanny ability, both then and now, to predict in which direction the political winds were blowing brought a certain immediacy to the table no one else could capture." The Ashes series would end its run with more than thirty-four books and twenty million copies in print, making it one of the most successful men's action series in American book publishing. (The Ashes series also, Bill notes with a touch of pride, got him on the FBI's Watch List for its less than flattering portrayal of spineless politicians and the growing power of big government over our lives, among other things. "In that respect," says collaborator J. A. Johnstone, "Bill was years ahead of his time.")

Always steps ahead of the political curve,

Bill's recent thrillers, written with J. A. Johnstone, include *Vengeance Is Mine, Invasion USA, Border War, Jackknife, Remember the Alamo, Home Invasion, Phoenix Rising, The Blood of Patriots, The Bleeding Edge,* and the upcoming *Suicide Mission.*

It is with the western, though, that Bill found his greatest success and propelled him onto both the *USA Today* and the *New York Times* bestseller lists.

Bill's western series, co-authored by J. A. Johnstone, include *The Mountain Man, Matt Jensen the Last Mountain Man, Preacher, The Family Jensen, Luke Jensen Bounty Hunter, Eagles, MacCallister* (an Eagles spin-off), *Sidewinders, The Brothers O'Brien, Sixkiller, Blood Bond, The Last Gunfighter,* and the upcoming new series *Flintlock* and *The Trail West.* Coming in May 2013 is the hardcover western *Butch Cassidy, The Lost Years.*

"The Western," Bill says, "is one of the few true art forms that is one hundred percent American. I liken the Western as America's version of England's Arthurian legends, like the Knights of the Round Table, or Robin Hood and his Merry Men. Starting with the 1902 publication of *The Virginian* by Owen Wister, and followed by the greats like Zane Grey, Max Brand, Ernest Haycox, and of course Louis L'Amour, the Western has helped to shape the cultural landscape of America.

"I'm no goggle-eyed college academic, so when my fans ask me why the Western is as popular now as it was a century ago, I don't offer a 200-page thesis. Instead, I can only offer this: The Western is honest. In this great country, which is suffering under the yoke of political correctness, the Western harks back to an era when justice was sure and swift. Steal a man's horse, rustle his cattle, rob a bank, a stagecoach, or a train, you were hunted down and fitted with a hangman's noose. One size fit all.

"Sure, we westerners are prone to a little embellishment and exaggeration and, I admit it, occasionally play a little fast and loose with the facts. But we do so for a very good reason — to enhance the enjoyment of readers.

"It was Owen Wister, in *The Virginian* who first coined the phrase *'When you call me that, smile.'* Legend has it that Wister actually heard those words spoken by a deputy sheriff in Medicine Bow, Wyoming, when another poker player called him a son-of-a-bitch.

"Did it really happen, or is it one of those

myths that have passed down from one generation to the next? I honestly don't know. But there's a line in one of my favorite Westerns of all time, *The Man Who Shot Liberty Valance,* where the newspaper editor tells the young reporter, 'When the truth becomes legend, print the legend.'

"These are the words I live by."